Carl Brookins

Bloody Halls

NORMANDALE COMMUNITY COLLEGE
LIBRARY
9700 FRANCE AVENUE SOUTH
BLOOMINGTON, MN 55431-4399

Echelon Press, LLC

BLOODY HALLS
A Jack Marston Mystery
An Echelon Press Book

First Echelon Press paperback printing / January 2008

All Rights Reserved.
Copyright © 2008 by C. Brookins
Cover illustration © Nathalie Moore

Echelon Press, LLC
9735 Country Meadows Lane 1-D
Laurel, MD 20723
www.echelonpress.com

All rights reserved. No part of this book may be used or reproduced in any manner whatsoever without written permission, except in the case of brief quotations embodied in critical articles and reviews. For information address Echelon Press, LLC.

ISBN 10: 1-59080-570-4
ISBN 13: 978-1-59080-570-1

Library of Congress Control Number: 2007935065

PRINTED IN THE UNITED STATES OF AMERICA

10 9 8 7 6 5 4 3 2 1

Other books by Carl Brookins

The Case of the Greedy Lawyers

Inner Passages

A Superior Mystery

Old Silver

Notes and acknowledgements

The Shakespeare quotes are drawn from, "Shakespeare," compiled and annotated by Frederick D, Losey, A.M. International Press, The John C. Winston Company, 1926.

The epigraphs and occasional quotes in the play by Ibsen which forms the framework of this story, are from "Four Great Plays by Henrik Ibsen" translated by R. Sharp, pub. By Bantam, 1955.

While there is, or was, a unique college in the Twin Cities of Minnesota with many of the characteristics of the City College described herein, all of the characters and events in this novel are products of the author's imagination. I am, however, deeply indebted to my colleagues at Minnesota Metropolitan State College, whose heroic efforts to establish a successful institution of higher learning for working adult students resulted in a wide range of learning experiences I never in my wildest dreams would have thought possible.

I am also indebted to my critique group whose ever vigilant criticism and suggestions made the manuscript better, to my touring partners in the Minnesota Crime Wave, and most especially to my outstanding editor, Kat Thompson.

CHAPTER 1

*You see, if you come an hour late,
you have to put up with cold meat*

Later, when I'd had time to think about it, I realized it was those banging metal trashcans in the lobby that marked my initial entanglement in the Marshall affair. Sometimes, when I dream about those noisy trashcans, I wonder what might have happened if I'd followed my first instinct, left the rehearsal, and gone to the theater lobby while the killer was still there. That thought makes me sweat, sometimes, in the quiet dark of an early morning.

The day of the murder hadn't been one of my better days. I'd stayed late in the college's Office of Student Services because that's what directors have to do to keep up with the workload. Now, well after the cocktail hour, I found myself in an uncomfortable seat, cold, bored, waiting. Waiting for my entrance in this creaky, drafty barn of a theater.

Weeks earlier I'd let my eagerness for the play get the better of my judgment. When the community theater group loosely associated with our college, City College of Minneapolis, announced they were going to produce Ibsen's "Enemy of the People," I couldn't resist the opportunity. I happen to like Ibsen a lot. Here was my chance, I told my friend Lori, to really stretch myself. If I landed a part, even a bit part, what an experience! Ibsen. Wow! So I auditioned. And I got a part.

"Wonderful," one would say. "Just what you wanted,"

another will say.

"Rats," I'll say. It was a much bigger part than I ever anticipated. Not to put too fine a point on it, it was too much part for me. Besides, I knew it would take up most of what little free time I already hadn't enough of. I should have declined, but I was the director's first choice, so pride entered into the equation as well as opportunity, and I was lost.

Dr. Stockman. Enemy of the people. That was to be my role.

That had been weeks earlier. Now here I was, facing an obsessed director, Delton, he said his name was, a graduate student from the big university across town. The small college for which I labored had no theater department so the acting company usually hired a grad student from elsewhere. Funny, this same director, when he'd called to offer me the part, had seemed pleasant, logical, even charming. No longer. I was fast becoming convinced that this mere child of a director knew no more about Ibsen's time and the dragons that drove the good Dr. Stockman than did that janitor, banging about in the lobby outside the auditorium doors at that moment.

What was it with that janitor? Didn't he realize the noise would distract us? I finally rose from my seat, intending to go to the lobby and snuff out the continuing banging. I had almost reached the double doors when the noise stopped. Silence fell on stage at the same moment. I glanced back and realized most of those in the auditorium were looking at me, or more precisely, looking in my direction.

"Well, Marston?"

"Well, Delton?" I shot back. Quick, that's me.

"I believe you have an entrance here," the director growled.

"*Ummm*... right. Sorry." I'd lost track of exactly where in the act we were when I started up the aisle toward the lobby. I was still curious about the now absent noises, but decided I'd better get on stage, playbook in hand. I trotted back toward the proscenium while Delton stalked off, deep in conversation with someone whose face I couldn't quite see.

As I approached the stage, I was conscious of the people scattered throughout the big auditorium. There were actors, stage crewmembers, set and costume people. Some were alone, some in small groups. All eyes seemed to be on me, but I couldn't positively identify everyone in the auditorium because the light was strongest from the stage, which threw many of their faces into shadow. The assistant director, a student whom I vaguely recalled from one of my counseling classes, fell into step just behind me and we made a short parade.

Because I was tardy for my entrance, everybody else had to wait. They didn't like it, although no one said anything. They were unhappy because we'd learned by this time that director Delton ran long rehearsals and delays added to the time. You'd think the guy was directing professional, paid actors. Professional actors probably wouldn't take the verbal abuse we'd already received, and it was still early in the rehearsal schedule. I found my place, did the scene, and we made it through Act I. It got on to eleven and just when I began to think Delton was going to have us start over or, worse, go on to the next act, he took a big, tired breath and kind of whooshed at us.

He stared slowly around at the assembled cast. That night he wore a frayed, shapeless green coat of some kind over a sweater and faded jeans. The coat might have been military surplus and it seemed to be about two sizes too large. His narrow shoulders slumped forward below his receding chin. He said, "Tomorrow night at seven, please. Do-not-be-late." He punched the words for emphasis. Another thing about Delton I didn't like was his eyes. At times they seemed to bore into you, as if there was a recording machine inside his skull instead of just a brain. Maybe that was just me. He'd made it clear from the start that he considered me a distraction to his art. It was unclear to me why he'd chosen me for the role of Dr. Stockman.

Dismissed, we collected our belongings and wandered through the backstage area, past old flats left over from God knew what ancient production. Backstage was a vast cavern inadequately lit by a few dim unshaded bulbs hung on long black snakes that descended from somewhere overhead. The grid of lights, sandbag weights, ropes and other trappings of live theater resided about twenty feet above us. The ceiling of the building was somewhere above that. We left in a group through a back door, into the cold November night, and somebody locked up. As I shrugged into my jacket and went out, I remembered the noises from the lobby.

The tiny space where we were allowed to park was just a narrow gap between the tall dark buildings. It felt oppressive, confining. I hunched my shoulders. I left my fellow thespians and turned the other way down the alley. I walked around the building to the marquee on Eighth and peered into the dark interior. Nothing. "All's well that ends well," I muttered aloud.

I didn't try the doors. Later I wished I had.

CHAPTER 2

*We shall proceed with the
greatest moderation, Doctor–*

Late fall in Minneapolis is not my favorite season. It's a time when I occasionally question my sanity in that I am still, after ten-plus years, living in this city with its extremes of heat and cold. In Minnesota, seasonal changes seem to occur almost every week. Of course I knew the answer to the why of it. I had a good position with a department boasting an excellent staff, in a college whose mission I thoroughly admired.

City College is an urban institution that operates from several administrative spaces in the middle of downtown Minneapolis and rents classroom sites throughout the city. We granted what was known in academic circles as an 'external degree.' External to what, I still wasn't sure.

At ten that particular morning, the view from my sixth-floor office window was depressing, but at least I had a window. You'd think a college that leased space in commercial buildings could insure that everyone who wanted a window could have one, but not this college. However, I didn't complain. Some staff didn't even have office doors they could close.

If I didn't care for fall in general, November is my candidate for the worst month of the year, Thanksgiving notwithstanding. By now the ground is frozen and the leaves have long since blown off the scraggly trees along the avenues. Not enough snow had fallen to cover the dirt and dead brown grass, not to mention the trash.

There is something to be said for a campus-based college with broad, curving walks, vine-covered brick or stone walls, crumbling turrets and stately old oaks, or elms, or even cottonwoods. A nice mature birch tree is an asset. A good full-time groundskeeper is another.

In addition to the depressing weather and scenery, the Vikings were in the midst of blowing another season. I sighed. Golf puts me to sleep and I'd rather watch the grass grow than a baseball game. Professional football and college hockey are my sports, along with theater. I peered down at the busy street through my soot and dust-streaked window, thinking life was pretty good right now.

I was waiting for a report from the registrar on the status of four students who'd been involved in an altercation at an after-hours joint earlier in the week. This quartet was known to hang out together. If I discovered that even one was in academic difficulty, I might be able to break up the little group before they got into more serious trouble. I'd always believed early intervention was better than punishment. This quartet was at the low end of the range, age-wise, for our students, all in their early twenties. We mostly attracted an older, more mature individual. Most had full time jobs and had been alive for around thirty years.

I went back and sat down at my littered desk. What I waited for was a report, what I got was something else. The door to our office suite suddenly banged open. Rapid footsteps approached, surrounded by raised voices. What was going on?

My door was thrust open and the assistant director of student services, my second in command, loped in. "Ranae? What's the matter?" I looked up at her in astonishment.

"Jack! Haven't they called you?"

"Who? What about?"

"The murder!" Her voice rose. She leaned over me and

planted both hands on my desk. A sheet of crumpled paper trembled in her fingers.

"Whoa, hold on. What murder?"

"A man was killed last night. Oh, God, Jack." She paused, rocked back on her heels, then took a deep breath to steady herself. "They found his body in the theater lobby this morning!"

"Theater! Who? My God, that's terrible. Here, sit down. Can I get you a glass of water?" I gestured her to a chair.

I looked at her while she took deep breaths and stared back. Tears made silvery tracks down her brown cheeks. I grabbed a tissue from the box on my cluttered credenza and handed it to her. She wiped her eyes. While she composed herself, I crossed the room and closed the door. Poisonous gossip was endemic at City College. The dispersed condition of our offices and faculty spaces scattered across the city presented no noticeable hindrance to the almost instantaneous transmission of rumors. Sometimes even facts, and that was before the advent of email.

This, I thought, was one of the drawbacks to a college without a campus in an urban setting. We had too little control over who came into the buildings and spaces we leased. Dead bodies on our doorstep weren't conducive to a healthy learning environment. Ranae's next words pushed me hard into my chair.

"One of our students was killed, Jack. His name is Stuart Jamison. God, I knew him. Had him in a class spring quarter. A really good student." That explained her tears. She was usually very cool, even in highly emotional circumstances.

I stared at her, stunned. "A student? The theater?" For a moment my mind shut down. Then last night returned to my memory and I gulped, "I was there, you know. At the theater. We were rehearsing 'Enemy of the People.'" The sounds of banging trashcans came back to me.

Ranae gulped, "That's awful! It could have been around the

same time." She took another deep breath. "We have to do something." She waved her hand, the one with the piece of paper still clutched in her fingers.

"Here," I said. "Give me that." I leaned forward and snatched the piece of paper. It was a memo from our president about the next in an apparently endless line of fund-raising events. I handed it back at her. "You're right. We have to figure out what to tell students, and quickly. Keep the gossip from running rampant. You'd better arrange for some grief counseling for anyone who wants some comfort and support. I'll call Lori Jacobs. She'll help. Who was this Jamison?"

No image of a Stuart Jamison came to my mind. With a staff of over a hundred, a faculty, including part-timers, numbering twice that, plus administrators and other assorted hangers-on, not to mention more than eight thousand students, it wasn't surprising I didn't recall this particular individual.

"Last year he won an award for his computer math project. Faculty voted him the most exceptional math student of the decade."

I sat silent for a moment. Then it began to come back. Sure, Stuart Jamison, a brilliant mathematical and computer wizard. He was articulate, good-looking, and he had the most acidic personality of any individual it had ever been my misfortune to encounter. His social graces were noticeably absent. The faculty hadn't cared about any of that when they had voted him the award. Since the faculty was chary with its accolades, he probably deserved the recognition. For a moment neither of us said anything.

"Family," I said. "The cops will make an official notification, but we have to be there too. What else? Do the police think it was a robbery? Drugs ? Maybe just a random attack?"

"I don't know much else. I suppose it was a robbery. But why d'you suppose he was in the lobby?"

I shook my head. "Maybe he ran in there trying to escape his attacker. Faculty and staff may need counseling as well."

Ranae nodded. "Okay, but I want to get help for the students first."

Trust Ranae to consider our students above anyone else. "How'd you hear about Jamison?" Outside my office people moved back and forth and distant telephones rang. I even thought I heard someone pouring coffee. Apparently the news of Jamison's death hadn't reached very far. Yet.

"'Nita called me from AV. She didn't say where she heard."

I nodded. It figured. Anita Talbot was one of the worst gossips in the place. You'd think she had enough to do trying to get projectors, TV sets and other machines delivered to our far-flung classrooms. She was efficient, well organized, and divorced, which was probably why she had so much time to hang on the phone talking to her network of contacts. Anita Talbot was a thirty-five year old busybody.

"You and I are going to have to do some serious damage control," I said. "There'll be media questions and the prez is not gonna be happy if he thinks Jamison's murder will be detrimental to the current capital drive. We should remember, though, that adults like Stuart Jamison have lives outside the college. This may turn out to have nothing directly to do with us."

"Of course, but somehow I don't believe that," Ranae said. "If we're not careful, Jamison will just get lost in all the damage control. I'll get started on his file, if we have one." I nodded and she went out, carefully shutting the door behind her. I ground my teeth and thought about what was to come. I hadn't bargained on anything like this.

Here I was, in my early forties, a veteran, ready to settle in, in my hometown, into a nice situation. I'd been other places, done my graduate program. Now I was ready for a management position in a small college that would see me to retirement. Murder was not on my agenda.

Right after I accepted my position, Ranae Jannard and I had several lengthy and intense discussions. It helped us establish a clean division of responsibilities and I thought we'd worked well as a team ever since. Rebuilding student and faculty trust in the Office of Student Affairs had been an important part of our efforts.

Ranae had gone to graduate school, obtaining an advanced degree in counseling and psychology in record time at the big public university across town. It was the same university that was supplying our current theater director. She got her degree while working full time at City College and she'd pretty much single-handedly held our office together during the final failing years of my immediate predecessor. I suspected she'd been passed over for the director's position because she was black and female, and because she'd been at City College for several years. Ranae had a reputation as a strong student advocate, which must have irritated some members of the staff and faculty. In academia, paybacks come in many forms.

In the conservative, largely white, upper Middle West, Ranae's taste in clothing, which ran to the flamboyant, probably didn't help. Today she was wearing a bright, shimmery, silky blouse of ivory, printed with huge reddish flowers. The sleeves were loose and billowy, caught in tight cuffs at each slender wrist. Her skirt was plain, dark, and quite short. The effect was spoiled by the tears and mascara that had been running down her cheeks when she burst into my office this morning.

What had I been thinking last night when I left the theater? Oh yeah, "All's Well that Ends Well." How ironic.

CHAPTER 3

I stick to my tea and bread and butter

I called the president's office. Since Student Affairs would probably be involved at some level with the media, I figured I'd better touch base with the top of the administrative ladder. Besides, over the years the president had developed a habit of using me as a sounding board.

President Arthur Trammel was once a forceful, dominating presence at City College. It had been a real coup to get him, a nationally-known figure in college administration, to take over the reins of a brand new experimental college with few assets. But that had been a couple of decades ago, and Trammel's career had peaked. Now in his declining years, facing retirement, he was mightily concerned about leaving a major legacy, a lasting monument to his administrative genius. Anything that might disrupt his agenda would be of intense interest. He wasn't in yet, but our press officer, Micky Nelson, was. Nelson assured me that they knew about Jamison's death and they were on it.

"We're on it, Jack," is the way he put it. "Jamison's body was found by a coed about six this morning."

A *coed*, I thought? What kind of talk was that at the beginning of the twenty-first century?

"She found a street door open to the lobby and decided to take a shortcut through the building to the restaurant where she works," he went on.

"How'd that happen?"

Bloody Halls

"Dunno, Jack. I haven't talked to the janitor. I've got the girl's name here somewhere." I heard the rustle of papers.

"Micky," I interrupted his search. "Save the woman who found the body for later. Right now, just tell me what you can about Jamison's murder. When do we expect the police to show up for the investigation?"

"Ah... well, it's apparently pretty gruesome. Positive ID, of course. I don't know who made it. The story is Jamison was badly beaten in the face, and somebody tried to take his head off."

"You mean decapitate him?"

"I guess so. His throat was cut from ear to ear. There was a lot of blood."

"Jesus!" The phone in my hand grew slippery with perspiration. There was a long silence while I tried to construct an intelligent question.

"It apparently happened sometime after ten," Mikey went on. "I suppose sooner or later the PD will tell us more precisely."

With a shudder I realized I didn't need to wait for the police. I knew when Jamison's life had been snuffed out. The noise of banging trashcans last night in the lobby, while I'd been waiting for my cue, echoed in my head. If I'd gone out through those double doors, I might have encountered the bloody murderer. It was not a pleasant prospect.

Micky continued chattering in my ear. "The cops haven't called me yet and I don't guess they'll tell me when they're gonna show up."

I wobbled out a question. "What about the newspapers and TV? Do they have it yet?" I pulled out a handkerchief to wipe my palms.

"I couldn't do much about that, you know. They heard the police call and showed up right behind the squad car. I think they got pictures before the body was covered."

"Christ. Well, Ranae is working on Jamison's background and we're going to arrange for counselors to be available."

"Look, Jack, besides that award he won and all, there are some odd questions about him. I don't know exactly what...."

I waited. Finally I said, "And?" I couldn't figure what Micky was driving at.

"Well of course, we're giving the police full cooperation, but we have to be really careful. Trammel wants...our office is supposed to see anything about Jamison before it gets released to anybody, anybody at all, especially to the media."

"Wait a minute. What do you mean there are odd questions about him? First I've heard of it."

"Geez, Jack. I just don't know. I guess I shouldn't have said anything. Better ask Trammel."

I sighed. Obviously, Nelson wasn't going to be any help on this subject so I switched gears. "Okay, Micky. We'll pull together information on Jamison's college activities. As soon as we have a rough draft I'll call. Then we can get together."

Normally, whenever a student did something newsworthy, our office supplied a background file to Micky for media distribution. My assistant or I checked the files and roughed out something about the student's academic program, extracurricular stuff, all routine. The draft passed through at least one other administrator in order to avoid potential problems with data privacy, current college policies, things like that. This was our first murder, but still, why was Nelson making such a point of reminding me to route everything through his office? And what was that mumbling and hesitancy? I talked to Ranae and related the substance of my conversation with Micky.

"That seems a little strange. What do you think?"

"I have no idea. Let's just follow our regular routine until we know more."

"Jack, it's beginning to look like he didn't have anything to do with student counseling. No records of any contacts. I may have something left from the award process though. I'll look."

"Okay, I'll print out his computer records."

We have this computer system in which all general student and staff data are stored, but we don't have enough terminals, so some departments, like ours, maintain supplemental paper files. But if the student had no contact with us, we had no files on said student.

I took a deep breath, turned to my computer and punched up the central student record database. The index gave me Jamison's social security number and an ID number. When I keyed in his ID, up popped his main demographic screen. I clicked through several additional screens to retrieve his academic record. The system was organized so we could quickly get a student's registrations, grades, or name and phone number; stuff like that. One of the dubious perks of my job was complete access to every student's file.

I waited for the screen to fill after keying in the appropriate codes. The screen came up promptly, but stayed blank.

What the hell? The system was occasionally slow but never like this. I tried the codes again, going through the steps very carefully. Still nothing. I tried another student file and the machine worked perfectly. Then I tried to access other parts of Jamison's file.

It didn't matter. If the computer was to be believed, Stuart Jamison had never registered for anything at City College. Ever. Furthermore, significant elements of his personal record were missing, pieces that should have been there, especially since I knew for a fact that Jamison had been a student at City College for at least two years.

Concerned, I called our computer center. Fred Coper came on.

"Jack Marston, Fred. I need to access a student file and I get blank screens. What's up?"

He sighed in my ear. "I suppose you tried Stuart Jamison."

Startled, I admitted he was right. "How did you know?"

"Because, the minute I heard about the killing, I went to look him up. Blank, null, nada." Coper's deep basso voice reverberated through the phone. "You will note," he said, shifting to his pedantic lecturing tone, "that Jamison's file is unlike those of unregistered individuals, those who were at one time students, or who stopped after being accepted, but are not current students. In those cases a screen comes up with information across the top and a legend that says NO REGISTRATIONS FOUND. But his screens are blank."

"Yeah. So what does it mean?" I was starting to sweat again. "How could this happen just when the student in question gets murdered? An active student, I might add."

"It means some slicker went in there and erased the records."

"What about the back-up tapes? What about the archives?"

"Nope," Fred sighed again through the phone. I sensed he was feeling some strain. "Somebody did something clever so when we went to back up the system last night, or maybe even earlier, it wiped out his files. Plus we don't have the equipment or the budget to archive everything. Costs a bundle, you know.

"Because the index shows all the appropriate screens for Jamison, and because the screens themselves are there, I think some kind of virus or trapdoor was stuck in there so the records would disappear when they were accessed without a special code of some..." His voice trailed off and I suspected he was beginning to consider ways to protect the system against a repetition of the problem.

I took a deep breath and gently hung up the phone.

CHAPTER 4

Oh, you mustn't take me too literally

I stared vacantly at the dull beige wall of my office.

"Jack?" Teresa Knowles stuck her shining blond head around the door. "The Jamison thing is likely to take a lot of your time the next few days. Why don't I draft those staff evaluations that are due? You can review them later."

I looked up at her. "My God, I'd forgotten all about them. If we don't get those things done today, I'll have the union on my neck and that'll bring Trammel down on us as well. Please do, and thanks for offering."

I smiled at her departing back. Teresa was another asset to our operation. In addition to her competence, her long service to the college gave her a vast store of favors owed her, favors she called in for us from time to time. She knew where more metaphorical bodies were buried than anyone else at City College. Few weeks went by that I didn't thank whatever gods look after me that Teresa Knowles remained our office manager.

She claimed my attention again a minute later. "The council rep from D. C. is on the phone about our revisions of the grant proposal. For the building fund?" she said. "Since you're the chairman of this particular grant committee...." she shrugged expressively.

"Okay," I said. "I better talk to him."

After I answered the representative's questions, I stepped into the main office. I could hear a steady murmur of conversation. The college was trying to shut down as much rumor and gossip as possible, but Jamison's death was the number one topic of the day. I wondered if the regular work of the college was getting done.

Ranae's office was on the other side of the reception area. Her door was open and I raised my voice so she'd hear me.

"Teresa, we'll need more people on this. Take our student workers off whatever they're doing. Ranae, you and Teresa will have to make some calls as well. Divide up the lists. After I see the Prez, I'll do some calling too."

"Old fashioned research?" Ranae questioned from her desk.

"Right. Call faculty, staff, and everyone else you can think of for any information about Stuart Jamison. We'll even take anecdotes."

"What do we tell people who ask questions?" It was our redheaded student file clerk, Eddie.

"Nothing. Say you don't know why, just that we need the information in a hurry. If they persist, tell 'em to call me. Any other questions?"

Teresa was already up and headed for our small copier with the staff telephone list in hand.

"We have nothing in our files on him, Jack. I can't locate anything on the math award either," Ranae said. "My kingdom for a horse," I muttered and went back to my desk.

A few minutes later there was a light tap at my door and before I could respond, it swung inward and my favorite vice president appeared.

"Hey, Marsh, how're things on mahogany row?"

Anton T. Marshall, academic vice president, shrugged once and dropped his two hundred plus pounds into my visitor's chair. He plucked at the knees of his carefully creased, dark charcoal trousers. His taste in clothes ran to pure white dress shirts, dark, well-tailored suits and conservative ties. Today he'd really branched out. He was wearing a dark green paisley tie.

"We got a problem here, Jack."

Knowing he usually got right to the point, I waited.

"This Jamison killing has got to be dealt with quickly."

"Well, Trammel and Micky are handling the press and I hear the police are being reasonable and discreet. Haven't met 'em yet, though."

"Uh huh. One problem is the deep hole of computing into which Jamison's academic records seem to have been sucked, right at the time we need them most."

"It's an interesting coincidence."

"Jack, I assume you're already building a file from your paper records on Jamison. We're going to have to put some special attention on this, give it a little extra, you catch my drift? We think you're the one for the job."

Marshall scratched his chin. His hands, well proportioned and noticeably larger than the average man's, had been one of his assets. He'd had a full-ride athletic scholarship in college. He'd been a star end and was intensely recruited by both the NFL and the Canadians. Sportswriters all over the country moaned in print and on television about the loss to professional football when he chose a graduate school scholarship instead.

Marshall's other asset was his intelligence. Not that he wasn't good-looking in a direct sort of way. He was. His smooth, unlined brown skin was the color of warm molasses and his regular features hadn't been rearranged on the football field. Unlike many former athletes, he stayed in shape and it showed in his trim waist.

I looked at him with a steady gaze. "Marsh, are you suggesting I get involved in the police investigation?"

"Not just me, bucko. I come as an emissary from on high." He pointed theatrically at the ceiling. "Trammel wants to see you. I'm here to suggest that you give his request serious consideration.

If you turn him down, he'll just get somebody else who might be a lot less discreet."

Interesting, I thought, watching Marsh spring lightly out of the chair. He still moved with the lithe economy and quickness that had distinguished him on the field, though he was years from the football stadium. Above average height, Marshall's long arms gave him an advantage in other athletic activities besides football, as I had reason to know. We competed at racquetball once or twice a month. He was still fast and very powerful. Only my legs kept me close.

He caught my look and smiled gently, "Trammel and I discussed this, and I volunteered to make the first probe. Sort of soften you up."

"Look, Marsh, I have a pretty full plate here and just last night we had this little `incident' over on the west side."

He merely raised his eyebrows and continued to gaze at me.

"Why do I have this feeling I'm not getting through to you?" I said.

"Jack, I know all about the incident, as you put it. I know that you're the best choice for this particular job. Also that you'll keep quiet about whatever you turn up."

"Just exactly what does that mean?"

Instead of replying, he smiled and left, calling over his shoulder, "Thanks, Jack. I told President Trammel we could count on you."

When I went to the outer door of my office, he was already out of sight down the long hall toward the elevators. It was a calculated exit. The hallways of the old building, with dark wooden wainscoting and marble floors, made wonderful sound chambers. By now practically everybody on the sixth floor thought they knew I'd just agreed to some important Presidential Assignment. Well, we'd see about that. I pressed the intercom button on my phone console. "Teresa, I'm going across the street to talk with the President and Mick Nelson."

I swung down the hall past Ranae's office and hit the down elevator button. I was struck by the seeming emptiness of the place. We usually had a steady flow of students in and out of the counseling offices. Most of our students are adults with family and job responsibilities, so their needs and their timetables are different. We don't have the disciplinary problems that seem to be a growing problem among younger college students.

The elevator didn't actually creak, but it was old and not very sprightly. It finally arrived and down I went to the lobby. Across the street in the presidential suite, all was subdued bustle. Here was a much grander sixth floor than mine. There was never a sense of crisis or impending disaster on this sixth floor. Such realities rarely touched this sanctuary of intellectual calm. A couple sat side by side in the President's reception area. They could be reporters. Or, I admitted to myself as I knocked on the press officer's door, they could be alumni, or just casual visitors.

"Come." Micky Nelson had a high lilting voice. Hearing his voice and looking at the shock of flaming red hair on his head, hair that never seemed to be combed, one might suppose that here was a true Irish tenor. Nelson couldn't carry a tune if his life depended on it. It wasn't for lack of trying. His light voice apparently kept him from realizing his dream of being a network television anchorman. He was shorter than average which didn't help but he was 'cute' according to a significant number of the female staff around the college.

Now, here he was, beating out press releases and representing the college to the media anytime old Trammel didn't want to joust with them himself.

"Hi, Mick, how's the press release on Jamison coming?" I sauntered into a cluttered space, projecting I hoped, a casualness I didn't feel. Nelson's office was so filled with untidy piles of magazines and newspapers, I wondered if the fire safety inspectors had ever been inside his door. He flapped a hand at me, and didn't look up from his typewriter. Micky had a good electric typewriter, in addition to one of the terminals in the college computer system.

"Word processors are great," he'd say, "but when I have a problem, it really helps to be able to beat on the old typewriter." The electric typewriter squatted on a rolling stand behind him, whereas the terminal occupied a prominent place on the corner of his desk.

"To tell you the absolute truth," he said, and hit two more keys. He swiveled around at his desk and curled his upper lip at me. "To be perfectly honest, that is not to say totally clear, this is a miserable situation."

"Why? It seems straightforward to me. Journalism one, two, three. Last night, blah, one Stuart Jamison, blah blah, was brutally killed, etc., etc. When asked to describe the unfortunate Jamison and reveal details of the victim's academic record, college officials were strangely silent. Rumors that Jamison's files were mysteriously erased sometime prior to the discovery of the deceased's nearly headless body are being emphatically denied. College officials, when questioned about the loss of the records, revealed incompetence, poor system security, and a total lack of concern." I smirked at him. "Hey, what could be simpler?"

Nelson grinned. "You got it. We have to be cooperative, give them all they need and avoid saying much. Did you know he lived downtown?"

I hadn't and said so.

"Yeah, it turns out he lived in a really nice apartment in the Towers. But the little we have on his personal life so far doesn't give any indication of his income, and his application in the file indicates he has no family. This guy was really unattached. No roots at all. I don't suppose your office has anything of substance for me, have you?"

"Did you know I was at the theater when Jamison was killed?"

"What!" Nelson's eyes got round and he stared up at me.

"Yeah, we were rehearsing "Enemy of the People" in the auditorium."

"What happened? Did you see anything? Jesus."

"Wait, wait. Late in the rehearsal I heard a terrific banging from the lobby. Trash cans, I think. I was about to go out and talk to the janitor when I had to go on stage."

"They found his body in a pile of empty garbage cans next to the south wall." Nelson's eyes still looked larger than normal. "You might have seen the murderer if you'd gone out to the lobby."

I nodded wordlessly. Brief service years ago in the criminal investigation unit of the U.S. Navy had not prepared me for confrontations with killers. I changed the subject.

"To answer your question, Ranae tells me we've got nothing at all on Jamison, but there must be information in some file the committee put together during the selection for that award he got from the faculty last year. They certainly had a printout of his academic record and maybe there are some notes. I'll try to run that down. I guess you realize there're too many coincidences happening around this guy. This whole thing is starting to smell like the lower end of Fulton Street." Mick stared at me. He'd probably never heard of the famous Fulton Street Fish Market in New York.

"Anyway, here's what I've got so far. It's just enough for an initial press conference." Micky handed me a sheet of paper filled with typing. It was a standard release, saying little but giving an impression of substance. I shrugged and gave it back.

He picked up a pencil to edit the piece and I strolled to the window where the afternoon sun had finally broken though the overcast. It streamed down on the buildings across the street. Weak rays illuminated the huge pile of rubble in the next block as well. I watched the men and their machines, intrigued by the distorted shadows thrown across the tumbled, jagged chunks of concrete and the random-appearing piles of unidentifiable detritus.

No sound came through the window, which added an eerie dimension to the scene. In the center of the block, where once had stood a seven-story hotel, a huge yellow-bodied boom crane chewed away at one wall. From my angle the machine looked like the end result of some genetic experiment gone bad. The tall black boom swiveled slowly forth and back, swinging its steel-jawed clam bucket at the end of a thick steel cable. Each time it was positioned, the bucket dropped about ten feet onto the raw end of a still vertical third-floor wall. It must have made a terrific noise. Plaster dust spurted out in big puffs of white smoke every time the bucket landed, smashing the walls inexorably into still more rubble.

Wood beams, wire, and chunks of concrete and stone littered the site. Three enormous dump trucks stood in a row ready to receive their loads. The interior walls of the rooms in the hotel had been painted in no particular scheme. I could see every imaginable color now exposed to the cerulean sky. The gray concrete became a kind of painter's base from which the blue, pink, yellow, beige, and ochre walls rose in shattered, irregular peaks and craters.

I'd been watching the destruction of some of my boyhood memories for several weeks. The city council wanted our college to remain downtown and since they'd already decided that the problem of rising street crime was centered in this particular block, it was a marriage made in heaven, or at least in city council chambers. Destruction of the block dispersed the criminals concentrated there to other areas of the city and made space for the erection of an administrative tower and specialized classrooms for City College. The original architecture of the block was a series of commercial buildings, most built around nineteen hundred. They exhibited the vagaries of vision of each builder or architect, so we had an uncoordinated mélange of two-, three- and four-story facades, in almost every architectural style, or pseudo-style in vogue, at the time of construction. Even in its rundown later years, the block presented a visual feast. Unfortunately it also presented feasts for other senses. Many illegal.

I wondered how Mathew Jellicoe, our eminent professor of business, felt, walking past the destruction every day to his office. He'd risen on more than one occasion in faculty and all-college meetings to protest the location of the new administrative tower and thus the destruction of the existing buildings. It was about the only time we saw him at such gatherings.

The hotel had, at various times, sheltered commercial travelers, tradesmen and even hard-working ladies of the night. Over a period of years, as the buildings sank slowly into the morass of slumness, those businesses that leased space, or entire buildings, came to have questionable value to the city. Several seedy bars had located in the block. It was rumored that substances other than alcohol were readily available within their walls. The bars were interspersed with theaters sporting gaudy, brightly lit marquees that advertised an endless succession of films that would never be nominated for Academy Awards. There were bookstores housing coin-operated video machines and selling magazines that catered to all the incredible fantasies of which the human mind is capable, frequently of a sexual nature. The block seemed to breed crime the way rats breed disease. Day or night, there'd be one or two patrol cars parked at the curb while officers dealt with the latest outrage. I looked over my shoulder at Micky, still editing his press release, and then back to the street.

Men in bright blue or yellow hard plastic safety helmets scuttled about the base of the big crane. They dragged pieces of cable and other objects into untidy piles. A huge steam-driven ram in one corner methodically smashed through thick chunks of concrete slab. Grimy dust rose over the scene. I'd observed that with crane and bulldozer, the wrecking crew pushed rubble over here and made big or little piles of other rubble over there. At times they seemed to be just messing about. The scene brought to mind small boys playing in a very large sandbox.

Discernible pattern or not, I knew that in time the trash would disappear and a paved lot would temporarily ease parking problems downtown. Inevitably, the lot would attract a certain patron. This would be a parking lot where hands containing small envelopes of white powder and other hands holding paper bills would extend from automobile windows. The hands would touch briefly as their cars paused, to make transfers that would help some individuals exchange their present hell of life on the street for the hell of the addict. Then the lot would be dug up again when the construction of Trammel's tower began, assuming a successful capital fund drive was completed.

Wind blew down Hennepin Avenue in random billows, like the passing of giant unseen feet. It stirred up dust and sent it ballooning into the air. The dust coated surrounding buildings and added more streaks to Micky's window. No, I didn't like fall in this place, and I didn't care for the 'progress' happening across the street.

"Well, whaddaya think?" Micky Nelson's high voice cut into my reverie. I turned and he handed me his edited piece. I scanned the single page again.

"I think it will fly." I went back to the window. "I hope no one thinks this murder is somehow significant except to the victim and his family. If we don't let it get out of hand maybe it'll go down as just another senseless killing of an individual who happened to be a student at this college. I realize I sound insensitive, Mick, but the college doesn't need a big scandal right now."

"What if the killer turns out to be someone here at City College?"

"So long as the motivation was personal, or the killer was deranged, we'll be all right, I think. But if Jamison or the killer, for that matter, turns out to be somebody important...." I shrugged. "Micky, how about adding a paragraph that says college officials are still checking Jamison's background and we'll have more information in a few days. Maybe that'll deflect any impertinent questions for the time being. Time is on our side. Try to work in something about our heavy adult student population, which is why there are fewer facts, other than the basics."

"Good idea," he responded, "I'll add that and get it next door." He threw his thumb over his shoulder in the direction of the presidential suite. Just then someone knocked on the door.

The President was ready to see me.

CHAPTER 5

*We consider it absolutely necessary
that you should make some public statement–*

Arthur Trammel, President of City College, sat behind his massive desk, watching me cross his rich green carpet. The desk had been donated by somebody, a grateful alumnus, I guess. If he hadn't been so big the desk would have dominated the room and dwarfed the man. Our President stood over six feet six inches in height and must have weighed over two hundred and fifty pounds when he was in his prime. Now he weighed more than three hundred and possessed a truly massive belly. His flabby jowls shook whenever he moved. We all expected him to have a heart attack at any moment. There was even a rumor that someone had started an office pool on how the medics would get him out of the building when the inevitable heart attack laid him low. Ah, the sweet, high-minded, academic world.

Behind his high polished dome and all that flesh, President Trammel possessed an incisive, well-trained mind. He'd studied the classics in England, at Oxford, if I recalled correctly, and he'd had a distinguished career as a professor. Then he moved on to academic administration where his rise had been meteoric. Now, here he was, a decade into his reign as our beloved president, facing the twilight of his career. But that was history. For years, his ego, almost as large as his corporeal self, had blinded him to the more obvious problems of his administration, such as my dysfunctional and incompetent predecessor. The more subtle and convoluted actions of certain of his administrators apparently also went unnoticed. He'd always been sheltered by his ego and by our adoring alumni. His ideas were on the money just often enough, as successive heads of our faculty union were able to testify. The present staff had evolved a series of coping strategies, a precise gavotte of damage control when the president got too far out on a limb.

President Trammel also fancied himself something of an amateur thespian, having indulged himself in theater at graduate school. He liked me because of my interest in theater, and we frequently wasted time talking about what he'd like to do on the stage after retirement, now within sight of his increasingly restricted vision.

I occasionally envisioned him as Sir John Falstaff in Shakespeare's King Henry plays, especially when Falstaff was played as a complete buffoon.

My advantage was translated into an occasional series of onerous events when I was required to explain to him that the staff had ignored yet another of his directives, because it would have disrupted some significant function of the college. A messenger from reality, that was me. Now I feared I was in trouble. I was about to refuse a direct request. In the past, such refusals had been tantamount to professional suicide for other administrators.

"Sit. Sit, Marston," he roared. He almost always roared. One of the marvelous things left about the man was his voice, basso-profundo with a vengeance. He should have been in grand opera in the 'thirties. He glanced out the corner window after I entered, looking toward the site where, if his current vision was realized, a great glistening monument to higher education and Arthur Trammel–the Arthur Trammel Central Administrative Tower–would rise above the rubble of Urban Renewal Project D.

His great, high-backed chair creaked and groaned in protest

as he slowly swiveled around until he stared at me across the polished oak football field that masqueraded as his desktop.

"Marston, I'm going to save you some time here. I know what you intend to say. You want to say that there is no way you can find the time to do a decent investigation of Jamison. And, you are going to add that it is because you received a bigger part in "Enemy of the People" than you anticipated. Then you are going to tell me that you weren't hired by the college to be a police liaison, and so on and so on." He stopped, drew in a breath, and continued to stare at me.

Christ! I couldn't believe it. I had just heard my semi-prepared speech issue forth from my esteemed president's mouth, a speech I hadn't even thought about in any detail until I was crossing the street from my building to this one.

"Ahhh, Dr. Trammel...I, ahh...."

Trammel watched me squirm. God, I'd almost called him President Trammel. It would have been a sure clue he had me backing up. Then he said, "You are also about to tell me you've worked too hard and too long to rebuild student and faculty trust in your office and to repair the damage done by your predecessor, to get involved in this unfortunate occurrence. Your arguments have considerable merit. Nevertheless, I cannot accept your refusal, although under normal circumstances, I would consider it."

My arguments? I hadn't said anything!

"You are, as usual, accurate and cogent. However, there are times when one is called upon to go beyond the reasonable, when one must respond, as it were, to a higher call."

I didn't believe what I was hearing. We were only talking about keeping tabs on the police investigation and fending off the media so they didn't blow an unfortunate murder into the sensation of the year, weren't we?

With scarcely a pause for breath, my president rolled

ponderously on.

"I know there are those here at City College who believe that Arthur Trammel has lost his administrative skill and that our only concern these days is for the successful conclusion of our plan to break ground in the next fiscal year." He waved a big hand at the window in a grand gesture. He had this annoying habit of referring to himself in the third person when it pleased him to do so. It so pleased him far too often for my taste.

"Marston, I know your record and I know what you have done for student services in this college. We needn't review ancient history."

He paused, breathing hard. I rose and walked to the window. Being president of this urban college, I noticed, didn't get you cleaner windows.

"Marston, I have to tell you in the strictest confidence that this task I am assigning to you has another dimension. It is so sensitive a dimension that I cannot reveal, even to you, what that is. Our objective is for you to assist the police force in their task, and to do it in such a way that they will complete their investigation quickly, calling as little attention to City College as possible. By so doing we should have few if any negative problems regarding the ongoing thrust of our capital campaign. I want you to be the college's principal contact with the authorities and to assist them in every way with their investigation. I want you to be with them whenever they find it necessary to come here and interview staff or faculty. The fact is, you are the only one in this entire college whom I trust to do this job, and to be discreet about it." He waved his meaty hands dramatically.

I didn't voice my immediate reaction, a line from "Love's Labors Lost." 'He draweth out the thread of his verbosity finer than the staple of his argument.' I stood with my back to him, staring out the window. I was turning around with another argument I had just conjured up when I realized that all activity in the renewal block had stopped and the machines were shut down. It was early afternoon and it wasn't unusual for them to quit then, but the dozen or so workers weren't leaving. They were standing in a cluster beside a dark hole, perhaps a door, in what was left of an interior wall of the old hotel.

A blinking blue light traveling up the street caught my attention. A police car made a run along Hennepin. It turned into the cross street, Seventh Avenue, a block away. Then it swung immediately into the open gate in the high chain link fence that surrounded the site. There must have been an accident. The driver parked beside the idle crane and got out. When the officer approached the knot of demolition workers one of them pointed at the hole. The cop bent at the waist and peered in, unhooking something from his belt.

"Marston?" Trammel sounded impatient. His voice had shifted from that intriguing almost-plea to his more usual peremptory tone. He wanted an answer and he wanted it yesterday, as usual.

"Excuse me, President–Dr.–Trammel. There seems to have been an accident across the street."

"What?" he roared. He lunged to his feet and waddled across the office. I moved aside at the big window to give him room. His interest was understandable. Any real or perceived threat to his current project drew immediate attention.

Around his big shoulder I saw other cars arriving. Some blue and whites had their lights flashing. Curiously, none of the vehicles was going very fast, nor was there any agitated movement around the opening in the wall. From several of the sedans, police officers stepped out and went to peer into the dark hole. Two uniforms moved the workers farther away. Another started unrolling a spool of bright yellow plastic ribbon. The ones that said DO NOT CROSS and CITY POLICE SITE. And sometimes, CRIME SCENE. CRIME SCENE ribbons sealed the doors to the theater lobby, just down the street. Two paramedics stepped out of an ambulance. One unloaded gear from the rear, the other went into the hole. A minute later he backed out again.

The medical examiner's black station wagon rolled into the block and stopped beside the ambulance. The policemen and the workers stood in a shifting knot, obviously discussing the event with some intensity. I could see policemen doing something that looked like writing. I turned back into the office as Trammel waddled back to his throne. The chair protested again as he eased his black-clad bulk onto the dented leather-covered padding.

"I don't like it, Marston. What's going on out there? The situation is getting out of control." I held up a hand, forestalling more oration.

"It's probably nothing, some poor homeless soul who got into the site looking for shelter and died of exposure. I'll check with the authorities and let you know. It seems appropriate, since I have this new title of official police liaison." Trammel looked keenly at me and I thought he was going to call me on the sarcasm I couldn't keep out of my voice, so I rushed ahead. "I'm already assembling background on Jamison so we don't encounter any more surprises."

"I'll give you a memo, Marston. Shift some of your routine work to others or delay it." He nodded with satisfaction as I left, but he didn't thank me. He knew, of course, that I had spent some time as a field investigator in criminal investigations with the Navy. I supposed that was why he and Marsh had chosen me.

On the way out, I stopped in Nelson's office again. "Micky, I'd appreciate it if you'd drop that part about college officials investigating the boy's background. We don't want anyone thinking we're doing the police's job. Just say that he was murdered and that he won an award last year, that the authorities are investigating and to call them for progress reports." I turned to leave, then stopped at the door.

"Did you see that the police have cordoned off part of the work site across the street?"

"What!" Micky came half out of his chair.

"Yeah. The only thing I can imagine that would cause them to do that is if someone found a body. Why don't you check it out and let me know what's up." Crossing Hennepin back to my office, I considered walking over there to see what I could learn, but decided Micky could handle it.

Questions kept bubbling up. Why this special concern about Jamison? Who'd want to murder a student? Except for the coincidence of the missing data from our computer, Jamison's death might turn out to be the tragic consequence of city living. The missing data coupled with Trammel's reference to something special linked to Jamison made the whole thing a little strange. At that moment, I had no inkling just how strange.

CHAPTER 6

*But there is life here–there is promise–
there are innumerable things to fight for*

Back in my office I asked Teresa to locate Alissa Constant, Dean of Adult Continuing Education. She'd been a member of various awards committees, possibly the one that made the award to Stuart Jamison. If I was right, she might have a copy of his student file.

Teresa walked into my office and shrugged.

"Dean Constant is gone, out of town, apparently."

"Due back when?"

Another shrug. "Two weeks at the earliest and as usual, nobody knows where she is."

I sighed. "Rats. Okay, call Talbot and get somebody to bring Alissa's master keys down. I'll have to go into her office." Teresa nodded and went out.

The dean never seemed to tell anyone at the college where she went on these semi-annual disappearances. She wasn't exactly secretive, just close-mouthed.

Dean Constant's office was on the fourth floor, almost directly below mine. I didn't like the idea of going into her office but time was important and we were moving into crisis mode. She was a private person and insisted on keeping her office locked whenever she wasn't in it. I assumed her files would also be locked, but I didn't think that would be a barrier. We had a long-standing rule that at least one extra key for every lock in the college was filed with our audiovisual director who was responsible for the various office spaces we leased.

Teresa poked her head in again. "Someone will bring Dean Constant's keys down."

"Any idea how soon?"

"Within the hour was mentioned as a probability."

I nodded, deep in a report of data on student disruptions, lack of academic progress by the miscreants, and their involvement, if any, with student counseling services. Some graduate student or other from the big university across town was always doing research on our activities and writing the inevitable report.

I dictated a memo to the student author suggesting she show it to her psychology department head. I gave the disk to Teresa, then went off to find Lori Jacobs for coffee.

"Hi, honey." Her sunny smile when I walked into her office immediately lifted my spirits.

"How're you doing?" I smiled back, absorbing her attractiveness. The faintest hint of some subtle perfume crossed the threshold of my awareness. Every time I saw her I was reminded of my good fortune that this intelligent woman was interested in me. I sometimes wondered how long I could manage to retain her interest.

Lori shrugged noncommittally in response, her straight auburn hair worn unfashionably long, shimmered in and out of the pale light from the window. Today she wore some kind of loose-fitting, shimmery peach blouse, with a large floppy bow at the collar.

"Are you free for coffee downstairs? For a little private chat?" The college maintained a small staff lounge with coffee pots and vending machines on the second floor, but it was almost always busy and there'd be several people at the big round tables we'd acquired from a hotel sale. There was a Tex-Mex restaurant in the basement offering decent food at only slightly inflated prices. On the plus side, the place stayed open late in the afternoon to accommodate the college and they served good, fresh, coffee all day long and until our evening classes were finished. Lori raised her eyebrows and switched off her cell phone which she placed in her desk. She rose from her chair to follow me to the door.

CHAPTER 7

*It is one of those beliefs that are
put into circulation in the world.*

Downstairs, I picked up two big ceramic mugs of black coffee and dropped some change on the counter for Bruno, the afternoon counterman. Lori continued on, choosing a booth against the back wall of the place. It was out of the sunlight that filtered in from the windows over the long cascade of steps leading down from street level to the restaurant. I put down the mugs and slumped onto the opposite bench.

The restaurant owners hadn't bothered to do much to decorate the basement when they opened the place. Its ambience was what it was. The walls were bare brick with lumpy, random pieces of concrete sticking out. The lumps were mixed with voids of various sizes and shapes where stones from the aggregate had fallen or been pried out. A row of big rough-poured square concrete pillars marched down the center of the single room. A thin plasterboard partition separated the kitchen and the wait stations from the tables and booths. Tables and benches were darkly stained and thickly coated with glossy urethane. The whole effect gave rise to the restaurant's unofficial name, the Caves. Only a few booths were occupied.

Lori looked up from under her bangs when I put down the coffee. A sonnet fragment came to mind, so I quoted it. "Thy gift, thy tables, are within my brain, Full character'd with lasting memory, which shall above that idle rank remain..."

"Meaning what?"

"I guess it means I think you look great among these tables."

Lori laughed aloud. "Some scholar you are. Well, how is our hard-working savior of student souls and purveyor of sundry helpful services?"

"I've had better days. How 'bout you?"

"Similar answer," she said, reaching for her coffee. "How 'bout those Vikings?"

I made a face at her and let one finger trail over her wrist. "I have just been through an arm-twisting across the street. A new task I don't relish in the least."

"Ah," she teased, tasting her coffee. "And what, pray tell, can this new task be? Seems to me you're pretty involved with the play right now."

"A. T. wants me to front for the college with the police while they investigate Stuart Jamison."

"Trammel does? For whom? Oh, Stuart Jamison, the student who was murdered. Oh, Jack, that's too bad. Unless they find the killer quickly, you could waste a lot of time with this. Trammel must know you already have plenty to do. Why you? Why didn't he pick on Micky, for heaven's sake?"

"Interesting questions. Or Marsh, for that matter. Something's going on, because even before Trammel called me in, Marsh was in my office practically pleading with me to agree to do it. I have this niggling feeling they are going to want more than just occasional contact with the cops."

"Do you think they're going to want you to conduct an investigation of your own? Whatever for?"

"I think you've called it, and I don't know why they want me."

"Well, sweetie, if this is your first interview, forget it. I don't think I ever even met Stuart Jamison, much less had him as a client in the counseling center, and I sure don't have an inkling why someone would want to murder him." She cocked her head in thought. "Do we know if the murder is even connected to the college? This could be a problem for you if you're pressed to do an internal investigation. It could have a negative effect on the gains you've made here about attitudes toward your office. But why the games? Marshall and the President should be up-front with their concerns."

"Maybe I'll get lucky. Alissa Constant was on the math award committee. She might have everything I need on Jamison."

"Isn't she out of town?"

"Apparently."

"I think it's interesting that she never says where she was. No pictures, no little tales of things that happened. Nothing."

I nodded. "Last summer I asked her point blank about her trip, but all I got was a smile and a vague geographic reference. 'Oh, out West,' or something like that."

Lori laughed. "Maybe Personnel knows where she goes."

"Good luck getting anything out of them," I said. "Our personnel officer has a thing about privacy."

"Such gossips we're becoming. There is one thing about the good dean that could help you, Jack. You know she seems to be available for almost every special task force and committee that comes along."

"You're right. Particularly search committees for new hires."

Lori looked at me. "Hey," she said. "If Alissa's out of town won't you have to wait until she gets back?"

I shook my head. "No. I'm going to her office later when Anita Talbot sends me the keys."

"Jack, I think that's a mistake. There's got to be a better way to get what you need."

One of Lori's attitudes that I admired a lot was her forthright approach to life. She was always direct and straightforward, had little patience for political games. It was probably because she matured early and went through an unpleasant adolescence coping with horny boys. Her family fortunately recognized her fine mind and supported her developing sense of self, including her college aspirations. The rising feminism of the nineteen-sixties, and the encouragement of some of her teachers, led her to counseling as a vocation. Now at thirty-six this trim career woman had forged solid dual careers.

In addition to teaching at City College and supervising the student psychological counseling service, Lori maintained an active professional practice with a private counseling clinic in Minneapolis. Most of the problems she handled there manifested themselves in sexual dysfunction, although she also dealt with child and family abuse situations. It seemed pretty grim to me, but she retained a wonderful sense of humor which, she insisted, helped keep her sane.

"I'll tell you something else that's odd," I went on. "Jamison is–or was–a math wizard and, I gather, something of a computer buff besides. Do you remember talk last year that Jamison was showing other students stuff about computer hacking? How to break security barriers, that kind of thing?" Lori nodded. "I don't know yet if anyone really investigated, or if they did, what they found out. But when we went to look at his records, they were erased."

"Erased? Do you mean someone went in and deliberately cleared out his records? What, everything?" The small frown-crease that I loved to kiss appeared between her eyebrows. She looked up from her coffee and stared into my eyes.

"That's the main reason I'm willing to go into Alissa's office. Fred Coper tells me the back-up was erased at the same time as the primary, apparently without anyone even realizing it had happened."

Lori reached out and touched my fingers. We were still finding our way together and neither of us wanted to create a lot of gossip. We avoided physical displays in public. I appreciated her gesture of sympathetic support.

"Someone must have inserted a trap-door or virus in the system," she mused. I nodded.

"Poor Fred. He's already in trouble with the college ethics committee over that soft-porn graphics program he imported. Now there'll be all sorts of new accusations, won't there?"

"I suppose so, although I don't think he's to blame for the erasures. Fred seems genuinely puzzled about how they happened. He's asked admin council to discuss the question of higher security levels several times in the past year."

"Well, there are all the old records. You'll just have to root through the stuff in the attic." She grinned. "Of course no one goes up there very often, so I bet you won't find much. All you'll do is mess up your nice suit." Her grin widened.

"Dammit," I groused. "Why me?"

"Rotten timing, too," Lori went on. "D'you suppose this will affect the building fund drive? Is that why Trammel wants you to investigate, or whatever it is you're doing? That's it, isn't it? He hopes you'll help get the job done quickly so the whole thing is smoothed over with a minimum of bad publicity. Save the fund drive. Save Trammel's erection." She waved in the direction of the construction site.

"Something seems to have happened over there this morning. While I was with Trammel, the police arrived. It looked like they found a body in the rubble."

"God," Lori shook her head and put down her coffee mug. "More problems."

I finished my coffee, careful to leave the inevitable grounds in the bottom of the mug. "So, that's how my day has been, how's yours, so far?"

Lori shrugged, reacting to the somber news of another possible death. "No major problems, thankfully. We have our normal load of students with anxiety or paranoia, a drinking problem or two, and our usual clients at the clinic. At the moment, our client load and our resources dovetail rather nicely.

"Classes are going smoothly, too. I have a super bunch of students this fall in both general and abnormal psych. Here's a bit of gossip," she smiled. "You understand, this is a long way from original research. I got it from one of the counseling associates, who apparently heard it from a student worker. She apparently overheard Anita Talbot."

I waggled a hand at her. She smiled and said, "Yes, I know, but it's just that this is so out of character from my picture of Professor Jellicoe."

"So tell me," I nodded.

"Anita was complaining that Jellicoe hasn't returned video equipment he had on loan. It's way overdue." She stopped and looked at me expectantly.

"And?" I prompted her.

"And? That's it! Don't you get it?"

I shook my head.

"Think about it! Of all the people at the college, who comes instantly to mind as someone you would never expect to be interested in television, much less video recording equipment? My vote would be old Jellicoe. I don't think he even has a desktop computer."

"Ahh. You think this is a clue?"

"A clue? To what? Where's your head?" she smirked. "There's no scandal here, this is just a bit of gossip about a colleague. It isn't even juicy."

I smiled at her. "I get it. It is interesting, because, of course, you're right. Who would suspect Jellicoe of even knowing that camcorders or cell phones exist?"

Lori looked at her watch and slid out of the booth. "I've gotta run," she said. "Department meeting in a few. Does this new assignment mean I don't have to read you your cues? Are you coming over tonight? Do. I'll try to take your mind off your troubles. And you can tell me all about what you found when you burgled Alissa Constant's office."

I smiled up at her. "An offer too tempting to refuse. I just don't know exactly when. What time are you planning to eat supper?"

She laughed her low, sexy laugh. "I love the way you manage to get that in. Supper is it? Well, we'll see. Serve you right if I just order in some pizza. Jack," she said then in a serious tone, "save some time for us, just me and thee. Not just tonight, but over the next few weeks, okay?"

Before I could respond, she flipped her fingers at me and sailed off in that long-legged, loose gait of hers, with a slightly exaggerated hip-wiggle for my private benefit. While I watched, I considered her parting remark. We hadn't been a couple long enough so that oblique remarks were usually interpreted correctly.

I got another cup of coffee and carried it back to my office. Constant's keys had been delivered with the usual stern reminder that they were checked out to me personally. I should not relinquish them to anyone else on pain of death or dismemberment. I took the keys and walked to the elevator.

Our building had been built long before secure office space became common parlance. The layout of the building contributed to problems of security. All the offices were built around the outside of the building. In the center, surrounding the central elevator shaft, was the marble-floored hallway. Two back-to-back stairways were built at one end of the building, so you couldn't walk entirely around the shaft. The stairs opened on every floor through separate doors so it was possible to travel up or down without encountering other tenants. But sometimes, when the building was quiet, you could hear footsteps in the stairwells. Creepy. The stairway fire doors to each floor were left unlocked during the day. Anyone off the street clever enough to figure it out could walk up or down to any floor, unless the security guard happened to be in the right place. One stairwell opened into the lobby, the other onto an alley beside the building. More than once a secretary had looked up from her terminal and found a tattered stranger silently watching from the hall. The hallways were not well lit. In many of the suites, there were interconnecting doors so one could go from office to office without using the hall. Only a few of the suites had locks on their interior doors so privacy was at a premium.

    The elevator seemed to have stopped running so I turned to the stairway. I jingled the ring of keys in my hand. Somehow it made my slow trip down the lonely stairs more pleasant. I wondered if I could tell Lori about Trammel's odd remark regarding some kind of secret connected to the murdered student. I wanted to. I wondered about the commotion at the destruction site. Another body linked to the college? Trammel would be seething. I realized my discomfort over what I was about to do was part of my hesitancy. I also wondered, as I went slowly down the empty hallway to Constant's office suite, if my role in Ibsen's drama of civic responsibility versus economic well-being was an omen.

CHAPTER 8

You must not misjudge me

Alissa Constant's secretary looked up from his book as I walked into thc CE suite. I imagined he had little to do right now with Alissa on leave and registration for winter quarter still a couple of weeks away. I smiled at him and continued across the room toward the inner office door. This corner suite was much like mine two floors above, although Dean Constant's outer office was smaller. It had always seemed ludicrous that admissions and other student services were near the top of this building and curriculum and the dean's offices were on the first and second floors, but I wasn't in charge, was I?

"She's not in, Dean Marston," said her secretary. He was a relative newcomer, or he wouldn't have called me Dean.

"I know that. I have a key." I didn't stop or turn around.

"Gee, Dean…er, Mr. Marston, Dean Constant gave me strict instructions not to let anyone in her office when she's gone." He cracked his gum for punctuation.

"I understand that, but this is an emergency. We need an important file she may have and we can't wait for her return." I had the door open and the lights on even as I threw my voice over my shoulder at the boy. He hadn't moved except to look up at my intrusion.

"Yes sir," he replied, cowed by my peremptory tone. Then he came to Alissa's door to follow me with his washed-out blue eyes.

I surveyed Alissa's desk.

Alissa Constant was a neat person. So neat that her office looked almost unused. No papers on her desk, only a brass bankers' lamp with its green-glass shade, a telephone and a black-handled letter opener, all in a precise arrangement. The office smelled slightly musty, as if it had been shut up for several days.

An impressive bank of matched tan metal five-drawer file cabinets filled the wall opposite the windows. They were standard-issue. I had a couple in my own office. These were unusual only because they all had locks and no labels on any of the drawers. With my occasional nasty turn of mind, I wondered if they even had files in them. I turned to her desk. It was also a standard-issue, large, double-pedestal type, with a fake wood-grained top. I sat down in her high-backed chair, also standard-issue, and pulled at the lap drawer. It didn't budge. I frowned up at the gum-chewing boy still watching me calmly from the door. He didn't dress much like a secretary, I thought irrelevantly; tight faded jeans and an oversized wide-striped shirt open at the neck.

"She always keeps it locked, and I don't have the key," he said in a quiet voice.

"I think I can solve that," I said, shaking the small ring of keys in my right hand. "You can go back to your book. I promise I won't bother the rest of her stuff."

I wasn't all that sure I had her desk key. If Constant's passion for privacy and security was strong enough, her desk key could have deliberately gone missing from the master key file. None of the keys I had fit the desk. I looked at the boy in the doorway, down at the desk and then back at him. If I had to force the lock I didn't want anyone looking on. After a moment he got my silent message and returned to his desk, just out of my line of vision.

Alissa Constant's desk had the usual locking arrangement. The lap drawer controlled the other drawers. It was a convenient situation for the errant desk-rummager like me, because I only had to force the one lock. Often with these desks, a small amount of downward pressure would separate the latch from…ah, there it went. I slid the drawer open, pleased that I hadn't had to resort to prying. Not being skilled at B & E, I might have wrecked the drawer. Besides, I didn't have a pry bar handy. The drawer still moved smoothly, so I hadn't bent anything.

The lap drawer contained the usual collection of miscellany, although her collection was better organized than mine.

On the left side of the desk was the double drawer that served as a small file cabinet. I pulled it open and skidded back until I could read the labels on the files. Most of them were run-of-the-mill, just what one would expect to find in the office of the Dean of Adult Continuing Education. But others carried the names of members of the college community. Here was Anton Marshall, our African-American Vice-president, Professor Mathew Jellicoe, small, fussy, a local man who got his Ph.D. at Princeton and now headed our economics department. Headed, right. He had the most awful wig or dye job I'd ever seen.

Here too was a file on Professor Emma Tidwell, our resident star, internationally renowned scholar, educated in the Ivy League, and professor of Victorian literature. A nice, brilliant, unmarried lady. Then I felt a tiny shiver run down my neck. There was a folder with Lori Jacob's name on it, and another with my name.

"Well well," I thought to myself, "What is this about?" Then I hit pay dirt. Behind Lori's file was another file with Stuart Jamison's name neatly lettered on the label. I pulled it out. It held several sheets of paper, and a quick glance verified I would find at least some of what I needed. I set Jamison's file aside. Now, I considered, was I going to look at those other files? I hesitated and then shrugged. In for a penny….

I plucked out the file on my sometime racquetball opponent, Anton Marshall. It held a single sheet of paper. On the paper, a neatly typed column of numbers, about thirty in all. I replaced the folder.

I checked some of the others. In Lori Jacob's file, the same, a single sheet of bond paper on which was typed a column of numbers and a few capital letters. I did note that some of the numbers were identical to those in my file, though not in the same order. This must be some kind of private code.

Professor Jellicoe's file was the same, except there were many more numbers in two columns on three sheets of paper and the file folder looked older than the others. I went back to Jamison's file. Yes, there was a sheet with a short list of numbers and letters here too. I reached for the Tidwell file and the phone rang. I must have lost five years off my life and I dropped Tidwell's file on the floor. My stomach did a flip-flop and the phone rang again. I heard the boy in the front office pick up. His voice was low so I couldn't make out the words, just the rise and fall of his tone. There was a short silence, broken abruptly by a sharp expletive and a clatter as he dropped the phone. Then nothing.

I grabbed the fallen file and went to the connecting door. The receiver lay on the desk emitting that peculiar series of pulsing sounds the telephone company inserts to warn of a handset not properly placed in its cradle. The secretary sat staring at the desk, mouth open. He was white in the face.

"What?" I said sharply.

My voice jarred him back to functionality and he looked up at me.

"It…It's Aliss…Dean Constant." He swallowed. "She's dead."

"Alissa? Good God! What happened?"

The boy gulped and said, "I don't know. That…that was Anita Talbot. She said they found Dean Constant across the street. Dead!" His voice rose to a squeak and he began to breath raggedly, gulping air like a fish. He put the phone back together and stood up abruptly.

"I…I, I gotta…I'll be right back. Sorry." He sobbed and lurched out the door, heading, presumably, for a bathroom.

Across the street? A sudden image of the police, the ambulance, and the form that had been taken from the ruined building flashed through my mind. The phone rang again. I grabbed it.

"What!" Not the best phone etiquette, but it got the job done.

"Jack? Jack Marston, is that you?" The voice was Micky Nelson's. "Tracked you down, didn't I?" His small triumph, apparently. "Listen, have you heard about Constant? What are you doing in her office, anyway?"

"Never mind that, what happened?"

"Well," Nelson replied, "we just got a call from the hospital. They've identified the body. From the demolition site this morning?"

"I just heard. Do you know how it happen?"

"Don't know anything else. I just thought you oughta know as soon as possible. I was with Trammel when the call came from the PD. I thought he'd explode. He told me to reach you right away."

We agreed this latest calamity was more of the kind of publicity the college didn't need and that Constant would be missed and broke the connection. The boy returned from the bathroom with beads of water in his eyebrows and I returned to Constant's desk. New questions raced through my mind. Why had the president wanted me to know about Constant right away? Did he think there was a connection to Jamison? I didn't like the implications.

I stared at the half-closed desk drawer. Subconsciously I had already decided what my next move would be. I also knew it was a bad idea that would trouble me for a long time. The staff files in Alissa's office were coded. I couldn't think of a single good reason for that. What secrets did they hold? I sighed and pulled all sixteen files from the drawer and bundled them under my arm. Then I forced the lap drawer back in place so it locked the desk and went back upstairs. I could tell the news of Constant's death was all over the place already from the murmurs and whispered conversations.

Back in my office, I looked around. I stuck the files I had retrieved from Alissa's desk under an untidy pile of other files on my side table and scratched my nose. Maybe I'd get lucky. Maybe the police wouldn't realize there were files missing. Maybe they wouldn't care. Sure. I looked out the window. The block across the street had changed little. There were still the piles of multi-colored rubble and the machines and men, pushing, dragging, and gouging. They were back at work now, ignoring the fluttering yellow police tapes that isolated the hole in the ruined wall of the hotel where Constant's body had been discovered.

Alissa Constant and I had never been what you'd call friends, but we had known each other as colleagues for the six years she'd been at City College. Her death touched me in ways I would not have expected. Jamison, on the other hand, I'd maybe met once or twice, so his death meant practically nothing on a personal level.

I remembered one of the last times I had talked with Alissa. It was at a meeting, one of those endless, frequent meetings which seem to take up more and more of our time at the college. A city representative had reviewed one more time the steps that remained before City College received title to Block D. He had just offered yet again to arrange a tour of the most notorious buildings in the block, the old hotel and adjacent bar. Several members of the vice president's council had promptly agreed it would be worthwhile.

I, almost as promptly, had suggested, with a large amount of sarcasm, that a tour wasn't necessary. Not necessary, that is, unless we were going to consider preserving the old hotel to be our first student dormitory. That led to another irreverent thought which I unfortunately also expressed. I hadn't wanted the old buildings torn down and everybody there knew it. So people weren't surprised when I suggested an alternative to the dormitory idea was to use the hotel as a source of revenue for the college. I believe I may even have made some passing, tongue-in-cheek, reference to the hot pillow trade.

There were snickers. Others had taken offense, including Professor Mathew Jellicoe. I recalled this committee was one of the few he sat on, and he never missed a meeting. From the beginning he'd been dead set against taking that block for the new tower. Now I saw him again in my mind, shifting back and forth in his seat so the slanting rays of the sun flashed through the hair on his head. We all had seen the reddish-green highlights when that happened. I remember thinking he looked like his head was generating a dichroic fog.

Alissa Constant had laid into me for several minutes, called me reactionary, a cultural snob, male chauvinist and other choice labels, until Marsh, who was chairing the meeting, banged on the table and restored order. A tour was arranged. Marsh agreed to get the word out. Now I wondered if he knew who went and when, because that meeting had taken place ten days ago, just about the time Alissa Constant disappeared.

I sat down at my desk. I pulled Jamison's file toward me, together with the telephone and a fresh tablet of paper.

By the time I closed the office at seven, I'd left four messages on faculty answering machines. I'd also interrupted three dinners and established that Alissa Constant had been on the last tour of the site and that no one remembered seeing her around the college after that. I also found that her file on the award presented to Jamison was helpful, except for the single indecipherable sheet of cryptic letters and numbers.

CHAPTER 9

Money has been flowing in-

Yes, Lori had pizza waiting, warm in the oven, when I arrived at her place in Brooklyn Park. I liked her apartment. She'd had it painted in off-whites with earth-color accents. The rooms seemed to radiate light, lifting my spirits.

I sighed, slouching in my chair. "I don't understand it. Even a frozen pizza tastes better here. Must be your deft touch."

Lori smiled at me over her glass of wine.

"I guess I haven't told you recently, babe. You're the best thing that's happened to me in quite a while. Maybe forever."

"You have said it before, but repetition is always welcome. Would it help to talk about Jamison and Constant?"

Lori was used to dealing with patient confidentiality in her work, so I wasn't hesitant about discussing things with her. Maybe it was a minor violation of my pledge to be discreet. But my leaders, Trammel and Marshall, had stressed discretion, not silence.

"I saw the news story about finding her body. It was a shock."

"Yeah. I didn't care for her attitudes about some things, but she was doing a fine job for the college. I sure hope she didn't suffer."

"Any information on how she died?"

"Nothing yet. I suppose she slipped on some rubble. But I don't see how she was missed if it happened while she was over there with a group and I can't think of a reason why she'd go there alone. My image of Alissa Constant doesn't run to hard hats, work shoes, and dusty jeans.

"I happened to see them discover her body." I added my long distance eyewitness account of that morning's scene.

"Didn't you tell me she went on one of the last tours of the block?"

"Right. The very last. I take it back. I can think of a reason why she might go over there alone. Maybe she went there to meet someone, someone she didn't want to be seen with."

Lori looked at me. "I don't know, Jack. Seems a little far-fetched to me."

Then we hashed and rehashed what I was starting to call the Jamison puzzle. "What baffles me is why someone went to all the trouble of deleting Jamison's computer records," I groused.

"Is it possible no information was ever entered?"

"Well, Fred Coper says the usual screens were set up. I suppose information could have been left out. But in the two years, someone would have noticed and complained. You know, we get those memos every so often requesting missing bits."

Once more during the evening, I had the feeling we were about to turn to more personal topics. But then Lori changed direction, as if she wanted to avoid talking about our relationship in the context of the two deaths.

"I hope this assignment doesn't screw up my credibility with the students and staff."

"In some ways, that's the most disturbing element," Lori said as we cleared the table and started turning out the living room lights.

We walked arm-in-arm to the bedroom door. "You'll have to be careful your role in the play isn't mirrored by real life." Lori smiled and put her fingers on my cheek. "Poor Jack Marston, enemy of the people."

She'd made it clear early on that she would welcome my presence for the night. We were relatively new lovers, still learning our way around each other, physically and emotionally. We went to bed in the big master bedroom. Our unspoken agenda in no way lessened our enjoyment of each other.

There was a stranger in my waiting room when I returned from a coffee break the next morning. I was spending more time than usual in the break room, walking the halls, dropping in on choice gathering spots, and listening or chatting casually with students and staff.

I buzzed Teresa. She came in and closed the door. I cocked an eyebrow in a question. The walls were so thin anyone trying to listen wouldn't have much difficulty overhearing. "Cop," she whispered. I nodded thanks and went to the door.

"Good morning. I'm Jack Marston, director of student services. Can I help you?"

The stranger rose from his chair and pulled a worn leather folder from an inside pocket, which he extended so I could see his badge and ID.

"Good morning, Mr. Marston. I'm detective Swanborg, Minneapolis police department. I'm assigned to the Alissa Constant case. May we talk for a few minutes?"

I gestured to my office and we settled ourselves. I examined the man. He was taller than my six feet plus, and thin. Even his hair was thin, brownish, just this side of mousy. Ordinary looking was the phrase that came to mind. He looked like almost every other male Caucasian in the world. I saw no distinguishing marks. His ordinariness probably came in handy in his line of work. The man looked bone weary tired, as if he'd been working overtime most of his life. I had a sense that he'd seen and heard too much in his time. It was in his dark brown eyes. There was more in those eyes, an alertness, an awareness. Or maybe I was just projecting.

Economy radiated from every gesture. He smiled slightly and opened his dark wool overcoat a little wider. From a breast pocket he produced a small wire-bound notebook and a pen. "How well did you know the dead woman, Alissa Constant?" he began, settling a little deeper into the chair, flipping pages in the notebook.

"Only as a colleague. We didn't socialize, except when we both attended college functions. Even then it was casual."

"Ever have a fight with the woman?"

"Once, in a meeting."

"Tell me about it."

So I told him about the cracks I'd made when the building committee was discussing the old hotel in Block D, and about Alissa's response.

"You do that a lot? Make cracks about serious subjects?"

"Well, Detective Swanborg, I do admit that. I have a tendency to try to lighten the mood from time to time. It's a habit I've acquired."

"Any other bad habits you'd care to admit to?"

I looked at him for a silent moment. "Interesting question. The usual, I expect. My close friends tell me I'm a little nosy, sometimes ask too many questions. Occasionally quote Shakespeare. On the other hand I can keep a confidence and I don't gossip. And, I'm a Vikings fan."

"Probably some of the reasons why you were named police liaison."

"Ah. You know about that."

"I got a briefing before I came over. Get to many games?"

I shook my head. "Watch 'em on the tube. Try to make some Gopher hockey games, though."

"Violent sport, even at the college level," he remarked. "Where were you when the last tour, the one Alissa Constant joined, was taking place?"

"At another meeting. We do a lot of those."

"You didn't want to join the tour?"

"No sir. I've seen that block of buildings off and on for nearly forty years. It's no secret I've objected to this penchant Minneapolis has for indiscriminately tearing down old buildings."

"So even though your remarks might have generated that last tour, you weren't interested in seeing the inside of some of those places."

"That's right, I wasn't."

"Who would you say were Alissa Constant's closest friends here at the college?"

I thought about that. Alissa hadn't been really close to anyone I could come up with at that moment except...

"For instance, what can you tell me about her relationship with a man named Anton Marshall?"

He'd caught me there. The man had obviously been doing his homework. "Almost nothing. In fact Marsh is the only one I can think of who was what you'd call `close' to Dean Constant. She operates...*operated* in one of his primary areas of responsibility, so it's natural they'd spend time together. There'd been talk that linked the two of them romantically, but I wasn't aware of any trouble between them. I supposed they'd have been concerned about the attitudes that always seem to crop up among the lunatic fringe when a black man and a white woman are seen together, even in this day. Why this interest in Alissa's unfortunate death? Is it just because we've had a recent murder?"

He looked at me silently for a moment. "Two murders, Mr. Marston. Dean Constant was hit on the head, a blow that crushed her skull before she was put in that hotel closet where the demolition workers found her."

I stared at him. Murdered? Alissa? Another murder in a couple of days. My breath came faster and I suddenly felt a little queasy. Never mind she wasn't one of my favorite people. Murdered! Great God, Trammel would have a fit.

"I'm a homicide detective, didn't I mention that?"

I recovered slightly. "No, I don't think you did."

Detective Swanborg had several more questions, all of which related to my knowledge of Marshall and Alissa's relationship. It raised my suspicion that the police might be considering Marsh as a suspect.

Then Swanborg said, "You better understand something.

We're perfectly capable of handling the investigations into these murders without outside help. Your superiors and mine have talked and we've agreed to `liaise'. But that doesn't mean you get to play detective. So let's try to keep things on a reasonable plane here. We'll tell you when we're coming and we'll tell you what we can. My chief says you'll get better access during the investigation after we're sure you and your friend Ms. Jacobs aren't involved."

So he knew about Lori and me as well. No slouch, this detective. We were polite and agreed to be as forthcoming as we could manage. But I think we both had reservations. I know I did. I was thinking more like a college representative than a regular citizen. Swanborg left me to my private thoughts and for a time, I got back to routine. It wasn't easy. Jesus, two murders in such a short time. Then I remembered Marshall's words and his tone of voice when he urged me to accept Trammel's charge to handle the police investigation of Jamison for the college. Was there a connection? I tried to call him, but his line was busy.

I hung up and the thing rang. It was the president's secretary requesting my immediate appearance.

I walked into Trammel's office and found that Marshall had preceded me. He nodded and I nodded back. I thought about Alissa and Marsh. Would the police fit him for the murder? Could he do something like that? I'd seen flashes of his temper in the past. Maybe I was biased because of our long friendship, but the image of Marsh as a murderer was preposterous.

The president was visibly upset. His eyes bulged. Beads of perspiration stood out on his prominent forehead and tracked down his fleshy cheeks. He drummed fat fingers on the arm of his chair. He didn't remind me of Falstaff.

After thirty minutes of verbal dancing and some fruitless speculation, Trammel and Marsh came to the point. I'd had an inkling in the last few minutes of the real purpose of this meeting, but I wasn't going easily to the slaughter.

"Jack," said the president with a great sigh. Easy for him,

with all that bulk. "Jack, we called you over here because I have to ask you to add an internal investigation of Dean Constant's demise to your ongoing investigation of the Jamison situation."

Ongoing investigation? Wait a minute! Lori had certainly made the correct call. "Excuse me. My recollection of our earlier conversations didn't include my conducting any investigation! Liaison with the police was the phrase I think we used. Do I have to remind you the police don't look kindly on amateurs messing about in homicide investigations?"

Marshall stuck in an oar. "Jack, we don't expect you to do anything dangerous, but we, President Trammel and I, would feel a lot more comfortable knowing that someone we trust is close to the investigation, that someone with the best interests of the college at heart was keeping abreast of things. We also feel it would help the college and the police if that someone was doing a little independent research." It was a long speech for Marsh. I hadn't missed the glance that passed between him and the president, a glance that suggested an unspoken subtext. Was this more of what the president had mentioned the other day about me having to operate partially blind?

Of course we came to the foregone conclusion. I was designated college liaison with the police on both murders. At the same time, I was specifically directed to do a little discreet investigating on my own. Rats. I returned to my office with the opening scene from Macbeth in my head 'When shall we three meet again in thunder, lightning, or in rain? When the hurly-burly's done, when the battle's lost and won.'

Well, by God, I thought, if I'm to be official campus snoop, I'd better get it in writing. I started roughing out a memo to me from President Trammel. The door opened and Anton Marshall appeared. "I thought we just finished our business, across the street." I looked up at him.

Marshall's face was not exactly grim, but he sure wasn't smiling. "Jack, we have to talk. I want to know what you found in

Constant's office."

I shrugged. Now there was an interesting question. I made one of those spur-of-the-moment decisions. It hadn't come up but I didn't tell Detective Swanborg about the files I'd swiped from Alissa's office and I wasn't going to tell Marshall, either. Not just yet. I'd purloined those coded files and they were my secret for now. "Nothing, really. Just the file on Jamison and the award. `Course, I didn't go over the office with a fine tooth comb, as they say. Should I? I expect the police to seal it at any moment, if they haven't already."

Marshall stared at me. "What was in the Jamison file?"

"Marsh! I just told you, information relating to his award last year. What are you looking for?"

He hesitated. "I…I'm just not sure. I don't know how far to go here."

"Look. It's pretty obvious something is bothering you, but I haven't a clue what it is. And what's the connection with Alissa's office? Why don't you just tell me what's on your mind?"

"I thought I could. Talk to you, I mean. That's why I pushed Trammel to have you look into things instead of hiring a private investigator. That was his original idea. But now, I dunno."

I was surprised. He rarely lapsed into sloppy language. I held up a hand. "Marsh, we've been friends since you arrived, and we've always been straight with each other, but you must realize that when you and Trammel ask me to investigate and liaise, I'm not going to try to thwart the police. I still don't want to do this investigation. I don't even want to be police liaison. It's partly because I might learn some things I'd rather not know about some of my colleagues. That includes you and Trammel. Another reason is my position with students. I've managed to re-establish this office as pro-student and essentially fair, and I think we've been able to keep the problems pretty well in hand. I worry that when it becomes known I'm snooping around, a lot of that trust will erode and I'll be placed in the same group with the rest of you anti-student administrators." I smiled at him but he didn't respond to my needle.

"Jack, it's the first reason I'm concerned about." He hesitated again, looking down at his hands. "I got into some trouble in college…in spite of the football. I was lonely and immature. I guess I'm embarrassed about what you may find out." He looked at the floor and shrugged his big shoulders.

"Two things, my friend. First, whatever I might learn, about you and anyone else, stays with me unless I see a direct connection to the murders." Mentally I was excluding Lori from my promise. I knew I'd need someone to bounce ideas off.

"The second thing is that whatever I learn that's connected to the murders goes to the police. You understand that? But I'm not a gossip and I'm not about to pass on to the police, or anybody else, irrelevant information. Listen, Marsh, it would sure help if you'd explain the undercurrents I'm feeling about Jamison."

There was a long silence. Marsh sighed heavily and got to his feet. "Okay, Jack, I guess I knew that's what you'd say." He turned to the door and then looked back at me. "It's true that I was seeing a lot of Alissa. It's also true we fought sometimes." He stopped.

"Anything else? What about our other small problem?"

"Jamison?" He paused again, then he said, "Nope. I can't say anything else. I don't really know anything else. I just hope we'll still be friends when this is over." With that he strode out of my office.

So do I, I thought, *so do I*. His repeated unwillingness to tell me about Jamison confirmed in a way that there was something odd about the student. But what about Alissa? In spite of our friendship, I knew I couldn't keep Anton Marshall off the list of suspects.

I called the personnel office and requested their file on Alissa Constant. Yes, I knew I could get basic stuff from the computer. Yes, I knew it was against policy to remove files from the office. Yes, I also knew I wasn't supposed to have access to the personnel files of employees of the college except those who reported to me.

"If you people have a problem with my request, call the president, and if you want to do the work for me I will happily accept copies of everything in her file." Everything? Yes, every last little thing. The file arrived thirty minutes later by student messenger.

I intended to take steps to keep certain information from disappearing the way the computer files had gone.

I buzzed Teresa. "Will you run a printout of everything in the computer on Alissa Constant, right away? Fred will give you access to the private material. I want copies of this file as well, just as soon as I read through it. Then send the original back to personnel and lock the copies in my cabinet. If you have any problems, yell."

Alissa Constant had been with City College for six years and her file was thick. President Trammel believed in religiously following the college policy of making annual evaluations of administrative staff, just as we were required to evaluate our departments. I scanned the pages, just to see if anything leaped out at me. Unfortunately, nothing did. Half an hour later, I gave the file to Teresa and turned to my playbook. I needed some time to study my lines. I found my place, a scene between my character, Dr. Stockman, and his brother:

To tell you the truth, Peter, I can't say just at this moment—at all events not tonight. There may be much that is very abnormal about the present conditions—and it is possible there may be nothing abnormal about them at all. It is quite possible it may be merely my imagination.

Yeah, right.

The hours slipped quietly by, and again I was struck by the sounds of activity I heard in the building. Every time the heating system fans shut down, I could hear a coffee maker gurgling, footsteps on the marble floor, windows rattling. Creaks, groans. Was the building ever completely silent?

CHAPTER 10

*I am so heartily happy and
contented, you know.*

Lori and I had a date for Friday evening, which made two evenings in a row. I found myself thinking about marrying again. My first marriage of ten years had ended in a mutually agreed to divorce, after a long period of acrimony. I'd come to believe that I wasn't marriage material. Several aspects of my failed marriage, with the exception of our daughter, a bright, lovely, well-adjusted young woman, now interning with the Justice Department in Washington, D. C., had led me to that conclusion. My semi-addiction to Sunday afternoon pro football was only a minor aspect.

Lori was changing my mind. When I examined our relationship, I discovered that part of my attraction to her was certain similarities to my ex-wife. Both women were intelligent feminists with successful careers, and both, naturally, adored or had adored me.

But of course I am adorable.

Now I was going to dinner at Lori's apartment, and I wondered if tonight we'd have that intimate discussion about our relationship. We were overdue.

I stopped at a small liquor store on Central Avenue I often patronize. George, the owner, waved a big hello when I came through the door. He catered mostly to the beer-and-a-chaser crowd. A few years ago I discovered some Amstel beer in his cooler which he gratefully sold me at a discount since the stock hadn't moved. We got to talking and George began to carry a modest selection of French and German wines plus some of the better California varieties. Now I was after some sauvignon blanc. Lori had told me we were having an exotic fish creation of her own design this evening. She's the better cook, although I know my way around a kitchen. Tonight my responsibility was to bring the wine. I bought two bottles and included a single fresh rose from a bunch on the counter.

I left the store and suddenly shivered when the door slammed shut, though it wasn't cold out. I glanced around but none of the few pedestrians nearby was paying any attention.

Lori lived in an older apartment complexes not far off a main feeder to the freeway system, so, although it was ten miles from our offices, it took only fifteen minutes to get there from the college parking lot. Tonight was special because it would be my last free evening for some weeks, due to the rehearsal schedule for "Enemy of The People." We still had an enormous amount of work to do and opening night loomed inexorably closer. Lori had promised to give me my line cues, at least for the first act, which was all I had memorized.

I arrived to wondrous odors wafting down the hall from the open door of her second-floor apartment. She wasn't inside, but I could hear her laughing voice coming from the place across the hall. I went in and put one bottle of wine in the freezer to chill. Lori disliked really cold wine. Steam rose gently from two pots on the stove. In the refrigerator I found a cold beer which I popped at about the same time my lovely companion returned from next door. Her cool hands slid around my neck just above my loosened collar and her mouth ever so gently touched my cheek.

"Hi, handsome." She says that because I'm not.

"Hi, beautiful," I responded. I say that because she is.

"Hard day at the plant?"

"Aww, shucks, Mabel. You knows we aren't s'posed to call it that. Makes it sound like a factory, or something."

She released me from the soft prison of her arms and slid across my body to check the progress of dinner. I took a swig of beer, my free hand moving in a long gentle caress over her shoulder and back, down to where her hips began their flare. She wore a bulky, fuzzy red sweater which effectively concealed her generous bosom, and tight faded jeans that effectively delineated the curves of her bottom. Her free hand dropped below my belt line and brushed across the front of my slacks in a frank and possessive manner. Then she chuckled.

"What's funny?"

"I was just talking with Dave and Evelyn." She chuckled again. "Jenner, downstairs? His parrot got loose in the back stairwell, apparently all day. When the UPS deliveryman showed up, the parrot squawked and scared the delivery guy. He slipped on the parrot caca, and packages flew everywhere." She laughed out loud. "He didn't get hurt, but Evelyn said it was a pretty funny scene."

Lori lifted the covers from the simmering pots and peered inside. Then she checked the oven.

"Can I make you a drink?" I asked. I turned and adjusted the volume on the Brubeck CD playing on the stereo.

"No, thanks, but do pour the wine. Dinner will be in moments. I have one request."

"As always, you have but to ask."

"For tonight at least, can we leave Jamison and Alissa out of the conversation?"

"Amen to that."

After dinner we relaxed on the large divan in the living room facing the empty fireplace. The orange roughy sautéed and bathed in some sauce of Lori's own creation had been exquisite.

She rarely had a fire. Carrying wood up and ashes down didn't appeal to her sense of neatness. I had offered to fetch and clean, but ever independent, she declined.

Now with wine glass and playbook in hand Lori was reading me my cues from the middle of Act One. After a half-hour of cues and lines, she called a break and went to her bedroom. When she reappeared, she had dressed down for the occasion, bundled in a ratty throat-to-ankle chenille robe firmly belted at the waist. She snatched the playbook from my hand and said in an odd accent, "Okay. I vill cue you now. Is you rrready?" And she launched once more into "Enemy of the People."

"Oh, is it you, Peter? Now that is very delightful."

"Unfortunately I must go in a moment—"

"Rubbish! There is some toddy just coming in. You haven't forgotten the toddy, Katherine?"

"Of course not; the water is boiling now."

For upwards of another hour Lori strode about the room, bellowing cues at me.

"The problem with Ibsen," she complained then, "is that he hated women. Is that why you wanted to play him?"

"Hey, wait now. I'm not playing Ibsen. Ibsen isn't a character in this play." My protest was met with a scornful sneer that would have done any melodrama heroine proud. Then she disappeared down the short hall. My next cue came from the bathroom. I responded. When Lori reappeared at the doorway to the living room, she'd removed the robe and was attired solely in a lacy, red teddy, cut very high on her hips and low across the bodice. I choked and blew my line. She smirked evilly and spun around. The straps fell off her shoulders and she did something at the front of the thing that I couldn't see. Over her bare shoulder she gave me another cue which I remembered. Then she turned around and the teddy fell to her waist. She grinned at me. I grinned back. Another cue. I blew another response.

I reached for her but she backed quickly away, jumped through the bedroom door, and slammed it shut in my face. Through the wood panels I heard,

"Ibsen was a horse's ass!" The door hadn't latched and I pushed it open after a moment's hesitation. Only the small bedside light was on. Lori was on the bed, neither the playbook nor the red teddy anywhere to be seen. I moved toward the bed, unbuttoning my shirt as I went.

CHAPTER 11

*–there are innumerable things
to work for–*

The weekend passed as most of them do for me. I spent a few hours at the college, got some laundry done and waved the dust rag over my apartment. Sunday I watched the Vikings blow another one, this time to Detroit. Things improved considerably when Lori agreed to a light Sunday supper at her place. After that, well….

Very early on a Monday morning, as pre-dawn light began to sift down through the clouds, highlighting the windows of the bedroom in pale gray, Lori and I engaged in some unusual pillow talk. We talked of murder. We murmured of police investigations and friends and colleagues, and all the difficulties I would likely encounter. Lori suggested that I start my investigation of Alissa Constant by considering her a candidate for an important administrative post at the college, and I a member of the search committee. I would interview her references and either evade or lie about the real reason I was calling, at least until word of her death reached beyond our local community.

More lying, I thought. Great assignment, this was. I hadn't told the police about the files I'd taken from Constant's office and I'd lied to Marsh, one of my best friends.

I'd have to move fast. That news of Constant's demise quickly spreading was inevitable. Faculty and staff have friends and acquaintances at other institutions and they frequently talk to each other. E-mail, the telephone, the Internet, and all.

Human nature being what it is, some of those who knew Constant would alter their recollections of Alissa to delete or at least soften certain details. Some of those details could be vital to my investigation. There was also the matter of her family. Should I talk to them? I was undecided. They might know something significant. Given the distances involved, her family lived in North Carolina, I doubted they'd have much to contribute.

Even though it was still early, after a quick, cold breakfast, we drove separately to the college. Lori elected to make a side trip to the cleaners, while I returned to my city apartment for a change of clothes. When I arrived at the college parking lot, I found a not-exactly-welcome committee. Five black students stood around the lot, trying to appear casual. They looked about as casual as wild elephants smelling lion and almost as large. I wheeled into my assigned spot and watched them saunter toward my car. The nearest, Caleb Williams, was the only one I could put a name to. I remembered Caleb from my advanced academic counseling seminar last quarter. He was bright, articulate, and argumentative.

I rolled the window down. "Good morning, Mr. Marston," he said, in a flat expressionless voice. The absence of inflection made the simple greeting more menacing than if he'd snarled at me. Caleb leaned down and stared in the window at me.

"Good morning, Caleb." I waited.

"Word is you doin' a number on Marshall. Investigatin' Constant. The brother's already tapped to take the fall." I must have looked a question at him. He made an abrupt dismissive gesture and said, "It's all over the college, man." I heard murmurs from the others as they moved in behind him, crowding my car. One leaned over the hood and stared at me through the windshield. The view through the rear-view mirror was suddenly limited to a dark windbreaker. "And don't be quoting Shakespeare at me."

I pushed Caleb back with the door and got out of my car. Locked it. Several words came unbidden to mind, but I resisted the impulse to spit them at him.

I took a couple of deep breaths and managed to say in an even tone, "I don't know what you've heard, and I can't speak for the police. I'm doing an internal review of the victims' records and keeping in touch with the police. No one," I stressed the words, "no one has suggested or even intimated that Vice President Marshall is a target. I have no agenda, and I damn well resent your implication that I'm trying to railroad anybody! And as for brotherly connection, Caleb, the fact that he's African-American will in no way affect my actions." My voice was rising and I was starting to get a little hot. Breath bloomed in the crisp air. Caleb raised a big hand.

"Be cool, man, be cool. We just want you to know where we at."

"All right, Caleb." I took another deep breath and waved a hand at him. "Marsh is a friend of mine, remember? So, no railroad, but no special consideration, either." He backed away a step, still looking me in the eye.

"You need help with your review, you know where to come."

"It isn't needed in this corner, and I doubt I'll have much of anything to do with the outcome. The fuzz don't like amateurs snooping around."

Caleb grinned then, a brief flash across his face. He and the others were gradually moving back, drifting away, appearing almost as casual as they had when I first drove in. I glanced around and saw that the parking lot had become busier as more late-arriving staff and faculty appeared. The sun lifted above some of the lower buildings on the east side and long rays and shadows struck across the lot, warmed the asphalt, and chased away early morning vapors.

In the office, I encountered a surge of turmoil. The telephone rang twice and Teresa had three questions, all in the space of a single hour. There wasn't even anything in the mail. I don't mean there was no mail. Mail we get lots of. Every day. The mail-person frequently brings a whole cartload just for our office. We get tons, but it's mostly advertising, or the ubiquitous *Chronicle of Higher Education.*

The file on Jamison I'd lifted from Alissa's office helped some, but not as much as I hoped. He seemed to have been a singular individual with no discernible roots, who arrived on our scene from somewhere else. Why he'd come to City College was not apparent. When I called his former high school, I learned it was out of business, a victim of Pittsburgh's urban renewal. The district education office didn't offer much help. The voice on the other end of the line agreed to try to find the records of Stuart Jamison, who probably graduated in nineteen-seventy-one or two, or perhaps it was 'seventy-three, but I got a sense that the person attached to the voice was not exactly thrilled with the idea of looking into old student records.

"Of course, if we knew his high school graduation date; if City College could supply that simple piece of information, if we could provide a transcript, for instance, or a student ID number, things would be so much easier," the voice scratched in my ear. I was reminded of fingernails on a schoolroom blackboard. "However, we will do our best," the voice continued. "If you'll call again in a few days…."

I assured the woman I would indeed call again. More calls to other possible sources, based on sketchy information in the file, were of no help. Having accomplished next to nothing the entire morning, I adjourned to the basement caves for a quick sandwich and a small salad. Returning to my office, I found Teresa absent and an unknown male student-type seated at her desk, the telephone receiver stuck in his ear. A second line was blinking, signaling a holding call. I waved a finger under his nose to get his attention and pointed at the blinking light. He shrugged a negative at me so I continued into my office. When I sat down, my keen powers of observation immediately registered that someone had been here while I was out.

Remember my table? Neat was never my forte. There were piles of documents stacked untidily on my desk, along with some three ring binders and, well...things. There was also a telephone and memorabilia of past speaking engagements, like a gold lion on a faux marble stand. Now, in the center of the desk, on top of everything else, was an envelope that hadn't been there when I went to lunch. I knew I'd never seen this nine by twelve white envelope before. In bold letters printed with a black marking pen, I immediately noticed my name.

I returned to my office door and looked out at the young man still sitting at Teresa's desk. He looked vaguely familiar. He hung up the phone and Teresa walked in.

"Who are–"

"Jack, this is–"

"Hi, Mr. Marston, I'm–"

We were all talking at once, so I stopped. Then Teresa stopped. She laughed. The boy at the desk continued, "...David Knowles. David. Teresa's brother. I came to take her to lunch and she asked me to answer the telephone for a minute." He smiled and waggled the receiver.

I nodded and smiled back. "'Much ado about nothing,'" I said.

David looked blank.

"He does that sometimes," whispered Teresa, smiling behind her hand.

"Does what?" said David.

"Quotes Shakespeare. Other plays too."

"Teresa, who left the envelope for me?"

"What envelope?"

"The big one on my desk." She frowned and walked by me, stopping short when she saw it.

"Well, it certainly stands out in that mess, doesn't it? I guess it came when I went down the hall. It must have been just before David got here. Sorry 'bout that."

"Too bad. I wonder why it was so prominently and anonymously delivered, is all. Well, have a nice lunch, you two."

They left and I stared at the envelope. It wasn't very thick and I doubted I was on anybody's list for a letter bomb, but still...the anonymous delivery, after my morning confrontation with Caleb and his friends, gave me pause. I decided I'd paused long enough, so I took my college-issued letter opener in hand and slit open one end, holding the envelope by its opposite corner. Since the letter opener came from the lowest bidder and was many years old, it chewed the paper fibers apart, rather than cleanly slitting the paper.

The now-tattered envelope contained a single sheet of paper, also white. I fished it out by its edges and looked at the heavy block lettering. Black ink. Same marking pen, same hand, it appeared.

AS SHE SOWETH
SO SHALL SHE REAP
ALISSA CONSTANT
MURDERED HERSELF

It wasn't signed. It was neatly printed. I was willing to bet the police would find it a useless clue, but I was going to give them an opportunity to examine it. I called that homicide cop, Swanborg. Murdered herself, I thought, waiting to be connected. Interesting concept. It sounded vaguely biblical. I didn't recognize it, but then,

I'm more familiar with Shakespeare.

"Detective Swanborg. I have here a mysterious envelope, delivered by unseen hands. It appears to be connected with Alissa Constant's murder."

"Really. I'll have it picked up right away."

"Good. Tell me, Detective Swanborg, I trust members of the college community are cooperating fully in your investigation?"

I heard a sigh. "Look, Marston, I've been reminded that you are the designated police liaison on this, and I'm supposed to 'relate' to you, so I will. But let's not get in each other's hair. Okay?"

After gaining some vague assurances that he just might keep me filled in, if he had the time, I hung up. Then I copied the contents of the envelope on our office copier.

A policewoman arrived with reasonable alacrity and went off again after carefully protecting the piece of paper and the envelope. She quizzed me and then Teresa, after Teresa returned, about the mysterious delivery. It was all very inconclusive.

It was now nearly four in the afternoon on the East Coast. I called one of Alissa's references. After a short delay I reached the personnel office of Atlantic University. Yes, they remembered Alissa Constant. Yes, they had a file, according to their computer, would I wait please? I would wait.

A few moments later, a new voice purred in my ear, amid the sighings and creakings of long-distance satellite telephonics. The new voice suggested politely that personnel records were private and unless I could demonstrate a compelling need, I had all the information I was going to get. I explained that I was conducting a background check on Dean Constant, who might become a final candidate for a new position at City College, and I needed to verify employment dates and positions. I further suggested in that my contact on the other end call me back at City College to verify my legitimacy. Fifteen minutes later, Ms. Georgine Harris was on the phone to me from Atlantic. Yes, Alissa Constant was their assistant to the director of continuing education for three years between 1979 and 1982. Yes, the director was still in that position, due to retire shortly. The woman mentioned two other people on the campus who might have known or had contact with Alissa, but refused to give me anything more. I waited because she hadn't hung up and I heard her turning pages in the file. Then I heard a soft "oh!" I waited some more.

"Excuse me…Mr. Marston…." There was a strange hesitancy in her voice. "I really…I can't tell you more. But I'm pleased to hear City College is being thorough in its…ah, its background check. Good-bye." Before I could respond, she hung up. What was that about? Apparently she found something in Constant's personnel file that was at least mildly upsetting. The telephone rang. It was President Trammel's office and did I have anything to report?

Without hesitation I quipped, "'I must confess that I have heard so much, But, being over-full of self affairs, my mind did lose it.'"

"Excuse me?" said Trammel's secretary. She waited.

Should I tell Trammel what I had learned so far? About the note? I decided against it. He wasn't always the most circumspect in a tense situation. In any case, I wasn't going to pass information to him except verbally and directly. I said so. It was not a satisfactory answer.

I called Alissa's former boss, the Director of Continuing Education at Atlantic. He'd given her a decent if somewhat reserved recommendation. After several minutes of verbal sparring, he agreed to consider a few additional questions. He told me that there'd been some vague student complaints about her. I raised the possibility of talking with someone else at Atlantic. He questioned my persistence. I explained we were in the habit of branching out from listed references to others. These were usually people suggested by the original references, in order to flesh out search committee reports. I assured him that applicants at City College were informed before the fact that we might do that. It didn't help.

The next two institutions from her list of references had nothing to add, except for Southern College, which professed no knowledge of the woman named in Alissa's file as a reference.

The same thing occurred twice more. These were all secondary references, individuals who were supposed to know Constant in a context other than direct employment circumstances. They were members of a couple of national or regional committees; another shared time and space as elected or appointed members of the board of a professional organization to which Alissa belonged–had belonged. It's a level too often never checked by search committees. I would have been unconcerned over one discrepancy, but three seemed too many. Were there others? I knew Constant to have been careful and exacting. She sometimes irritated colleagues with her persistence over inconsequential details. So it was an inconsistency in character for her to be sloppy about her own resume.

The phone rang. My direct line. When I picked up, there was no one there. Not even any heavy breathing.

CHAPTER 12

*Have I ever at any time
tried to go behind your backs!*

I called Indiana State. It was easier to establish my bona fides this time. The man I talked to had a whistle, as if there was a gap between his front teeth. He quickly confirmed the glowing recommendation which they originally provided us when Alissa was first hired. "So the summary is, everything in the recommendation is okay?"

"Of course, Dean Marston." I didn't bother to correct him; sometimes titles ease the way a little. "Is there any question?"

"No sir. I just seem to be finding a few discrepancies and want to be sure of the facts." There was a pause and I heard him sigh.

"Well, actually, there were some questions, but I'm not sure how relevant they were."

I assured him again that this was a confidential inquiry.

"Well, I guess it's all right. She was the project director for some sort of soft-money, special education project during her last year here and it seems there were some ...*hmmhm* ah…disciplinary problems associated with the project." I could almost hear distaste in his voice.

"With students? Exactly what was the problem?"

There was another pause. "Well, I'm not sure I should mention this, but, the project was terminated a year early. It seems a security guard found some of the students in…ahh some sort of…ah, *hmmhmm*…questionable circumstances. I recall that Ms. Constant was reprimanded for inadequate supervision and the project was terminated."

Silence. I probed further. Mainly I wanted to know why she got such a glowing recommendation in light of the reprimand. The more I questioned him, the slipperier he got and finally he pleaded urgent business and practically hung up in my ear.

I made one more call to Indiana. I knew a former graduate student at the U during the time Constant was there.

"Hey, Jack! How they hangin'?"

"Hey, Fred. Long time. What's going on, now that you're out of academia?"

He proceeded to tell me in more detail than I cared to hear. Finally I broke into his narrative. "Fred, I called you because I have a situation here and I need a little help. It's not a major problem, but I want you to think about your last year in graduate school at Indiana. Is there anything you recall that might have been a little out of the ordinary?"

"Hell, Jack," he rasped, "that was ten-twelve years ago."

"I know, but think about it. I'd appreciate it. I'll call you back later."

"Naw, I can only think of one thing. Some sort of scandal in the education department, I think. The campus rumor mongers had a field day for about a week. Lemme see if I can remember any details. 'Course, I don't know how much of what I heard was fact and what was garbage, but…oh yeah.

"There was this project in ed psych and one night a security guard found some of the project kids, minors, I heard, having a party with a couple of grad students. There was some booze and maybe drugs and sex? Geez, Jack, it's hard to…yeah, the project director lost her job over it, somethin' like that." He paused. "But, she wasn't at the party. You know how it goes. The crap always rubs off on whoever's in charge. That's about it." I could almost hear him shrug.

"I don't know, Fred. That doesn't connect with anything here. Anything else?" I was becoming a facile liar.

Another pause. "No, that's it. Dull year, I guess."

"Thanks, Fred. I'll probably be down your way next year for a conference. If it works out, I'll call you. Maybe we can get together for a drink."

"Hey, great! Nice talking to ya."

I hoped Fred would pass off my call as unimportant, and not mention it to anyone. Now I had Alissa Constant linked to some kind of minor scandal, perhaps. I called Indiana back. When I reached Alissa's former supervisor, the dean of education, he was surprised. He said so.

"I'm surprised, Dean Marston. And I'm just leaving the office. What is it now?"

"Can you confirm as true or false that Constant directed a special ed psych project that was terminated for allegations of improper supervision?"

There was no answer. I sensed I had struck gold. "Dean? Are you there?"

A long sigh came into my ear. "I have no more to say to you, Dean Marston." The phone clicked in my ear and we were disconnected. Hah! I went to supper.

The next day, I called three other institutions that had employed Constant. In each case, now that I had some experience, I was able to detect a similar pattern. I was building a picture of Alissa Constant significantly different from the woman we thought we knew. At the third institution another, disturbing dimension was added.

"Dean Marston, is it? Odd that you should be calling. I just got off the phone with another gentleman from your college asking many of the same questions."

"Really? What is the gentleman's name?"

"McKenzie, I think."

It was more than odd. A quick scan of the staff list revealed what I was already sure of; there wasn't anyone on our staff named McKenzie.

After two more such incidents, I called the PD and tried to reach the detective who had interviewed me. When they finally ran down Detective Swanborg, he assured me they weren't calling and didn't need to.

"We're pretty sure we know who killed Constant. We just have to wrap up a few loose ends before we make an arrest. Furthermore, if we were calling her references, we wouldn't be telling anyone we were from City College. That's ridiculous," he snorted. "Incidentally, why are you calling her references?"

"You know, background stuff to tie up the file and for any press questions that may arise." It was crap and he knew it.

The week slid by. I went to rehearsals when my character was needed, which was frequently, and continued to make calls. In between I talked to a few students the staff turned up who claimed to have known Stuart Jamison. There weren't many. The picture that emerged was that of an intelligent individual with an extensive understanding of accounting and business practices and computers but not much else. He appeared to be a loner. Almost unapproachable. One or two more perceptive students told me they thought Stuart was lonely. He seemed to want friends at times, but at other times he pushed people away.

Because of our more mature student population, there is no student life, as it's commonly known. The chances for social interactions at the college are relatively small. There was one woman, a divorcee with a reputation for being something of a predator, who cheerfully admitted she'd made a determined play for Stuart, but she had been firmly rebuffed. She remarked that she thought he hadn't really wanted to sever their budding relationship. For some reason, I mused, Jamison isolated himself from everyone at the college. Why would that be?

CHAPTER 13

*I have investigated the
matter most conscientiously–*

After all that time spent calling people who knew, or knew of Alissa Constant's prior employment, I began to feel as if the telephone was grafted to my left ear. Rehearsals for "Enemy of The People" continued, interspersed with office routines. The weekend had come as a welcome respite, but now on Monday morning, my frustration rose.

What was all that defensiveness? Why did so many of the contacts I'd made sound as if they weren't being frank with me? Maybe it was just my suspicious nature.

Even more perplexing was the occasional reference by people I was reaching out to, that someone had been there before me. If the police weren't calling about Alissa, who was, and why? Then a possible answer came to me. Alissa must be under consideration for some new position at another institution, and they weren't prepared to go public just yet.

I called Fred Coper. I remembered something he'd mentioned about his service background. He answered on the third ring. "Fred."

"Yes, this is Fred Coper." His distinctive, familiar voice was something of a comfort.

"Jack, Fred. I have a little project here that's right up your alley."

"What, you think we have nothing to do over here? Geez, Jack, I don't need you making work for me."

"Didn't you tell me once you were in cryptanalysis in the

service?"

"So?"

"I've run across a file that appears to be in code of some kind."

"Really?" Hah. I could hear interest in his tone. A nibble. Now to set the hook.

"Fred, this is highly confidential and you've got to swear to keep it private before I tell you any more."

"Geez, Jack. Don't play games. Just tell me what you want and I'll tell you if I can help." So much for hook setting. I told him about the coded files in Alissa Constant's desk. I didn't tell him where they came from. Maybe I could avoid revealing that and maintain some semblance of my promise to the president.

"Haw. Jack, I was only in for three years and change, and naturally I don't have the manuals. Number codes with a one-time pad are impossible, even with a computer and then you need a program."

I held the phone away from my ear until Coper ran his complaint list and stopped for air. One-time pads? I didn't want to know about that. "Okay, okay. I understand. But you're the one who told me you acquired a reputation for flair and creativity. I'll give you the complete story as soon as I can, but meanwhile, help me out a little, will you? And keep it under your hat."

He sighed. "Well. Send it over. I'll have some time later in the week."

Great, I thought, hanging up the phone. I'm getting nowhere on all fronts. Maybe I'll open an office as a slow sideline– "Marston Investigations: Missing Persons. Our motto is, you lose 'em, we'll look for 'em. No guarantees."

Outside, the clouds hung closer to the ground, obscuring the upper floors of some of the city's taller buildings. Rain spattered the window and ran in random patterns down the streaked pane, smearing the view even more. It was the kind of day when nothing good would happen. I longed for a cigarette. The door opened and

Teresa walked in. She stood on the other side of my desk, looking down at me for a long moment.

"I just got a call from Marie in the president's office," she said quietly. "The police arrested Vice President Marshall early this morning."

I closed my eyes. Even though I'd half-way expected it, it was still a shock. Now what? I had no hard information on either the Jamison thing or on Constant's murder. What I had learned was that we probably had some bad information in the files about Alissa Constant and that several academics around the country had either lied or avoided the truth in making recommendations for her.

I couldn't imagine Anton Marshall as a killer. He had a killer instinct on the racquetball court, but that's a long way from murdering another human being, even in the heat of anger. Or passion. However, I couldn't prove he didn't do it. Worse, it looked more and more as if I was conducting an investigation that would help convict my friend. Terrific. Teresa's voice brought me back.

"Marion Lester is on his way up here, Jack."

"What for?"

"I think he knows about your investigation."

"Great. Well, I have to deal with him sometime. Thanks." Lester is head of the local faculty organization. Since his cooperation or at least his acquiescence was important to gaining help from the faculty, I didn't object to his peremptory demand to see me. He showed up ten minutes later.

"Well, Marion, what can I do for you?" He stalked into my office, dressed in a gray, off-the-rack, single-breasted suit. The collar button on his white shirt was undone and his tie was askew. There were random spots on the tie that might have been gravy. He also wore a stern look on his sharp-nosed face.

I speculated once again that his diminutive stature and his loss of hair at an early age had led him to thrust himself into whatever leadership roles he could find. As president of the faculty organization, he had both influence and power and I wanted his help. Lester wasn't noted for his cooperative nature, although he and I had never had any serious disagreements. Now, however, he was sending signals that his prominent nose was seriously out of joint.

"What you can do for me is this," he said, falling into the chair beside my desk and immediately cocking it up on its back legs. "I should take this right to the president, but he's so worried about his precious building campaign that he wouldn't hear me if I did get to see him. Not to mention that his academic V.P. has just been arrested for murder."

"You know about that?"

"Oh, hell, Jack, everybody knows. You know how well the rumor mill works around here." He dropped the chair to all four legs and leaned toward me. "The word is you're doing some kind of internal investigation of the murders, separate from the cops. I want to know why." He reared back again in the chair.

"More noise from the rumor mill, right?"

He nodded.

"All right, I'll tell you. This time the rumor is fact. I'm doing it because President Trammel and Vice President Marshall requested it," I said evenly, resisting an urge to stick out a foot and tip him over backward. "Strongly requested it."

Lester looked surprised at my frank answer. For a moment he was silent and I could almost see wheels turning in his brain.

"As a matter of fact, I was about to call you. I need your help." He rubbed his beak and stared at me. I paused, but when he remained silent, continued. "I need to interview faculty who knew and worked with Jamison and Constant and it will help if you'll issue a memo urging general cooperation."

He raised his heavy black eyebrows and said, "Why should I? Seems to me it's strictly a police matter."

"Look, I didn't ask for this assignment. I'll give you whatever assurances you want that nothing I report to Trammel will compromise anybody unless I'm absolutely sure it's relevant to the murders. Besides, nobody will tell me anything they don't want me to hear."

Lester had some reservations about going public with complete support, but he finally agreed to be agreeable. Something, anyway.

"Personally, Jack, I hope your investigation helps clear the air fast. Nobody wants to think of a colleague as a murderer. Still, it must be tough, investigating a friend and knowing you might unearth information that will help convict him."

I nodded. "Would you be willing to check faculty association minutes for me?"

"What for?"

I shrugged. "Bits of gossip. Something odd. Maybe the minutes will trigger a recollection."

Lester thought about it. "Seems like a long shot, but I'll see if anything turns up."

After he left I called some faculty members I knew well. Questions and a little anticipatory fence mending were in order. I knew I was going to have to work with these people after the killers were caught and I wanted it clear I supported the faculty organization.

I got lucky. Five of the first six were in their offices. I discovered two similar characteristics between Constant and Jamison. Neither seemed to have had much contact with other members of our little community, except normal ones. Faculty members didn't know much about Jamison. He did his work, he was a bright or above-average student. He came to class, did his number and left. Nothing suggested the two victims were connected. I still thought the murders were the work of two killers.

CHAPTER 14

I should think he would be very glad that such an important truth had been brought to light.

Faculty members I talked with indicated that Alissa Constant was always pleasant, sharp, got her work done on time. She disappeared at irregular intervals on vacations to places she didn't talk about, and apparently didn't socialize within the college community. Except, of course, with Marshall. Most people knew about or suspected their intimate relationship. She always attended the appropriate college receptions and other semi-social activities, but she left early, and always alone. Late afternoon receptions were often preliminaries to dinner or drinks or both for couples or small groups of faculty and staff. Burgeoning romance as well. Lori and I had become an item as a result of one such event, after a rough start.

Lunchtime came and my string of successful calls collapsed as I reached out to more and more empty offices. I called the police department and discovered that detective Swanborg was out. I also learned that Marsh could receive visitors that afternoon. Lester reappeared

"What news, Borachio?" Lester just stared at me. He hated it when I quoted Shakespeare.

"I skimmed our minutes for the past two years. Nothing."

"Well, it was a slim chance. Thanks, Marion."

"The only odd thing at all was when Matt Jellicoe showed up to insist he be put on the site committee."

"Jellicoe? Oh, right, I remember that. He never does anything he doesn't absolutely have to."

"Well, it's no big deal."

"That it?"

"Yep. But I'll issue a memo, ask faculty to cooperate." I thanked him and heard my stomach growl. The phone rang again. This time it was Marsh.

"Listen, Jack. I guess you know where I'm calling from. This is crazy. I didn't kill her."

"I know you didn't, buddy." I said it automatically. I believed it, didn't I? "I'll come down later. What can I bring you?"

"No, don't." His voice was flat and tired-sounding. "That's why I called. Don't come down here. I don't want to see you, or anybody else while I'm locked up."

"But…"

"No. I've arranged for a lawyer. I'll talk to you after I'm out." He hung up.

Dammit! He shouldn't shut out his friends. On the other hand, if he had killed her, I was the last person he'd want to see. I stood by my desk a moment staring at the wall. Then I went to a lunch I didn't feel much like eating, my stomach notwithstanding. I pantomimed eating motions at Teresa, hanging on the phone, as I left. She nodded and waved me away. The telephone, I reflected in the elevator, ruled our lives. Downstairs I went through the buffet line and took a chair at a large round table. I was a quarter-way through my taco salad when several faculty joined me.

"So, Jack. Chicago is already leading the Central Division by a game. I figure we'll be in second when December rolls around." The speaker was a woman who lived in Hudson and was a rabid Green Bay Packers fan. She was the only faculty member I knew who admitted to an interest in professional football. "That leaves your hapless purple Vikings with only an outside chance for a wild card spot."

I glanced her way. "We'll see, Lona, we'll see."

The conversation turned to Marshall's arrest and speculation about his chances. Emma Tidwell quietly sat down. Hers was one of the names on that group of coded file folders. I nodded to her.

Our table filled and the restaurant became more crowded. Two of my tablemates started an argument about the merits of the police case. Since neither of them had the slightest knowledge of the case, it was mere speculation.

A sociologist, Myles Anderson, who was sitting on my left barked out, "Well, hell. Jack here knows Marsh pretty well, let's ask him."

"Ask me what?" I swallowed the last of my salad.

"Regardless of the case against him, could Marshall have killed Constant? Is he capable of it?"

"Of course, he's capable of it, Myles," snorted his antagonist, a short, heavy-set woman from the business department. She wore a carefully tailored dark suit that set off her thick, close-cropped hair. "All men are capable of violence."

"Just men? What about women?" someone else interjected.

"Never mind that," Myles interrupted. "Answer the question, Marston. You know him as well or better than any of the rest of us," indicating the table.

"Now entertain conjecture of a time, when creeping murmur and the pouring dark fills the wide vessel of the universe…." I couldn't help it. Conversation stopped and they all looked at me. Before I could continue, another voice filled the silence.

"They certainly fought a lot." It was the low, husky voice of Emma Tidwell. She'd had a throat infection as a child and the operation that saved her life had scarred her larynx. It gave a throaty, sexy quality to her voice. "My office is just around the corner from hers on four, you know, and some trick of the heating system makes it easy to hear raised voices from her office." She paused. Was she blushing? I couldn't tell in the subdued lighting of the place.

Emma Tidwell was a tall, spare female, with average looks that would have been improved if she hadn't always worn her dark hair pulled tightly back in a severe knot. She habitually dressed in long, loose, dark-colored dresses that didn't seem to change much with the seasons, except they appeared to be heavier in the winter. Emma Tidwell, internationally renowned scholar and tenured professor of Victorian literature, had just confessed to eavesdropping.

I looked over my coffee cup at her. She looked back, and gestured dismissively. "I don't mean I listened in," she said, "but sometimes, when Dean Constant or Dr. Marshall raised their voices in her office, they were difficult to ignore. Last summer I finally put a piece of cardboard over the vent."

I was about to ask her a question and was wondering how to put it discreetly, when a loud voice intruded from the entrance.

"Marston! By God, what's the meaning of this?"

I looked up at the man striding toward me. The people between us scattered before the tidal wave of his indignation. Harvey Johnson was holding a piece of paper in one hand. He gestured widely, so the paper fluttered and drew the light in the room. It became the focus of everyone's attention. Johnson was a tall, florid historian who favored tan wide-wale corduroy jackets with dark leather patches. We frequently saw him stalking through the building with a huge black pipe clenched in his jaw. He reached our table in long strides, coming up hard against the edge. The table jerked, slopping coffee. Several people slid their chairs back in alarm. Johnson didn't appear to notice. His attention was fixed on me. I wondered absurdly if he was going to take a swing at me.

"What's the problem, Harve?" He hated to be called Harve. His face got a little redder. Maybe he'd hyperventilate and forget his question.

"This!" his voice rose a notch. Motes of dust from the ceiling, disturbed by the vibrations, filtered down. "This memo from Lester confirms that you're conducting some sort of investigation. And it suggests that faculty cooperate with you. What the hell gives you the right to snoop around? I think we'd better have an association meeting. This is unconscionable!" His voice got louder. There were murmurs from the crowd and several more people, attracted by his bombast, came toward our table. Johnson was said to have his eye on Lester's presidency and sometimes took the opposite side of an issue. So much for my hope for quiet interviews among the faculty without a lot of argument. On the other hand, maybe it was as well we got this out in a casual rather than a formal setting. A line from King Lear came to mind. I stood up instead.

"Dr. Johnson," I said loudly, overriding whatever his next statement was going to be. He closed his mouth and the crowd quieted. I dropped my volume to a more conversational level. "President Trammel simply asked me to look into the backgrounds of Jamison and Constant. That memo from Marion just asks you to cooperate a little. It's really not a big deal. It's obvious I can't force you to talk to me." I saw several people nod their heads.

"We want to protect the college, and Dr. Trammel seems to think the best way to do that is for the college to stay in close touch with the police investigation. You know this is a crucial time for the fund drive. I guess Trammel thought having someone in the administration keeping track would help. He tapped me. But why me instead of Nelson or someone else, I don't know. Maybe you ought to ask him."

Someone I couldn't see said, "Johnson, you're out of line. If you don't want to talk to Jack, don't. Personally, I think it's a good idea. There's a legislative session coming up in January and we need the bonding bill."

There was more, some favored Johnson, some favored the president. I knew quite a few faculty and staff didn't think spending money for a stone and glass monument to President Trammel was worthwhile, but a lot of them liked the idea of fresh new offices and a more upscale image for the college. At this time I'd rather they argued about the new construction instead of my inquiry.

Johnston stuck to his point. "Why you? Why not Marsh? That would have been more logical. Did Trammel expect Marsh to be arrested?"

I'd wondered the same thing, but wasn't about to say so. Questions and comments pro and con flew back and forth like shuttlecocks.

"Look," I finally said, "you all know how I feel about arbitrary invasion of students' privacy. Why should I feel any different about faculty? Or staff?" There were continuing grumbles and some affirmative head nodding, but I sensed the initial uproar was over. Now I wanted to talk with Emma Tidwell. When I looked around for her, she'd already left the room.

Later that afternoon I glimpsed her going into her office suite on the fourth floor. I followed. When I entered the open door to her office, she looked up, startled. I had the immediate impression that I wasn't a welcome visitor.

"Yes, Mr. Marston? I'm very busy and due to leave shortly."

"This won't take long, Professor. I just want to follow up on your comment at lunch."

She sighed. "I knew that remark was a mistake the minute I said it. Frankly, it just slipped out."

"What can you tell me about conversations in Alissa

Constant's office?"

"Nothing. Oh. What's the use? I am neither a gossip nor an eavesdropper. However, when Alissa and Dr. Marshall quarreled, which was not frequently, mind you, their voices were sometimes raised and I overheard them."

"What does 'not frequently' mean, exactly?"

"Oh, perhaps three or four times in the past school year." She sighed again and sank down in her chair. I sat beside the desk and looked around. Unlike Alissa Constant's office, which betrayed little of the occupant's personality or interests, Tidwell's office told me that it belonged to someone with an intense love of books and literature. Shelves filled one corner, the back wall and extended around the single window. In another corner, a delicate side chair covered with some dark fabric sat before a floor lamp with a pale buff-colored shade. Beside the chair, a dark wood table held a heavy book and a pair of reading glasses. There was only a little room on the shelves for more books.

"I'm not collecting gossip, Professor, but whatever you tell me may help. I assure you, unless it is relevant to her murder, I won't repeat it." She gazed at a sheet of paper on her small dark wooden desk and didn't say anything. Then she pointed at the ceiling where I saw a piece of cardboard wedged into the vent.

"I heard a good deal. Too much, actually. Alissa Constant was not a nice person." Suddenly, there was venom in her husky voice and I realized she was deeply angry. Her shoulders went rigid and her face stiffened. "Alissa Constant connived, manipulated, and used people. I think she was using Doctor Marshall. At first I think there was a genuine attraction between them. I…I heard them making love, once, but that was a long time ago," she hurried on. This time there was no hint of color in her pale cheeks.

"She was pressuring Dr. Marshall for something. I'm not sure what it was. But I have the impression this was nothing new, that she was practiced at it."

"Pressuring? How?"

"I can't give you a specific example. It was the way she used words. Being elliptical, not saying exactly what she meant. She was…manipulative. Smug."

"You obviously didn't care for her. Still, I expect you want her killer caught, especially if the police have arrested the wrong person." I said it softly, making it a question, but Professor Tidwell, after her one small outburst, retreated into her more usual taciturn shell.

"I have told you all I know. More than I know. I refuse to say any more on the subject. I won't speculate. I know nothing of young Jamison. He never took one of my classes. I don't believe I even know what he looked like. Now, Mr. Marston, if you'll excuse me, I have to get home to a stack of student papers."

I had learned a little more about Alissa, and that Professor Emma Tidwell had detested Constant. I had never known her to exhibit such emotion before, except on the subject of Victorian literature, her life-long interest. If Constant had offended Tidwell, there might be others, besides Marsh, who had been pushed too far.

CHAPTER 15

*There may be much that is very
abnormal about the present conditions–*

The stage was dark when I entered the theater from the rear. A single dim light swayed gently on a long pigtail from an unseen connection above the curtain, where a tangle of wires, ropes, and cables looped like some giant, demented plate of spaghetti left behind by the gods.

The theater where we were rehearsing and would perform Ibsen's "Enemy of The People," had survived a multitude of urban renewal attempts. Its twenties-style art-deco marquee and lobby showed their age. Like a dowager with memories of a kinder, gentler time, when servants were a constant buffer against the perils of the world, the old theater persevered into the late twentieth century, peeling paint, water stains, and all.

It started life as a vaudeville house, then suffered a clumsy conversion to motion pictures in the twenties. Most of its interior plaster romanticism and the great marquee projecting over the sidewalk survived from that period. The plaster was a dingy gray, badly in need of either serious scrubbing or a new paint job. When the movies fled the central downtown entertainment core of Minneapolis along with many upwardly mobile residents, the place stayed empty for years, except for an occasional itinerant evangelist. Now it had reverted once more to legitimate theater. Once again aspiring actors trod the boards, learning their craft and hoping for that big break, the chance to make it to Broadway or

Hollywood.

I was not among the aspirers. At age forty, I had long ago lost those fleeting dreams, briefly nurtured by encouragement from the head of the theater department during my undergraduate years. He cast me in a lot of second-level parts whenever strong support for the leading man was needed and amateur theater had nurtured my long-standing interest in Shakespeare. The director also liked it that I was able to move about the stage without falling through the sets and I had a voice readily heard at the back of the hall.

This place, however, was something else. I walked off the stage, into the house, an auditorium that'd give pause to the most seasoned director. The proscenium-style stage was enormous, at least seventy-five feet across and who knew how deep. The arching ceiling soared high above the proscenium. There were more than 2,000 seats. I hoped to God the producer would restrict our audiences to the downstairs center section and close off the two balconies that hung over me in the gloom like monstrous gaping jaws. The only illumination came from that single work light and the four glowing exit signs over doors leading to the lobby where Stuart Jamison's throat had been savagely cut.

I made my way down a long side passageway that connected the back-stage area with the house. Midway down the dark hallway was a wood-paneled door that opened on a steep flight of stairs to the basement and the warren of narrow passageways, small offices, chorus dressing room, and acres of storage space, now mostly empty. The musty basement smelled of sweat, greasepaint, and moldy costumes, props, and pieces of old curtain.

My heels on the hardwood floor of the passage made sharp rapping sounds that caromed off the plaster walls and ceiling. I pulled at the door handle. Locked. My missing actors couldn't be down there. Now what? Maybe the cast was taking a break, although Delton wasn't prone to such common decencies. I stopped and listened. And of course, the building answered my question.

Most old buildings do that, if you give them the opportunity. They creak, they groan and they breathe. They whisper secrets. First, all I heard was the blood pumping in my brain. Then I heard people some distance away talking, walking. A door opened across the stage and a burst of happy sound washed over me. The cast had been in the basement catacombs after all, probably looking at the dressing rooms. My feelings of gloom began to dissipate.

Eleanore Temple, stage manager for the play and a member of our adjunct faculty, appeared and explained that Ted Delton had been called back to the University on urgent business and she was running the rehearsal. She looked at me. She knew about my special assignment.

"Ah, Dr. Stockman, Enemy of the People. Do you have a sense of your life running parallel to this play?"

I admitted the thought had occurred to me.

"Use it, Mr. Marston, use it. Now, let's start a stumble-through on Act Three, okay?" Her bright, insistent voice brought us all to attention. My biggest scenes occur in act three. I quickly became immersed in the words and the fabric of the play as we read lines and moved about the stage, following the rough notes our director had sketched out. Time flew. There were noises backstage, behind the musty drapes that hung morosely at either side of the great, dim stage.

"Begin, please," said Temple from the third row. We were doing the town meeting. Dr. Stockman continues his warnings.

What does the destruction of a community matter, if it lives on lies! It ought to be razed to the ground, I tell you! All who live by lies ought to be exterminated like vermin! You will end by infecting the whole country; you will bring about such a state of things that the whole country will deserve to be ruined. And if things come to pass, I shall say from the bottom of my heart: Let the whole country perish, let all these people be exterminated!

There was a clank overhead. I craned my head back and peered beyond the lights toward the upper catwalks.

"Jack! May we have some focus here?"

"Oh, sorry, I was just...." I waved vaguely at the unseen ceiling.

"Yes, I know," she smiled. "Project, folks, and always remember that if you can't be heard at the back of the hall, we're short-changing paying customers."

I wondered if we'd have any customers way up there in the second balcony. The rehearsal eventually ended. The security man went on overtime at 11:30 and the college couldn't afford that until we reached the last week of rehearsals. Then we'd have crews and actors almost 'round the clock to be ready for opening night.

I had a few words with the eager young man who played Billings, the editorial assistant in the play, and he trotted off, stage left. Alone, I turned and walked in the other direction, still thinking about the scene, and headed for the stairs that would take me to the backstage door. I paused under the single remaining work light hanging fifteen feet above the stage and looked back at the vast, dark auditorium. I turned and took another step toward the door.

There was no sound in the rafters, and I still haven't a clue what warned me. I leaned to the left, and so a hundred-pound sandbag, one of those big gunnysacks used to stabilize flats and counterweight backdrops, missed me by a hair as it fell. The thing hit the floor beside me with a deep, hollow boom and exploded. I felt the vibrations and a solid blow to my legs that knocked me to my knees. Sand stung my face and hands when the bag burst.

I crouched, listening to my pulse roaring in my head. My

stomach jumped and my fingers began to cramp. Sweat popped out as I began to realize how near a thing it had been. I would have been killed if that bag had hit me.

I cautiously stood up. My shoes were filled with sand and my knees shook, almost sending me back to the floor. Accident? A murder attempt? I stared upward. I assumed I was looking at the rafters and the catwalks. From what I could see, it might have been the Taj Mahal, the blackness was that complete. For a moment there was no sound. Then I heard raised voices and rapid footsteps as cast and crew came running back, attracted by the cannon-sound of the sandbag hitting the floor.

I looked at the rope tied to the top of the remains of the bag, my senses beginning to function again. It didn't look old. Had someone staged an accident? Was that someone still up in the rafters? I extricated my feet from the sand and tottered to the side of the stage. Somewhere here was a large switch that turned on all the work lights.

I threw the big breaker with an echoing clang. Lights appeared in random patterns, depending on which burned-out bulbs had been replaced. I found switches to other lights that dimly illuminated the fly area. If anyone was there, they were staying out of the light, or had already departed. I didn't even consider climbing the ladder to the first-level catwalk. I don't relish heights, and my knees were still wobbly. By now cast members were crowding around.

Eleanore Temple looked at me. "Nasty accident."

I nodded, unsure of my voice.

"We better call the police," said Eleanore.

"I don't think so," I countered.

"Why not?"

"I don't see anyone up there. Anybody see anything?" I called to the cast milling about. I got a chorus of nos. Temple looked at me, one eyebrow cocked.

"The college has enough trouble right now. Let's not stir anything up unnecessarily," I concluded.

At that moment our director, Ted Delton, appeared. "I thought you were busy tonight," I said.

"Huh," he said, ignoring my question. "We'll have to get the stage crew to look at the rest of those bags. Can't have accidents delaying our opening, although, God knows, some of you could certainly use the extra time! You especially, Marston. Get your lines down, people! It's impossible to do much with interpretation and movement while you're carrying playbooks!" He turned on his heel and disappeared as abruptly as he'd appeared.

"I thought you told me Delton wouldn't be here tonight," I said.

Eleanore glanced at me as we went out the door. "That's right. That's what he said when he called me."

CHAPTER 16

*Is there something going on that I am
to be kept in ignorance of?*

Midway through the morning Teresa announced she'd received and signed for a large package. She thereupon presented said package. It was another white envelope, this one a little fatter than the last. There was no return address. I took it into my office and sat down. I inserted my college-issue letter opener-cum-emergency-screwdriver under one flap and ripped off the end. Inside, between two sheets of plain gray cardboard, were several eight by ten sheets of laminated paper. I turned them over and looked at the first one.

"Jesus Christ!" Teresa came to the door, drawn by my exclamation.

"What?" she asked.

"Sorry, I was startled by the pictures. Somebody has favored me with color photographs of nude young men." Teresa came around my desk and looked over my shoulder. The pictures were copies, looked to be several generations from the originals. The definition was soft and the color was bad. But the subjects were clear enough.

In several, two naked boys grappled with each other in intimate fashion. The last picture was a threesome of nude, young-appearing boys. The backgrounds were all white with nothing on the walls.

Teresa picked up the pictures and shuffled quickly through

them. Then she dropped them on my desk with a look of distaste. "Jack, these are just kids. Some of them look only twelve or thirteen!"

"Yeah, I get the same impression. What's this all about? There's no written message."

"Do you think it's connected to your snooping?"

I glared at her.

"Excuse me, your investigation?"

"I don't see how, but I've never received stuff like this before Trammel stuck me with this damn assignment."

The telephone rang and I scooped it up. "Marston!" The president's bellow was probably detectable across the room. Teresa winced as I jerked the receiver away from my head.

"Yes, sir?"

In a somewhat lower tone he went on to detail several ways I could be of immediate assistance and ended with a terse reminder that I appeared to be making little apparent progress in my murder investigation.

"Teresa," I said after hanging up the phone, "I guess I don't have to remind you to keep mum about this latest delivery. Put these pictures in the locked file with the other stuff, please?"

"Gonna call the cops?"

I considered it. "Not yet. I don't see how these are related to the murders. Just more problems if they're connected to the college."

She raised an eyebrow and left with the envelope. Twice in two days I'd chosen to protect the college. I wondered if I was taking on too much responsibility.

I called Mary Tendun, the college's development person. "Good morning, Mary Tendun here." Her soft, pleasant voice was an antidote to the harder voices I had been coping with so far that morning.

"Mary, it's Jack Marston. How are things?"

"That's not a good question to ask today. We're already seeing a sharp drop in the flow of pledges and I think the week's tally of checks received will be below average."

"Ouch. What's the presidential reaction?"

"Jack, he doesn't know yet. And when he hears that these murders are at least partly responsible, he's likely to shoot the messenger."

"Maybe you can get a volunteer to deliver the report." She laughed briefly in my ear, then her voice took on a serious tone. "We really can tie the drop to the murders, you know.

"We've had phone calls from donors and alumni working on the drive. A couple of volunteers have quit because of Constant's death. They said so. But we're not talking about losing huge amounts of money. At least, not yet. None of the corporate or foundation donors have been in touch. 'Course, most of those are already committed. And I can't even begin to believe that any of the national donors who haven't sent checks yet will be affected one way or the other by the killings."

"What about the local foundations?"

"Oh, they're another story. If the murderer or murderers aren't found quickly, many will pull back. They may already have and we just don't know it yet."

"Mary, is it possible someone is trying to stick the college with a lot of bad publicity to kill the fund drive? Has anything been said that might suggest that?"

She paused for a moment. "Oh, heavens no, Jack. What an absurd idea! The murders will surely make things more difficult, and you know how much President Trammel loves difficulties." I could sense, though not see, her tongue firmly stuck in one smooth cheek.

"Well," I said, "murder and scandal might be one way to kill the fund drive. I'd appreciate it if you'd think about it some more. Anything that seems out of place might help me with this. You've probably heard that Trammel has me looking into the murders independently of the police. So far, clues are sparse and I can't imagine a motive that directly involves the college, except one linked to your fund drive."

"OUR fund drive," she corrected me. "Yes, the president mentioned your task, and I've heard some staff grumblings."

"Why should they care, if they're not involved?"

"Oh Jack, you're bound to kick over a rock or two in some lives that would be better left alone. In fact…" Suddenly I heard a different tone and a little hesitancy that reminded me of some of the phone calls I'd had about Alissa.

"Mary, please, I need all the help I can get. You know the longer this goes on, the greater risk there'll be real damage to the college."

She sighed. "Jack, lots of people at City College are very supportive of you. We know you're discreet and you didn't ask for this assignment. I really know nothing about these murders. I never met Jamison, but Alissa Constant…well. I have little doubt that a number of people are glad, or relieved, at least, that she's gone. Oh, I don't mean they're glad she's dead, you know, but there were many here who disliked and even feared her."

"Feared? C'mon, Mary. I know some people didn't like her. But isn't that a little strong?"

"No, Jack, it isn't."

"But why? She was a dean and I know she wasn't above a little political log-rolling to get her way, but we've all been guilty of that. What do you know that I don't?"

Mary sighed. "I hate this gossipy stuff. She's a very manipulative person. I've watched her at lots of different meetings. She'll use almost anything to get her way. And I'm not just talking about important issues."

"Go on."

"Alissa Constant always tried to use people. She did things just to get points, not because she cared. Think about how many things they tried and abandoned in her department. Manipulation was her middle name, Jack. It seemed to be second nature. And she was very good at it. I think that's how she got where she is– was."

"Are you trying to tell me she acted unethically at times?"

"I'm afraid so."

"Marshall?"

"Of course. She enthralled him. At least at first. I think he was tougher than she expected."

"Thanks, Mary, that helps." I wasn't sure how, except to give Marsh a stronger motive.

"Well, frankly, I didn't like the woman at all."

The day passed and I worked late. Lori came by and suggested supper out, but I begged off. Finally, I wrapped it up and went to jail.

Marsh looked uncomfortable when he saw me in the glass-walled room set aside for attorney-client meetings. I was uncomfortable. Jails are not pleasant places to visit. Mostly they are hard, steel bars, concrete floors, and walls, built to hold hard men. Hoosegow, lockup, slammer. Jail. Hard words. When the security check was finished, the guard let me through the barred door, then slammed it shut and locked it. My taut nerves twanged at the sound. Would he open it again when I wanted out? I looked at Marsh standing there in ill-fitting prison garb. The lighting was not kind. He looked haggard, tired, years older. His normally smooth chocolate skin seemed mottled and rough. We didn't sit down in the hard chairs.

"I wish you hadn't come," he said.

I said I'd heard from his aunt and asked if there was anything I could do for him. Marsh said no, his lawyer was taking care of everything. My face felt stiff. Our words came out flat, stripped of emotion. It was as if we were both afraid of revealing something, anything. For once I didn't make any wise cracks or quote Shakespeare. My stomach growled. I looked at my friend and knew he couldn't have killed Constant. I felt like crying. Later, when I described the encounter to Lori, I did cry.

Marsh talked as if his lips were frozen. Flat, cryptic. His lawyer, from a well-known city law firm, showed up and explained the final steps in Marsh's processing. He'd be released early tomorrow, she said, unless the judge decided to go against the recommendation of the prosecutor, but that was unlikely.

We didn't shake hands when we were through. Marsh turned as though his hips were locked and left through one door, his lawyer and I through another. She stopped me briefly in the hall outside the last security gate.

"You're holding out on me, aren't you?" Her harsh raspy voice didn't fit her slender physical persona. She was short and walked with a pronounced swagger, brassy hair swinging back and forth above her shoulders.

"Yes." I didn't see any reason to lie to this banty rooster of a woman, but I wasn't going to tell her about the note or the pictures. Not yet.

She kept strutting along. Then she put a hand on my arm. "You're trembling. Nasty experience, jail, isn't it? Do you think he's guilty? Why are you holding back?"

"No. No chance he did this. I don't know. I want to help Marsh. I promised a lot of people I wouldn't talk about what I found out unless it was relevant."

"And you're sure what's relevant?"

"So far, yes."

"Playing God?"

"I hope not. I think the other information I have has nothing to do with Marsh. But if I learn it does, you'll know about it."

"That could be too late."

"I'll keep that in mind. Are you a good lawyer?"

She grinned briefly as she turned down a corridor toward a side door, where she had parked her car. "One of the best."

I continued toward the main entrance.

"Sometimes, knowing bad stuff is important." Her voice floated back to me.

I reached the lobby and a familiar figure came down the stairs from the second floor. It was the homicide detective, Merrill Swanborg.

"I heard you were in the building. Rushing off or can we talk?"

"I have nothing on."

He smiled tiredly at me. "I'm almost off duty now, what do you say we grab a drink around the corner?"

This was interesting. Nominally, at least, we were on opposite sides. He was working on evidence to convict Marshall, and I was looking for proof someone else had killed Alissa. "Sure, if I can get something to eat at the same time."

He nodded and we agreed to meet at Richard's, a popular place a block away on Third. Twenty minutes later, we were seated at an isolated corner table in the dim restaurant. They had Amstel beer and I was working on my second bottle. Swanborg was drinking scotch, neat.

"So?" I glanced around.

"Let's order supper first."

Richard's was a longtime hangout for cops and newspaper people. The wood wall panels and the bar were almost black with the stain of years of smoke and fumes. Dark red cushions, colored glass hanging lamps, firm carpeted floor completed the look of the place. Richard's was big, low-ceilinged, crowded, yet always quiet. One could have private, undisturbed conversations here. Make deals.

Our conversation while we waited was desultory. We covered the weather, the latest Vikings football game, and whether the Gopher basketballers might make it to the Final Four this year, important stuff like that. I began to wonder if Swanborg was just lonesome for civilian contact and I'd happened along. Then he sighed, looked at me for a long moment, and said, "I hope this isn't a mistake. It's certainly unorthodox, but I want your help and I'm prepared to give you something in return."

"Why?" I said, surprised.

"Because there are some peculiarities in the Jamison case. It occurs to me that your civilian status may get you around some roadblocks I've encountered."

"I'm all ears. I won't break any confidences, but I won't hesitate to use whatever you tell me if I can help Marsh."

He nodded. "So, tell me what you think so far."

I looked at him and said, "I'm convinced Marsh couldn't have done it, killed Constant. I also think now that the murders are linked." Swanborg nodded slowly and took another swallow of scotch.

"About Marsh, I assumed that. Why do you think the murders are linked?"

I leaned back a little and watched him. "Frankly, it's a gut feeling." I had a coded file he didn't know about. I was tempted to tell him everything. I didn't. I still don't know why.

The waitress brought our supper and we dug in for a few minutes in silence. Then Swanborg resumed. "I think we have a solid case against Marshall. That's why we arrested him, of course. But it won't to be first degree premeditated. We think that he whacked her in a rage. Prosecutor agrees. Did you know he was accused of statutory rape in college?"

"Statutory rape? You mean an under-aged girl?"

"That's the definition, under the age of consent. And then in graduate school, he was arrested and later sued for assault." I was stunned by these revelations, tried, unsuccessfully, not to show it.

"How come none of that is in his personnel record?" I asked.

"The first complaint against him was dropped. Although Marsh was present, he didn't actually touch the girl. Because of his importance to the football team, since he didn't commit the crime, it was hushed up. It appears Marshall and some teammates celebrated a winning game and Marshall had too much to drink. He passed out. Other teammates collected some girl who shouldn't have been on the campus at that hour in the first place. One thing led to another and the guys took her to Marshall's room and raped her."

"Wait a minute. You're implying it was the girl's fault. Just because she was on the campus late at night doesn't make her guilty. They shouldn't have abused her," I snapped. "Even if she agreed to go to the room. Even if she was drunk." My voice rose. I was getting hot.

"Whoa, don't jump down my neck. I agree with you, as it happens. I'm just telling you what we've learned. Things were different then. In those days it was always the woman's fault. It's pretty clear Marshall was in the room passed out, but it's probable he never even saw the girl, before or after the rape."

I took a deep breath and realized Swanborg had set me up. He'd deliberately used provocative language to flush my attitude about rape, instead of just asking me. Why? Routine cop stuff?

"All right, what about the second incident?"

"A group of students got into a hassle at a roadhouse. Apparently some local tough guys objected physically to college kids coming on to hometown girls. When things got rough, Marshall jumped in to defend one of his college buddies. Things got out of hand. He's so big, he apparently wiped up the place with at least one guy and there was a lot of damage to the roadhouse. Later, the local guy filed assault charges. Since the locals started the whole thing, college and town folk made a deal and the charges were withdrawn, but Marshall had to pay a share of the damages."

"Seems pretty flimsy to me."

"That's just some of it. His dad died violently in an industrial accident of some kind. Football is a violent game. He's been around violence all his life. By itself, his past wouldn't convict him, but it shows patterns, links. He has no alibi for the time of Constant's murder. He was involved with her and they were fighting. So far everything is circumstantial, but there's a lot of evidence, and we're getting more all the time."

"Was Alissa raped?"

"No evidence of it. But she had skin under her nails and it isn't Caucasian."

"So, this is your way of telling me I haven't a hope in hell of doing Marsh any good?"

"Here's what I think. I think the two murders are unrelated. At first we considered the possibility that they were connected, even though the methods of killing are different, but no longer. We know you've made some calls about Jamison and that your computer information on the guy has been erased."

I opened my mouth to say something, surprised at his information, but he held up a hand and bored right on.

"I suspect you haven't had much luck with Jamison so you're concentrating on Constant, trying to help Marshall. But Jamison is the reason we're having this conversation."

"We're being stonewalled on Jamison. It's like somebody's

trying to bury the whole thing. We're feeling all sorts of pressure to back-burner it."

"Official pressure?"

Swanborg held up a warning hand. "What I'm telling you is that I hope you'll keep the pressure on. Persistent civilian pressure is harder for us to deal with. In return, I'll try to keep you informed of anything we come up with that you might use to help Marshall. See, when we decide a suspect is probably guilty, sometimes cops try to get evidence to convict and ignore pointers to other suspects. We don't mean to, but it happens."

"What kind of pressure are you getting on Jamison?"

"Don't ask. Just take my word for it." He belched suddenly, a short, sharp belch. "'Scuse me. I think it's stress."

I waved it off, concentrating on his words. "Jesus, Swanborg, do you realize what you just told me?" I jerked out of my chair and stomped up and down by our table.

"You're raising your voice again." Swanborg maintained his mild tone. "This has to be between us. If it gets out," he shrugged his big shoulders, "I'll be in deep trouble. Deal?"

I blew out my breath, sat down again, and looked at him. Now I could see he was seething. He just had himself under better control at the moment. "So you think you have a pretty good case against Marshall for Constant, but you're sure he didn't kill Jamison and you want me to help you on Jamison?"

"You got it."

"And in return you'll give me anything that might help Marshall?"

"Yep."

"Deal," I said. Swanborg smiled a wintry smile that didn't touch his eyes. We didn't shake hands.

CHAPTER 17

*Well, fortunately, we can turn the
situation to good account.*

Someday, I thought, I'll get it through my head there are only sixty hours in every eight-day week. I'd just received another brief but pithy tongue-lashing from director Delton for muffing my lines. Eyes on my playbook I was silently reading Act Three again in the dim light spilling into the auditorium from the stage. Few members of the cast and crew were about. Delton had changed his technique for Act Three after the initial stumble-through and rough blocking of the action. He was calling individuals and small groups to work on specific scenes.

Members of the crew were busy elsewhere, building sets and working on costumes. I was unnoticed as Ted Delton and one of the women in the cast walked by, focused intently on their conversation, which had to do with solving a computer problem the student had. They were staring at a pile of printouts the woman was holding.

"It looks like I'm gonna have to write a whole new section of code."

"You using the latest version of that application, Sarah?"

"Yeah, but the documentation seems to be screwed up. Every so often I have to run a series of trials to be sure I'm doing it right."

"And when it doesn't work, you can't be sure whether it's your machine code or something else, right?"

"Right."

"Okay. Try this. Copy the first section you showed me and add these lines of code. Then it'll flag the errors and even tell you what the error is, if you run the diagnostic in the other section."

"Oh. Wow. Sure, I see. Great. Thanks."

To my untutored ear it sounded pretty sophisticated. Delton, computers, Jamison. My tired mind jumped about. Was Delton capable of creating a trapdoor virus as Fred had suggested caused the erasures? And if he could, why would he? I decided to check it out.

Rehearsal ended before its usual ten P.M. conclusion. By previous arrangement, Lori was expecting me, and I arrived toward the end of the local television news.

"Well, lover," Lori greeted me, "how was rehearsal? Good, I hope, since your efforts as Dean Crimebuster of City College have so far borne little fruit."

"I got chewed out again for not knowing my lines, but, hell, that's becoming routine. Y'know, my little poppet, I don't think my grasp of my part is all that far behind several others in the cast. I wonder why he seems to be picking on me. Maybe that's just my own creeping paranoia."

"Would you like to go over the killings with me again? Maybe I'll spot something."

"You probably will, but can we just forget murder for tonight?"

"Hey, sweetie, I didn't mean to add to your discouragement. Let's watch the rest of the news. We'll worry about world affairs for a change."

As we settled together on the couch facing Lori's small color television, the reporter was saying something about reorganization in the Justice Department, where my daughter was employed. It was hard to concentrate on the announcer, good as she was, with

Lori's warm breath on my neck and her teeth nibbling my ear.

"Desist, desist," I protested softly, "I wanna hear this."

"Desist? I'm only trying to distract you from murder, my dear."

"Just pause a minute," I modified my original request, smiling into her eyes.

"According to a Justice Department spokeswoman, the dissolution of the Organized Crime units, originally established by former Attorney General Robert Kennedy, will not result in any layoffs." The newscaster went on to explain it was reorganization, and that money would be saved in the witness protection program.

The weather and sports passed with two fewer viewers, as Lori and I applied ourselves to the pursuit of mutual pleasure.

In the morning, your basically depressing, moist, and chilly morning, I read the mail, penciled a few notes for follow-up, and dumped most of it in the office wastebasket. For some reason, the conversation between Delton and the female cast member popped back into my mind. I went to see Fred Coper in the computer center.

"Fred, what does this sound like?" I related the substance of the conversation I'd overheard the previous evening. Coper agreed that both Delton and the student would need a fairly high degree of computer knowledge and experience.

Later that morning I ran into Fred loping down the stairs to the caves. "There's one other thing, Jack."

"One other thing?"

"Yeah. That conversation between the gal and your director? They were talking about a programming project here at City College. Did you know that?"

"No, but what difference does it make?"

"Probably none, but why would this guy who, you say, is not staff, but from the university, right? Why would he have such detailed knowledge of our admin systems?"

"Does he? I didn't get that from what I overheard."

"No, but I talked to Sarah. She's employed here at City College to develop this program for us. She told me the circumstance was purely casual. She was thinking hard about a problem. He noticed her distraction and she explained. He just sort of coughed up an approach."

"That sounds as if Delton might know enough to erase your computer files, right?"

"Right and I just finished testing his idea. It works just fine."

"Ah. But his ties to City College are pretty tenuous," I said.

"Yeah, but I wonder why he knows so much about us. I'm gonna look into this."

"Be my guest. But remember, we're dealing with killers here. If Delton is somehow tied in, we don't want to spook him." I continued up the steps. I was encouraged. Having Coper actively pursuing another angle to this mess might help me get answers sooner. The police had already established that Fred couldn't have killed either Jamison or Alissa Constant, so I was comfortable having him pursue the Delton angle on his own.

A lab tech from the police department called my office. My status as official liaison was paying off. She confirmed that the pornography was of overseas origin and that it appeared both the note about Constant and the writing on the envelope with the pictures had been printed by a marking pen of identical manufacture. She refused to speculate whether it was the same pen, but chemical analysis indicated it was the same kind of ink. I took that to mean the same hand was involved, thank you very much, even if the authorities weren't willing to be that positive.

Fred Coper called. "Jack?" His voice sounded excited to my ear.

"Yes, Fred."

"I called a friend at the U. He checked and insists Delton has never registered for any computer courses there."

"So?"

"So, there's something suspicious here."

"Fred, just because Delton never took a computer class doesn't mean much. Watch what you say to people. You don't want to expose yourself to any danger." With reluctance, Coper agreed to go slow and check with me before he did any other independent investigating.

That evening I went to rehearsal again and during a break asked the director about his computer background.

"Why do you ask, Marston?" He turned his dark, reptilian eyes on me.

"Idle curiosity, I guess. I heard you talking with Sarah and kind of got the impression you're pretty knowledgeable."

"Really?" He raised his eyebrows at me. "Shouldn't you be studying your lines?"

CHAPTER 18

I am a man with a conscience

Lori looked at me across my kitchen table. We were having a late snack after another rehearsal.

"I was thinking about that news report last night. D'you think it's possible," she said?

"What?" I was busy admiring the misty effect of steam rising in front of her wide-spaced eyes.

She winked, which always got my attention. "That Stuart Jamison was in a government witness protection program and somebody located him? That he was murdered by a mob hit man?"

"Sure. And I'm the reincarnation of J. Edgar Hoover, come back to set my boys straight. Wouldn't we know if he was registered under a false ID? I feel more and more inclined to the police view that Jamison was just a random victim. Two murders and two murderers."

"I take it you intend to concentrate on Alissa's murder then?"

I nodded in the affirmative.

The next day there was a message form taped to my telephone to call Detective Swanborg. When I reached out and finally touched him, probably by fiber optical cable, he was a tad irritated.

"Marston, I thought we had a deal."

"Yeah?"

"Part of that deal is that you keep me informed of anything

that might clear up these cases."

"So?"

"So, why did I have to hear third hand that you nearly got killed at the theater the other night?"

"Killed. Where'd you hear about that?"

"Thorough police work. We tend to talk to people who have contact with murder victims. You're connected, you're in a play, we're talking to people in the theater."

"Detective Swanborg, that falling bag likely was an accident. We looked, but didn't find anyone who shouldn't have been there. I admit, there are some pretty nasty characters in the theater world, but we don't have 'em." There were suddenly niggling doubts in my head. Was I too casually shrugging off the falling sandbag?

"Now, you listen to me." Swanborg snarled at me. "When we heard, we took a look at the frayed rope on that sandbag. The lab says it was definitely frayed, and deliberately done. From here on, you watch your back. And keep me informed!" He slammed the phone down. I looked at the instrument in my hand. Deliberately frayed! Attempted murder. My heart suddenly beat more rapidly than normal. I definitely should have paid closer attention to that exploding bag.

I spent an enlightening hour struggling with a proposal to expand our private psychological counseling services for troubled students. We already offered limited services, but we usually referred major and long-term situations to a private clinic in the city. Limited resources nearly always sparked debate over proposals for new, or expansion of existing, services. Unless they were directly related to teaching, which, after all, was the primary mission of the institution. When it came to curriculum, the debate was over which subjects were more important. At City College we were always debating something.

It occurred to me that I had a potential conflict of interest here. Since the proposal was for contracted services, Lori's association of psychologists could be in the running for the contract. I decided to talk to her before I went further.

The damn sandbag intruded again. I called Merrill Swanborg and told him of my suspicions about Delton. He was much calmer, or perhaps more tired when he came on the line.

"How about making a discreet inquiry into Ted Delton's background?"

Swanborg snorted. "The director? I never said we'd be your investigation arm, Marston."

"No, but you have to admit it makes some sense. You say the rope on that sandbag was frayed. That means someone in the theater, with more than just casual knowledge of backstage theater must be involved. Have you looked at those catwalks in the fly area?"

"So, you believe our lab report?"

"I'm just being careful. Isn't that what you told me to do?"

"Do you have something concrete to offer? Lot's of people have access to the theater. If you want to follow some random whim of your own, don't look to city hall for help." He hung up in my ear again. I was going to have to polish my reflexes so I could return the compliment the next time we had a phone conversation.

I called Fred Coper.

"Fred, it's Jack. Any progress on those codes?"

"Not yet. But remember, Marsh's a friend of mine too, you know, so I'll help clear him if I can. I can't believe he's a murderer. You know?"

Silently I agreed, except that anybody seems to have murder in them, under the right circumstances. "Yes. Well, if you turn up anything unusual about Delton, I'd like to know right away."

"You think Jamison's murder is connected to the theater?"

"I'm not aware of any such connection between Jamison and

the theater."

"Murderers come in all guises," he replied obscurely. "Jack the Ripper was maybe a doctor, or a prince. As it happens, Personnel requires quite a background on anyone who does high profile stuff for us. Before you came, we had us an adjunct faculty who was supposed to be really hot stuff. Degrees from one end of the country to the other. And, a real looker too. She had a pair of...."

"Fred!"

"Uh. Sorry, I forget sometimes I'm not supposed to say things like that."

"You'd better remember. You'll get into serious trouble."

"Okay, lemme finish. The woman was a total fake. In those days we didn't check much. After a while, funny stuff came to the surface. Like, she had gaps in fundamental knowledge. Eventually we found out her credentials were mostly faked and got rid of her. But it's been a policy ever since to require good background checks on everybody who does anything for the college. We'll have a file on Delton and I bet I can get some info from the U since he's local." Enthusiasm was growing in Coper's voice.

"Just be careful. We don't want an invasion of privacy suit."

I reflected that the background check on Constant had not turned up the negative feelings I'd unearthed. I collected some typescripts Teresa had prepared of my notes on three earlier staff interviews. She had two trusted student workers and one of our clerks asking basic questions about contacts with Jamison to help me avoid wasting time on people who had no information. The danger was, if someone lied, I might skip them. On the other hand, there was no guarantee my keen and experienced ear would detect lies, either. I was still considering redirecting their efforts to Constant.

Coper called again late in the afternoon. I could hear

discouragement in his voice.

"Nothing, Fred?" I was trying to be sympathetic.

"GIGO!" he said, firmly.

"GIGO?"

"Yeah, Garbage In Garbage Out. It's an old computer term, means if you don't enter good data, you don't get good answers. I got a pile of information on Delton but a lot of it doesn't fit. And there are gaps where somebody should have updated the files and didn't. I got his name spelled at least three different ways. They all show up because the files are keyed to social security numbers. The U does the same thing."

"And?"

"And, Doctor Marston, I have two different dates for his M.A., attendance at several undergraduate institutions, endless numbers of credits in nearly every subject imaginable. There are pages and pages of stuff, but no parental names. And this guy apparently doesn't have a thesis advisor, which I thought was required."

"So what's the bottom line?"

"They have very bad data entry and error-checking procedures over there."

"Great. Is it possible the data was altered after entry?" I was beginning to think we were all sinking into a bottomless swamp of computerese and incompetence.

"Sure. But that raises all sorts of other questions. What should I do with this? It's pages and pages of stuff."

"Put what you've got in a file folder and lock it up somewhere." Alarm bells were going off in my head. Maybe I was overcautious, but I didn't want to alert Delton to our interest. I remembered the sandbag.

My favorite president came on the line. That was unusual. He didn't ordinarily place his own calls. He was not happy.

"Marston, come over here."

President Trammel's abrupt summonses were not to be

ignored. I grabbed my jacket and went across the street.

He was enthroned as usual behind his barrier of a desk, fingers steepled beneath his fleshy chins. He merely looked at me as I crossed the acre of green carpet. The carpet must have been recently cleaned. I smelled that odd dead fish smell from the chemicals. At least that's what I thought it was.

"Well, Marston," he roared, when I drew within shouting distance. "What have you to report?"

"It's a little difficult to conduct this inquiry without offending people, so I'm moving slowly, President Trammel."

"Never mind that, get on with it," he roared. "Donations are off. I can't afford to worry about a few hurt sensibilities at a time like this." His exasperated sigh was like a change in the wind.

Maybe you can't, I thought, but I have to. What I said was, "I'll try to move things along a little faster, sir." A little gentle groveling never hurt.

"See that you do, see that you do. I also want you to think about how best to approach the possibility of getting Dr. Marshall to resign."

"*What?* I beg your pardon?" I was still standing at one corner of his desk. If I'd been sitting, I probably would have leaped to my feet. What was this? What had happened to innocent until proven guilty?

"Yes, yes, I know. It is a most unfortunate situation, but this college can't be saddled with suspected murderers at this crucial time. I think, for the good of the institution, we have to consider that Dr. Marshall may have become a liability."

Why the sanctimonious old bastard! My initial reaction was to tell Trammel to go to hell, but that wouldn't help Marsh. I thought about it and listened to his rasping breath. I'd have to play things carefully from now on. There was a moment of silence. Then he imperiously waved me out. My audience was at an end. I left wishing Portia was available to advocate for Marsh when the president demanded his pound of flesh. Quality of mercy, indeed.

CHAPTER 19

*–they have tried to rob me of my
most elementary rights–*

On the way to my car, in the twilight, disturbing thoughts intruded. Falling sandbags, dirty pictures, anonymous messages, telephone hang-ups. My mind was aswirl with random images. Yes, I was now calling it 'a case.' A more disturbing thought intruded. Was I being watched? I looked around. Not many people in sight, no one who seemed to be paying attention to me. When I got to my car I looked around again, tried to be casual as I fumbled for the door lock. Again, nothing looked amiss.

I had just unlocked the door to my apartment when the phone began to jangle. I swung the door shut and walked to my desk. My electronic slave dutifully answered after four rings and I pinched the volume up so I could hear the caller's voice.

"Daddy, are you there? If you're not, call me tomorrow night."

I grabbed the phone, spilling papers from the desk onto the floor calling, "Kitten! I'm here."

All in the same motion I dropped into my desk chair and bent to retrieve falling papers. There was a faint crack and a tinkle of glass behind me.

"Elizabeth. How are you, darlin'?" Over the years my daughter and I had developed the habit of calling each other once a week, for specific reasons, or just to talk. Sometimes our conversations consisted of no more than a few pleasant words. At other times, we had been a measure of support for each other.

"Hey, how's my favorite dad?" Her voice was warm and

sugary, like her mother's. Not cloying. It was warm and smooth, flowing like a shallow creek in the late summer sun.

We caught up on her recent life, then I said, "Listen, you work in the Justice Department so you must know about the witness protection program, right?"

She laughed. "Fraud, Dad, anti-trust, all the boring low-profile business things. We aren't into cement overshoes and disappearing witnesses. Besides I'm still basically only office help, you know."

"Sure. But what do you know about the program?"

"This is a very strange question, Papa mine. There is such a program. It was set up to provide a haven for witnesses against the mob, organized crime, you know. We'd give witnesses protection and a whole new identity, and move them somewhere else, but it was only for someone who could testify about major stuff or top bosses. That's about it. Everything else is classified on a need-to-know basis. The people who run the program won't even say how many witnesses are in it."

"Lose many?"

"Another question with no answer. What are you into out there in the sleepy Midwest, Daddy? There's no organized crime in your patch."

I laughed gently. "And therefore, possibly a good place to put witnesses, no?" I looked up at a black fly on the wall above my head.

"Dunno, but I do know this. If you ask the U.S. Marshall's office, they'll tell you nothing and then go through your life to find out why you asked."

Interesting, I thought. "And would they talk to you?"

"Nope, maybe to my boss or my boss's boss."

"Well, Elizabeth, I'll do nothing to jeopardize your career. You know how proud of you I am, and besides, I'm counting on you to support me in retirement, once you get to be a big time lawyer."

She laughed and then asked, "How's Lori?"

"Good. Good, as is our relationship."

A soft chime sounded through the phone.

"Doorbell, Dad, my current date, gotta go."

"Love ya. Don't stay out too late, y'hear?" Her laughter gurgled in my ear and she hung up. I looked thoughtfully at the phone, then reached up and brushed at the fly on the wall. It didn't move. Besides...flies in November? Now I realized it wasn't a fly at all, it was a hole. I stood up and put a finger on it.

Crack, tinkle! It was a replay of those earlier sounds. I fell right back down again, glancing off the desk chair as I dropped. My weight slammed the chair across the room, where it fell over when it encountered the edge of the small piece of carpet in what passed for my living room. I landed with a thump, sprawled on my backside beside the desk. I ignored the annoying howl of the telephone coming from the floor under the desk where I had dropped the damn thing, and rolled over. I looked at the window opposite my desk. There were two small cone-shaped holes side by side in the panes that hadn't been there when I left yesterday morning. I looked back at the wall. Now there were two black flies. A bead of sweat started down my left temple and my hands were suddenly slippery.

Jesus Christ! Someone had just taken a shot at me. Two shots! I grabbed the phone again, noting in passing that a piece had been broken out of one side of its case. Great. Two phones bashed in one day.

Fortunately, Swanborg was at his desk.

"I think you ought to come over here right away."

"Why?" Swanborg still sounded a little testy.

"Because somebody just took a shot at me in my apartment."

"What?" he roared almost as loud as Trammel. "Stay away from windows and et cetera. We'll be right there."

I gave him the address and sure enough, it took him hardly any time at all to arrive, even though I heard no sirens. He had several other cops with him. They came quickly and quietly into the room and began to examine the window and the wall.

"You aren't worried about him still being over there?" I waved at the wall in the general direction of the street.

"There's a team across the street. They checked out the general area before we came in here. Tell me again what happened."

He took me through the incident while another detective took notes. I watched as other officers dug the slugs out of my wall, traced a trajectory angle, and with the aid of a small telescope, pinpointed the probable location of the shooter.

My hands began to tremble again and I sat down on the couch.

Swanborg looked down at me. "You okay? You look a little green."

"Yeah, well, I don't feel so good. Getting shot at is hardly among my daily activities."

Swanborg's team figured out that I must have stooped at the instant of the first shot to retrieve the dropped papers, and moved again for the second. Pure luck or an inexpert shooter. The other detectives left and Swanborg and I looked at each other in silence.

"I never heard a gunshot, either time," I said finally.

"Two glass panes, a street, and probably a silencer. I'm not surprised," he shrugged. More silence.

"Merrill," I said then, "let me try something on you."

"Civilians," he muttered. "I should have my head examined for ever letting you in this far. What in Hell is going on?"

"Some facts and some impressions. You get a butchered man in our theater lobby. I didn't see Jamison's body, but I did get a graphic description of the scene. Could the murderer have been interrupted? What I mean is, could he or she have just killed Jamison and then been scared away?"

"From what?"

"From leaving a message of some kind. Put that aside. Now you start the investigation. We discover that Jamison's records at

City College are mostly erased. Information that should be there is gone."

"Or never entered in the first place," Swanborg grunted.

I nodded. "I get tagged to do an internal investigation, which I read as a way to keep the lid on. But the lid on what? I thought first it must be because of the fund drive, but then Trammel tells me there are unmentionable dimensions to Jamison, and Marshall intimates the same thing."

"What dimensions? What?" Impatience colored Swanborg's voice.

"More investigating." I held up my hands to keep him quiet. "Now you get pressure from upstairs, whatever that means, to go easy on the Jamison murder and concentrate on Constant, right? I call around about Constant, get some funny vibrations and I learn that I'm following a recently trodden path. Somebody else is calling about her. Somebody named McKenzie. I assume it's the cops, but you tell me you don't need to do that because you have Marshall and are satisfied. Okay so far?"

Swanborg nodded with a dour expression.

"What if you talk to the FBI? They aren't very cooperative with the local authorities, you'll tell me. Well, how about the U.S. Marshall's office? Will they talk to you?" I stopped and stared at him. He shook his head, and then became still, staring back at me from where he sat hunched on my sagging sofa. He leaned forward even more, slender hands dangling between his knees. He looked at me for a long, silent minute.

"By damn, you might be right, Marston. The Federal Witness Protection Program! I should have thought of it myself." His voice was a harsh whisper in the dark room. He rubbed his face with one hand. "It fits. I can make an official inquiry, but they'll just bury it. We'd never get a real answer and we'd never know for sure if we're right, but that's the only explanation."

"I'll bet Trammel and Marsh know Jamison's real identity. If we're right, Jamison was killed by a contract killer and his death is unrelated to Constant's, just as you said at the beginning. So we've got two killers, like I said. Remember, Marshall was still in jail the night the sandbag fell."

"Yeah, and one of the killers knows a good deal about you. That was a murder attempt at the theater and here's another one at your apartment. We ought to get you out of this. Can you take some vacation for a couple of weeks?"

"Whoa, I'm not going anywhere right now, especially since I'm sure you've tagged the wrong guy for Alissa Constant's murder."

Swanborg rose to leave and said, "Well, if you won't take a vacation, stay away from lighted windows. You better not say anything to your friend, what's her name?"

"Lori," I murmured.

He walked across my living room to the door. "Don't tell Lori about this incident. Not tonight. Not for a while. What I don't get is why the shooter is still around, if it's the same guy who killed Jamison."

"Maybe he lives in Minneapolis," I said quietly.

"Hard to believe." Swanborg shook his head and walked out with a brief wave of his hand.

Brave words, I thought. No vacation for me. What the hell was I doing? No answer came so I turned out the rest of the lights and had a drink.

CHAPTER 20

*I am neither more self-interested
nor more ambitious than most men.*

It was the beginning of another day in the trenches of City College. My parking place near the gargantuan new ramp going up, though just a block from our offices, seemed particularly lonely and isolated that gray, bitter morning when I drove in. At least my hands had stopped shaking. I was pretty certain whoever had taken a shot at me last night probably thought he'd hit me with his second. I was safe, until I turned up healthy at the college Was that a generic 'his,' or was I subconsciously sure it was a man? I wanted just to disappear for a while, but I wasn't willing to abandon my attempts to help Marsh. I looked around when I got out of the car, but I saw no one who appeared to be interested in me.

I crunched across the semi-frozen earth. Inside the ramp, small groups of men in white and yellow hard hats and an assortment of stocking caps and bulky outer clothing stood smoking, drinking coffee, and chatting. Most wore wide stained leather belts that sagged with the weight of their well-filled tool holsters. The external wire-framed elevator cage rose slowly toward an upper floor, its big electric motor humming loudly in the crisp morning air. Paper trash lay about in disorderly piles. My breath was a white plume.

It was quiet for that time of the morning in our building. I pushed open the door to our office suite, encountered Teresa's smiling face, and the blessed smell of fresh coffee from the mug in her hand.

"Oh," she said, "what timing. I just this very instant finished making morning coffee. Can I pour you a cup?"

"Great. That would be just great." When she brought it in, Teresa stopped, about to hand me the mug, but then drew back.

"Oh my. I'm not sure I should come any farther. Is this your desk? I'm afraid there may be a monster under all that ready to grab me. Are there any nests in there? Maybe a rat or two?"

She was more than half right. My locked file was filling as I gathered and created more folders of information on the people involved with Jamison and Constant, and other papers related to the more routine goings on of the college continued to proliferate in untidy stacks on every horizontal surface.

After last night I had a whole new perspective. There was no longer any doubt in my mind that we were looking for two killers and I, at least, was sure both were still out there. There was no conceivable reason for a contract killer to target Alissa. But Jamison was an unknown quantity. On to another name on a file from Constant's desk.

Mathew Jellicoe was a preeminent member of the economics faculty. He'd been with the college almost since the founding of the place. Educated at the London School of Economics, he had rubbed elbows with the likes of Alan Greenspan and Walter Heller. He was intelligent, but had no discernible personality, except possibly a total lack of humor.

Jellicoe could take the most arcane and obscure economic theory and translate it into basic, plain English so that even our dullest students could understand what it meant. Even more difficult, he could make me understand it–at least for a while. He was a short, rotund man who always seemed to wear the same dark blue, shapeless suits. I suspected he bought them in quantity.

Others, less charitable, suggested he only had one suit. He always wore a starched white shirt with a dark tie. In the winter he wore what appeared to be a good quality, heavy topcoat, sometimes with a white silk scarf.

Professor of Economics Mathew J. Jellicoe appeared to have no family, just like Jamison. Tenured, he ignored all but the most essential faculty and staff functions. He never won any of the clutter of awards made by students or organizations at the college; he never served on committees. He was never consulted on the hiring or tenure decisions that filled the lives of faculty, when they weren't teaching. He was a loner. Not exactly unpleasant, he just wasn't there, except in class, or when you confronted him with a specific question. Professor Jellicoe was also, I discovered, on sabbatical leave this year.

"When did his leave start?" I wanted to know.

"At the end of summer quarter," the dean's secretary told me.

"Do you know about his plans? Is he out of town?"

"Well, faculty have to submit a plan, you know, in order to be approved for sabbatical. I think he's staying in town doing research. Of course, if he decides to make a trip, he wouldn't have to notify us. Why all this interest in Professor Jellicoe?"

"I have an economic question for him. Thanks, Gail."

I dialed Marilee but there was no answer.

"Teresa," I called, "when Marilee gets back, ask her to come see me, will you?"

"Sure, but remember, this is the morning she goes to gourmet cooking class."

"Oh, yeah, that's right. You know, she's already such a good cook, can you imagine what she'll be like when she's through with this latest course?"

Teresa walked to the door and stood there smiling at me. "D'you remember that baked salmon she made last year?

Whooee!" I nodded. Our division had a reputation for throwing first class parties, mostly because of the quality of the food we provided. We'd had some outstanding successes, primarily due to our star, Marilee Jannard, although I had developed a specialty or two over the years.

I called Personnel and they told me where to locate Jellicoe's older personnel files. By now all the department heads had received a memo from President Trammel that gave me access to practically everything. The Personnel Office purged office files every few years and transferred older documents to a file cabinet in the attic. It meant grubbing around in a grimy storeroom, but if I was going to be thorough, I'd need to scan the records of everyone whose names were on those files from Constant's desk.

Two hours later I was back in my office with a page of notes and several documents lifted from Jellicoe's records. It was against college policy to do that, but I was becoming less and less careful about precise interpretation of certain college rules. After last night, who knew which were friendlies and which were not?

There were no great revelations in his file, except that Jellicoe had taught at an obscure Eastern college for a short time prior to moving to City College, and guess what? Alissa Constant had taken graduate courses at the same place. I also discovered that Mathew Jellicoe was a hometown product. He'd grown up in Minneapolis and graduated from a local high school. I decided that I was going to talk to Professor Jellicoe, sabbatical or no.

Mid-afternoon I met Lori for coffee.

"How are you?" I asked, coming up to her booth, trying not to sift attic dust into my coffee. The police had warned me not to tell anyone about the shooting, and I'd not taken Lori into my confidence as yet.

Lori smiled at me and then frowned, leaning away as I slid into the seat across from her. "Goodness, where have you been playing?"

"Attic. Personnel's storeroom." I smiled. "Don't you look nice today." She did, in a dark red jersey dress.

"Oh dear. Anything interesting turn up?"

"Not really. Did you know Constant took a couple of graduate courses back East from Jellicoe?"

"Really. I always find it fascinating how people's lives cross. Often in ways that don't seem real. For example, after we met I learned you grew up here in the Twin Cities. I was living in Riverview and I sometimes wonder if we ever attended the same state basketball tournament games."

"Doubt it," I smiled.

"Why?"

"Because of our ages. I graduated before you started ninth grade."

"Right, but Riverview was basketball mad. My brothers brought me almost every year from sixth grade on, on the town bus."

CHAPTER 21

*–it would be an easy matter for me
to set on foot some testimonial–*

I discovered that in addition to the econ course Alissa'd taken back east, she'd taken another course from Jellicoe here at City College. Since any of us could audit City College courses at no cost, several of us took occasional classes from our faculty, but she'd paid the fee. Did I care? Did it matter? I wasn't sure. I was sure I had to talk with Jellicoe. I punched the computer keyboard to bring up the professor's address. Then I grabbed my coat and left the office.

The scribble in my notebook told me I was close to the address, but I wondered if I had come across yet another glitch in our computer system. This didn't appear to be the kind of neighborhood where a respected senior member of the economics department faculty would live. I was driving through a neighborhood that was heading downhill. It was a long way from being a slum, but I knew what a tenured senior professor's salary was these days, and I would have expected he'd live in a tonier part of town. This area would soon show up in the newspapers as one of our 'problem neighborhoods.' Several curbs were cracked and the streets hadn't been repaired in years. I passed a couple of houses that appeared to be abandoned. White and pale weathered pastels seemed to be the predominant colors.

Still, my own apartment wasn't something you'd ever find in "House Beautiful." Lori had begun to make occasional disparaging comments about my place and we were spending more and more time at hers. Of course, her big, queen-sized bed was an improvement over my Hide-A-Bed.

Jellicoe's address was one of those ubiquitous ramblers built in the late fifties all over the northern prairies. The city was full of them. This one appeared to be in some better shape than many of its neighbors. A beat up old Ford sat in the driveway that I vaguely recognized as belonging to Matt Jellicoe. Lights shone from several windows, competing with the fading late afternoon sun.

I parked behind the Ford and walked up the frozen grassy path to the concrete block platform that passed for a front porch. My breath was plainly visible against the yellowish streetlights that had just blinked on. Jellicoe's mailbox had seen better days; it hung there as if tired of all the junk mail that had been stuffed into it over the years. Its door was bent out of shape so it wouldn't close tightly. Paint was peeling off the mailbox. Paint peeled off the white doorjamb as well. I didn't see a bell so I rapped on the door, a standard-issue plain-panel exterior door, painted, sometime in its distant past, a pale blue. It had three small lights of nearly opaque glass. There was no discernible response to my rap.

I turned my ring around and rapped on the glass, on the vertical pane set into the wall beside the door. I couldn't see in, a shade was drawn over the glass. After a moment I contemplated putting on my gloves and really pounding on the damn door, but then a light came on and a shadow loomed up. I heard the night latch rattle and Professor Jellicoe opened the door. His myopic eyes, magnified large behind thick lenses, peered out at me. I had heard students say that they sometimes felt like insects in collection boxes when he metaphorically pinned them to the wall in class.

"Evening, Matt," I said calmly. Was I being too informal? We weren't close colleagues. Indeed, most college faculty don't consider any non-academic professional staff to be colleagues. It was only five-thirty in the evening, but he had the look of a man who'd been belting them down for several hours. "I'm sorry to bother you at home like this, but I'm involved in this murder investigation, and I need your help."

He didn't give me so much as a flicker. Christ! Did he even recognize me? He stood there, light from the living room filtering through his hair, turning it dark maroon.

"Professor!" I said, raising my voice a little. "I need to talk to you!"

"You don't have to yell," he remarked mildly, swinging the door open. "Come in, if you must."

I walked into a clean, spare entranceway. I didn't smell any cooking odors. Maybe he ate out, or much later. To the left through a partly opened door I glimpsed a dining room with a dark bare table and matching chairs. On the other side of the small hall was an arch that led to another room. Jellicoe gestured half-heartedly toward the arch and I walked past him into the medium-sized living room. The furniture was old, also dark, but matched and obviously of good quality. I picked a comfortable-looking chair and sat down. Jellicoe closed the front door and turned toward me, but he hadn't followed me into the room. He just stood there under the arch staring at me. I smiled up at him. Try to put the suspect at ease, from my Criminal Investigation manual. The Navy had apparently assumed that their investigators only talked to suspects.

"You may not know that the president has asked me to be liaison with the police and to conduct a quasi in-house investigation. Of Stuart Jamison's death. I assume you read about that." I got a restrained nod.

"I just want to ask you a few questions, and since you're on sabbatical all quarter, I thought I'd better run out here to see you.

Trammel is pretty anxious to get this wrapped up as soon as possible. He's worried about adverse effects on the fund drive."

For a moment I thought he hadn't heard. "Why don't you all just leave it to the police?" His voice was flat and he sounded almost bored. There wasn't a flicker of anything in his pale eyes.

"Trammel seems to believe we can keep the college from getting hurt by bad publicity if I poke around a little."

"I don't know what I can tell you. I had Mr. Jamison in two, perhaps three classes during the past two years. He was a good student, not brilliant, but good. He certainly had some interesting ideas about corporate record keeping."

"Thanks. I don't need to see your class records, but if you remember anything about him that might help us fill in some blanks, I'd like to know, and I'm sure President Trammel would be grateful." We talked some more, mostly about Jamison, some about other recent happenings at the college. Jellicoe seemed to have only a bare minimum of interest. It took a mention of Alissa Constant's death to get any real reaction. When I asked if he remembered her as a graduate student, his gaze turned away from me and he looked down at the thin carpet.

"Oh, yes. I do remember her. She was brilliant. I talked to her about changing direction and going into economics, but," his voice trailed off and he gestured vaguely.

He came and sat down, perched, really, on one end of the sofa. He didn't offer me a drink, or coffee, he just politely and softly answered my questions. Yet now I was beginning to get a feeling he was concerned about something that wasn't apparent, perhaps something he hoped I wouldn't ask about.

After about ten minutes, the telephone rang somewhere toward the back of the house. Jellicoe flinched, rose with alacrity, and excused himself. He left the room in that peculiar shuffle he had, as if it hurt him to bend his knees. Arthritis maybe, I thought.

I stood up and looked around the room. There weren't any pictures on the walls. There weren't any books on the shelves or tables, just a few knickknacks scattered about. The room had no character. It was a bare stage. It almost felt as if no one really lived there. I could hear Jellicoe's voice, a susurrating murmur in the background, but I couldn't make out any words. They ran together in a low, confidential-sounding tone. A door in the living room wall opposite the front of the house was slightly ajar and there was a light on behind it. Being the inquisitive sort, I stepped across the room and pushed gently on the door. After all I'd come here to learn something, hadn't I? The door swung open a little further. Jellicoe could come back at any moment so I didn't go in, just stuck my head in. Very interesting!

The room was all white, ceiling, walls and floor. Semi-gloss enamel, it looked like. A white cloth tightly covered the single window. There was little furniture, just a low table, about eight feet long and three feet wide on sturdy white painted legs. A large white sheet was draped over the top. On the table was an empty white plastic easel. On either side of the table stood two black aluminum tripods, the kind photographers often use. Mounted on top of each was a silver-coated device–umbrellas, I'd heard them called. In one corner stood a larger tripod with a small video camera attached to it. Anita Talbot's bit of information by way of students and Lori was right on the money. I was sure I was looking at the college's missing video equipment. I turned back and stepped out of the room just as Jellicoe hung up the phone and returned.

"Well, Mr. Marston. Was there anything else?"

"Nope." I smiled easily at him. "Just think about Jamison and Constant and call me with anything that you think is helpful." Jellicoe didn't bid me good night when he closed the door and left me standing in the chilly night. Well, if I had thought I was going to detect some major new evidence, this interview was certainly a bust.

I drove home, mulling over the only piece of new information I had picked up, that Mathew Jellicoe had a functional video recording setup in his home. Why? He'd apparently been using the camera to copy something. As Lori had mentioned, it didn't seem to fit the man's image. But then, how well do we really know our colleagues?

I probably should have asked him about the camera, but then I would have revealed I had snooped while he was out of the room and something told me Mathew Jellicoe would have been exceedingly displeased.

CHAPTER 22

*–in any case, I shall have done
my duty towards the public–*

"Jack, Anita Talbot has called at least five times since I got in. I stopped keeping track after the first three. She knows I'll give you the message. She sounded upset, to say the least," said Teresa, a mite exasperated.

"Okay, I'll call her right back." What was the problem? Maybe one of our student workers had misplaced a precious projector. It was an uncharitable thought. Anita's line was busy.

Ten minutes later we connected. Teresa was right. "Can you come up here to my office right now?" Anita's voice was low, flat.

"Sure 'Nita, but what's this about?" I'd go up there, but it wasn't as if I had nothing else to do, God knew.

"Not on the phone," she hissed. "Just come up here. Now!"

I strode into the outer office to see Teresa deftly deflecting someone to Marilee. Her quizzical expression sent me a question which I read. I jabbed a finger dramatically out and up.

For reasons known only to building 'programmers,' I think they're called, audiovisual services and storage facilities were ensconced on the top, or eighth, floor of our building. I was forever encountering blank-faced student workers pushing large trolleys of equipment in and out of the elevators. This morning, the elevator was prompt and empty.

It was quiet on eight and I easily followed Talbot's penetrating voice down the long hallway to her office. This floor had been renovated so it was more open, if not brighter, than the floors below. The thin November sun washed through the grimy windows, its weak rays barely able to soften the gloom of the wide hall.

"…and I think we have to repeat orientation sessions. We'd better or there won't be an operating projector or VCR in the whole damn place!" She slammed down the phone, not bothering to listen to the reply.

"Anita." I remonstrated. "Such language." My tone was light and I smiled. The smile faded under the withering glare she turned my way.

"I know, I know. I don't usually flip out like that, even when I feel like doing it. C'mon." She lunged out of her chair so I followed her out of the room.

Office Manager and general factotum of audiovisual services, Anita Talbot was in her mid-thirties, voluptuous and divorced. Some called her predatory. She was a confirmed gossip. She was also possessed of a voice, her detractors said privately, that could break water tumblers at thirty paces.

"There's a store room down here where we'll have some privacy," she said over her shoulder.

Privacy? For what, I wondered.

I recalled that last year she'd had a run-in with Fred Coper, over some scatological computer graphics she stumbled across in the computer lab. Apparently the graphics were part of a large package of programs Coper imported from another college and he hadn't been familiar with everything supplied, or so he said at the time. Unfortunately, Coper isn't known for his sensitivity to feminist issues, or to females in general. I think he wishes we still lived in the early fifties. Except for computers of course.

Anita demanded deletion of the offensive material, a reasonable request, you'll say. Exactly, I'll agree. Unfortunately, Coper didn't see it that way and during their disagreement, he made some rude and specific remarks about a possible intimate void in Talbot's life.

The remarks got back to Anita and things were escalating into the stratosphere when others stepped in and resolved things. The offensive material destroyed, Fred and Anita agreed to withdraw their inflammatory remarks. A cold uneasy true between the two was still in effect. Since that dust-up they tended to avoid each other as much as possible.

Anita drew ahead of me, almost running in her tight blue skirt and high heels. I couldn't recall ever seeing her move this fast.

In the storage room, she already had a portable television unit set up. She reached down and unlocked a drawer in the long steel worktable and took out a videotape. She turned to me, eyes on the black plastic container. Her voice was low and had a hesitant quality I'd never heard her use before.

"Jack, I found this tape in one of the VCRs after it'd been checked in." Her head came up and her direct gaze met mine. I could almost feel it. She'd made a decision.

"I'll be blunt. I talked to a couple of people here, including Lori Jacobs, before I decided. She says you're all right and I can trust you. I have to trust someone. I…wanted to...just...burn it at first. Then I got really angry and I blurted out a lot of it to Lori. She told me you'd run into some porno stuff recently and maybe it was all connected with the murders. So, then…well, she persuaded me to let you see it. I can't just take it to the cops." She whirled and snapped the cassette into the slot in the VCR.

Snow, visual noise, and static sounds came at us from the television, then the sound went dead and the picture rolled and steadied. What I saw was a murky, out-of-focus, badly lit scene of a room with a bed. All the light came from one side, casting harsh shadows in places. The cameraperson had held the camera unsteadily and panned it randomly around the room.

There were five boys in the scene, all naked. They were engaged in a variety of sexual games, at the obvious direction of someone out of range of the camera. One or another would glance to one side, waiting to be told what to do next. As a result, instead of a more or less continuous flow of action, the thing had a jerky, start-stop feel to it. After I became used to the unsteady frame, I realized that the boys were quite young and appeared to be way under the age of consent. They were all self-conscious, acting with no apparent pleasure at what they were doing. I reached and hit the stop button.

"Anita, what…"

"Wait," she said hoarsely. "There's more."

Reluctantly, I turned back to the VCR and touched the play button. After a few more seconds of naked, stilted male games, the picture broke up, the screen went dark, and a different scene snapped onto the screen. This one had also been taped in a plain room with only a single forlorn poster stuck on one wall. This scene had only three participants and there was a sound track of sorts. To my untutored ear, it sounded real, as if the microphone was on the camera, or hanging from the ceiling.

There were two men and a woman in this little drama, all adults, all naked. They were racially mixed, the men being dark-skinned African-Americans, unlike the first segment in which all the boys appeared to be white.

The trio writhed and strained on a bed in various intimate positions, always careful to position themselves so the camera had a clear view. I noticed the video had been judiciously edited so none of the participant's faces were visible. We saw an ear, a nose, or an eyebrow, but never enough to identify the owner. Still there was something. Then it clicked. The woman in the picture could be–I swiveled my heard around to stare at Anita. She'd crossed the room and was standing just behind me, staring with obvious disgust at the screen.

Her breath came in harsh, irregular gasps. She wasn't excited, wasn't turned on, she was very, very angry.

"You see?" she cried, when she realized I was staring at her. "You see it too, just like I did! That woman looks like me! But it isn't!" Her voice rose in panic.

"Anita!" I said sharply. It had the desired effect. She took a deep breath and pressed her hands over her stomach. "Keep watching, pal," her mouth twisted bitterly. "It makes me sick."

I returned to the screen. But what was I looking for?

"One of those guys could be vice-president Marshall," she hissed at me.

I studied the rest of the tape. It only ran five or six minutes. She was right, one of the male participants could be Marsh, but I doubted it was. When the tape finished, I told her so.

"All right, Anita. That isn't Marsh, and I know it isn't you, but I can see why you're so upset."

"Jack, what happens if copies of this tape end up in the hands of somebody who has it in for Marsh or me? Or what if it gets passed around to students?" Her voice got low and intense.

"Okay, I understand. Just because I believe you, doesn't mean everybody else will. There's enough similarity to cause talk, especially with Marsh accused of murder."

She nodded.

"But why this tape and why here?" I scratched my nose.

"There are two possibilities," Anita growled. She paced back and forth, the way caged tigers sometimes do. "This is either a desperate attempt to embarrass me and cause problems for Marshall, or it's somebody's dumb mistake that the tape was left in our machine."

"How'd you find it? Who was the last user?"

She shrugged. "Don't know. The tape is unlabeled, see? I picked it out of the stock that's been returned the last few days. We do that, randomly check to be sure the tapes are still okay. There's no way to trace where it came from. It could just have easily been erased and never seen."

"Maybe we can figure it out. If you can stand it, play it a couple of more times. Don't watch the action, look at the rest of the frame. Try to describe anything you see in the room that might be a clue. Watch for jewelry. Look at their fingernails. Watch for scars. Write down everything you notice that might reveal where the tape was made. Or give it to me and I'll do it." I held out my hand.

She recoiled a step and shook her head. "No. I'll watch it." Then she locked the tape away again and we returned to her office.

"At first," she said, sitting behind her desk, "I though it was more stuff from Coper, bugging me again, you know?"

I nodded.

"But I've been taking some computer workshops. Fascinating stuff. I really love it, you know? Anyway, last winter Jeff taught a programming workshop. He was really funny and supportive. I was the only non-faculty person in the workshop. Funny, at one time I thought I'd never be able to stand the sight of him. I guess all that stuff last year is behind us." She sighed and shook her heard. "I still don't think he gets it, though. He's just one of those sexist pigs who'll never learn."

I smiled at her. "Maybe not. Maybe he'll change. He isn't stupid,"

"Maybe. Maybe. Computers are really interesting, you know? I got this book from the library about codes. I could hardly put it down. So we talked about it in class a little. Fred was a cryptologist in the Army, did you know that? He says I seem to have a natural talent for codes."

I nodded.

"Well, Mr. Marston, I don't have time to chew the fat with you, and I'm sure you have plenty to do." She was fast returning to her normal self. Dismissed, I left.

Later, after I considered all the reasons why it was a bad idea, I decided to trust my hunch anyway and I talked to Fred Coper.

"I was talking to Anita Talbot earlier today and she mentioned that she was developing an interest in codes."

"Yes, I remember when she brought a book to the workshop. We had quite a discussion. She seems to be one of those people whose mind has a natural bent for that stuff."

"What'd do you think about enlisting her help with the coded files?"

He looked at me for a moment. "Are you serious?"

I nodded. "Sure. She told me you said she has a natural talent for computers and codes. You're real busy right now, so maybe you'd like to see if she's willing?"

"Pushing your luck, Jack, but okay."

An hour later Anita called me. "I just talked to Fred Coper. What's the deal?"

"I'll send you one of the coded files I found in Dean Constant's office. It might help us solve these murders. But you have to keep quiet about it. Don't talk to anyone other than Fred."

"So he said. You really think this file has anything to do with Alissa Constant's murder?"

"I can't answer that until it's translated."

"But you hope whatever it is will clear Marshall, right? What if it makes things worse?" Her voice crackled in my ear.

"There's always that chance, but since I'm convinced Marshall didn't kill her, solving this code can only help. Of course it may be unrelated. Again, if you do this you have to promise to be real careful. You may learn stuff you don't want to know." There was a pause while we both thought about the implications of what I was getting her into, then she sighed again.

"All right, Jack. I'll give it a try. Fred was pretty insistent too. I dunno why I listen to you guys. But no promises, okay?"

"Thanks, Anita. I'll send a copy up right away."

CHAPTER 23

*Keep a very careful eye
on the manuscript–*

Temperatures for the next two days stayed right around the freezing mark.

Normal for November. A weak sun struggled to penetrate the constant, broken cloud cover. We still had no snow to speak of, although the weather service was predicting it at any time. The Vikings won two in a row and rehearsals for "Enemy of the People" continued to lurch along. Sometimes we made wonderful progress, everything came together, and we could almost taste the improvements. Other times it was as if we were pushing against an invisible wall through which neither words nor actions penetrated.

Student services at the college maintained an even tenor. Busy with mid-quarter examinations, students had no time to get into trouble or to seek our help with the larger issues affecting their lives. Once the testing period was over, we'd see several depressed students questioning the value of the education City College offered, and there would be a small number of incidents when other students acted out transitory frustrations. Ranae reported that the minority community still seemed to accept our denials of a racially motivated focus on my friend Anton Marshall and there hadn't been any demonstrations, so far. Marsh was out on bail and back at work, but he preferred to stay in his office. No longer did I encounter him, coffee mug wrapped in one of his massive hands, leaning against a wall in some hallway, having an earnest conversation with a faculty member, or sitting with a group of students or a staff member in the booths of the restaurant in the cellar of my building.

His arrest, Merrill Swanborg told me, had been based on several circumstantial factors. "Listen, Jack," he said at one of our infrequent meetings. "Everybody we've interviewed has one or two stories to tell about his temper tantrums."

"Isn't that an overstatement? Sure, even I admit that sometimes he's exploded about something. But he's never actually threatened anyone." I glanced at Merrill, a man I was coming to respect more and more. "I bet you haven't turned up anyone who's accused him of jumping on them in a personal way, have you?"

Swanborg shrugged. "No, you're right. But there's more, you know. He hasn't an alibi for the critical time. None we can verify. Claims he was at the health club in his building. The most important evidence is his fights with the dead woman. We've turned up several people who heard or actually witnessed Marshall and Constant arguing, sometimes storming at each other. There were scratches on her back. Fingernail scratches. They match his hand spread."

"Passion," I tried to pass it off. "Find any skin under his nails for a DNA test?"

"Nope. No sure motive, either. But we're working on that. Our theory is she was putting pressure on him to do something for her."

Merrill watched me closely. I shrugged. Sipped my coffee. That squared with what Professor Tidwell had told me. I hadn't related that conversation to Swanborg. Something else that bothered me, along with the purloined files and the mounting evidence that Alissa Constant was a master manipulator everywhere she went.

The police apparently had not yet examined Constant's background as extensively as I had. They hadn't unearthed evidence of the problems and questions that had swirled about her. If the pattern I thought I saw held true, others could point to it as evidence that she'd pushed Marsh too hard for a favor. Maybe he pushed back, too hard.

Was that it? Had Constant discovered the violent incidents in Marsh's past and tried to use them to advance her career? Or ruin his? I shook my head. I couldn't convince myself Marsh would hit her over that, even in anger.

Oh yes, President Trammel was on my back with ever greater pressure to resolve the investigation so the flow of contributions to the building fund would quickly be restored. After all, he pointed out, the legislature would meet in January and we had to show strong community support in order to get the needed bonding appropriation for the rest of the millions required to successfully erect Trammel's Tower. It was interesting to see how my perceived role had changed from that of liaison and unofficial spy to that of principal investigator. I was not encouraged.

Merrill stood up. He'd been sitting there quietly, just observing me. "I know it's tough, Jack. You and Marsh were good friends."

"Are," I nodded. He reached over and gently touched my shoulder as he left. Sensitive, Merrill Swanborg. He must have realized how miserable I was feeling. I'd have to watch myself.

After lunch, I sat at my desk a while and stared at the window. It didn't help.

The damn phone rang. It was Lori.

"Well well, he lives, he lives." Her voice was an instant tonic for my blues. We'd been separate for a couple of days, not even talking by telephone. Hearing her voice, I realized that was part of my ill feelings.

"Why yes, my little chickadee," I leered into the phone in a very bad imitation of W. C. Fields. "It is I. How may I be of service? Carnally, I hope."

"Uh, Jack," her voice turned serious. "Anita Talbot just contacted me. She's upset about something and wants to talk with me."

"Did she say what about?"

"No. I agreed to meet her in the Caves in about twenty minutes, so we'll have to skip our coffee date."

"Ah, well, I hope it isn't too serious."

"Call you after I talk to her?"

"Sure. I'll be in my office the rest of the day."

Thirty minutes later the phone rang again and Lori asked me to come to the basement. When I entered the restaurant I went first to the coffee line, then looked around for Lori, and saw that Anita was sitting with her. The place still smelled of the noon meals.

Lori and Anita had a corner table with a good view of the whole room. Lori sat with her back to one wall and Anita sat across from her. The only empty chair was against the other wall so that Anita sat between Lori and the door.

Talbot was a woman with a particular presence that seemed to give people a reason to talk about her and they did. After her run-in with Fred Coper over the dirty graphics in the computer, Lori told me she thought Anita often deliberately acted provocatively, but she wasn't a real tease.

She had a thin brown file on the table in front of her. She twisted in her chair and watched me cross the big room with a noncommittal expression on her face.

"Hello, Anita. I gather you're upset about something. Does it have anything to do with that file I gave you?" She nodded and I sat in the empty chair. There were a few other people in the place, all sitting some distance away.

"Lori has settled some questions for me, but I want to lay this out so you'll understand why I wanted to talk with her first. I guess I didn't fully realize when I agreed to look at this file of yours what I might find out. It makes me feel a little squirmy." She took a noisy sip of coffee.

I sat back, and gave her time to sort out her thoughts. More people in twos and threes were coming into the restaurant and the din of conversation grew steadily louder. It became difficult to hear her. She leaned forward.

"At first, I was pleased you gave me the file to decode. I hear the stories about me, you know. And I thought it would prove I'm not just a lightweight. Anyway, while I was working on it I remembered something. Stuart Jamison was in one of the computer workshops where we discussed codes. Actually, this is not a terribly difficult code to solve, once you figure out the patterns. It's a double substitution, using numbers and letters."

I raised my eyebrows. My tour of duty in the Navy had brought me into casual contact with codes, so I had some idea what she was talking about. Double substitutions are not quite as easy as she was making out.

"Anyway, I cracked it, stayed up all night last night to decode the whole thing," she twisted her mouth at me. "But it's makin' me nervous." She sighed. "I'll get to the point. Alissa Constant must have had you followed for many, many hours over the past two years, and whenever you and Lori got together, she made a record of it." Her bright red nail tapped the file. "I can tell you the dates and times of your dinners and other things. When you stayed overnight at her place and when she stayed at yours." Anita paused, took a deep breath.

I smiled, slouched a little, tried to appear relaxed. Damn Alissa, I thought. Who did she think she was, spying on Lori and me? My mind tried to fit this information into patterns of Constant's behavior. Anton Marshall's name was on one of the files I had taken from Constant's desk, along with files for several others at City College.

"I can't tell if she watched you all the time. But there's more. Look." She opened the file and shoved a piece of paper over to Lori.

Lori's mouth made a little moue of distaste when she read it, then she slid the paper toward me with one long tapering finger. "Read that. Apparently she had a snooper looking through my windows."

Lori was right. I remembered the incident on the living room floor described in the note. I looked up at Anita, with raised eyebrows. Damn the woman, I thought.

"Anita," said Lori, "there's an embarrassment factor here for Jack and me. I certainly don't like the thought of some weasel watching us make love." She reached over and took my hand. "But Jack and I are of age. We have a good, loving, relationship. We enjoy each other's company a lot and we give each other pleasure. It doesn't matter who knows it. I might have the urge to slap Alissa Constant's face if she were here this minute, but this information isn't a motive for murder."

I took a couple of deep breaths and nodded.

Anita nodded back. "I know that, but look at the last couple of lines on the bottom of this page. Unless I screwed up, it looks like there could be more, maybe another page. What's on the next page? What if you guys have been robbing banks or something?" She smirked to show she wasn't entirely serious.

"Well, there wasn't another page, and I certainly haven't been robbing any banks. 'Course I can't speak for my partner in crime, here," I cracked. "It won't be in that file, but both of us have alibis for the time of her death. We were at a boring conference in St. Paul in the company of several dozen other folks. The police know that."

She nodded, looking relieved.

"What you've done in breaking the code is terrific," I said. "I really appreciate it. If we've satisfied you, I have another favor to ask."

"Yeah?" Anita looked at me with a frown.

"As it happens, there are several other files. Are you willing to decode them as well?"

She groaned. "Jack, C'mon. I have real work to do, y'know? What are you gonna give me? More slimy stuff I don't want to know about? Why don't I just give you the key and you can do your own translation?"

Lori reached across the table and touched Anita's hand.

"Anita, you're right." A shadow fell over the table and we all looked up.

Fred Coper said, "You can't just give him the key, 'Nita. I'm about through with another file and the key's different."

Anita Talbot looked at each of us, then craned her neck to glance up at Fred. "Well, okay. If you'll help me, Coper."

He nodded, still looking at her.

Anita rose from the table. I said, "Just don't talk about this to anyone."

She grinned. "Yeah. I know what some people say about me remember? That I gossip a lot? I guess it's true, but I also know how to keep shut when it's needed. Did Alissa keep a file on me?"

"I didn't see one, and I doubt there is one. It appears that she concentrated on people directly in line with her responsibilities, people whom she expected to use one day to help her career. Too bad, too. She was bright and competent. Didn't need the extra leverage."

"People like her vice-president," said Lori quietly, looking at the table where her fingers traced aimless patterns on the surface. I nodded. Feeling positively conspiratorial, Lori and I watched Anita and Fred walk away, then we too left the restaurant.

I had new worries. For several days I had been considering trying to get back into Constant's office to look for other coded files. There was another aspect of it preying on my mind; it was almost two weeks since I'd lifted the files from her desk. If one of them contained a motive for murder and I'd been sitting on it all this time, Merrill Swanborg was not going to be pleased. What if I was responsible for letting a murderer escape?

CHAPTER 24

*It is no use falling foul of those
upon whom our welfare so closely depends.*

I decided to give Anita three files, Marsh's, Jellicoe's, and Tidwell's. I had no particular reason for choosing those three, except the one on Marsh, of course. I just hoped Anita would find something that would prove he didn't kill Constant. Grasping at straws is another way to put it.

When I returned to the office after taking Anita the files in an innocent-appearing brown interoffice envelope, I found a call slip from Merrill Swanborg. I reached him immediately, for a change.

"I thought you'd want to know, we located the place on the roof of the apartment building across the street from your place where we're pretty sure the shooter stood."

"Pretty sure?"

"Well, this guy was careful so we didn't find any cigarette butts or shell casings or skin scrapings, you know. A transit and some calculations plus a little disturbed gravel gave us the location. You were lucky. The only place with a reasonable view of your apartment is one story lower than your place so he, or she, had to be standing, which meant just a little less accuracy."

My hands started to sweat again at the renewed memory of the two black holes in my living room wall.

Swanborg changed the subject. "Marston, our inventory of Constant's office and a comment or two by an office clerk indicates there may be some files missing. You wouldn't know anything about that, would you?"

"Umm, I'll have to think about that. Anything else?" I didn't want to lie to him, but I didn't want to give up those files just yet, either. Any chance of getting back into Constant's office to look for other coded files had just disappeared.

"No. I don't know when the case will go to the grand jury. That's up to the D.A."

"Is there anything against Marsh that I don't know about?"

"What d'you mean?"

"Well, you have to admit," I said, "all your evidence is circumstantial."

"You have everything we have. The state won't go for first-degree murder. We don't think he planned to kill her."

"I don't think he killed her, period. Have you looked into her background? She was involved in several odd incidents as far back as graduate school and at other colleges where she worked."

He laughed softly. "Still snooping about are you? Yes, we know something about Constant, but most everybody has a few rough spots in their past. Haven't you?"

We left it at that. I wiped the moisture off my palms and thought about rehearsal. I also thought about Ted Delton.

The phone rang. My presence was required in the president's office, forthwith.

President Trammel sat erect behind his desk when I entered. He wore his usual somber expression. Micky Nelson and Mary Tendun, our development director, were already seated across the room.

"Good, good, Marston. Prompt. I always like that in a man." Trammel's weak attempt at jocularity had no discernible effect on the rest of us. "Let's get right to it. Marston, I want you to hear this." He gestured toward Mary.

"Jack, the news isn't good, we're experiencing a serious drop in donations, and in pledges as well. We're almost twenty percent below our projected collections for this date." She twisted her pale fingers nervously. Mary is a small, birdlike woman of great energy and tenacity who knew just about everybody who was anybody in town. Especially people with money. "I've made calls, of course, and donors are telling us they feel obligated to make the payments eventually, but they don't want to be linked to the college right now." She shook her head, short gray curls trembling. "You know we projected some pretty hefty interest income as a part of the campaign, so delayed donations will have a serious ripple effect." She looked at me.

"Micky?" roared Trammel. I knew he'd heard the bad news before, but any talk of reductions in the flow of money seemed to give him a bellyache. For Trammel a bellyache was major trauma.

"Can we issue some kind of progress statement?" Micky nodded eagerly and for a minute we lobbed the idea back and forth. The president wanted to call a press conference and blow things all out of proportion. Micky seemed to agree on the surface, but all the time he kept trying to deflect Trammel to keep the man from appearing foolish, not to mention the rest of us. He didn't want to expose our president to unanticipated questions from reporters. Had the situation not been so serious, I would have paid more attention to Micky's maneuverings, but I knew my time was coming.

I didn't want to give him everything I knew. In the past, Trammel had occasionally revealed other administrator's confidences, either inadvertently or when it served his own purposes. If that happened, I'd have violated promises made to those I had already interviewed. Another reason was that I didn't want to reveal all the information I was collecting. Airing the wrong piece of this now could alert one of the killers that I was getting closer, always assuming I was getting closer.

"Marston!" He barked at me. I'd missed his first verbal summons as he disposed of Nelson.

"Sir?"

"We gave you a tricky, but vital task. What progress have you made?"

I looked at him silently.

"Spare us any Shakespeare."

I decided to give him Constant. "President Trammel, it appears there is considerably more to Alissa Constant's background than we knew. I've discovered information of a rather sensitive nature about the woman from other venues which may have direct relevance." Damn, I was beginning to sound like him. I hoped he didn't realize it. Then I had another idea.

"It appears highly likely that the killer of Stuart Jamison was not the same individual who murdered Alissa Constant. I've also learned some things that lead me to believe Stuart Jamison was enrolled at City College under false pretenses." At this, two of my listeners snapped their heads up and looked at me with greater attention. Micky's mouth fell open. As I'd hoped, he was forestalled by President Trammel.

"Ahh, I don't think it's necessary to go into any greater detail, Marston." He held up one paw and swung his gaze to the others. "I don't have to remind you two that this is all highly confidential. Extremely confidential."

Micky started to protest, but the president cut him off. "Can we expect some kind of resolution in the next few days, Marston?"

"I'm not sure, sir. I've also discovered some information from Constant that appears to be in coded form. We're attempting to decipher it, but until that's done and we learn its significance, it's still a matter of finding and connecting all the small pieces."

Trammel scowled, took a deep breath, and waved us out. He didn't look up as we trailed out and closed the door. I could guess at his thoughts. If Jamison had been planted on us by the federal witness protection program, Trammel must be cursing the day he let the authorities talk him into it. There had to have been some profit in it somewhere. Now it was starting to look as if Jamison's murder was going to cost us some serious money, and we weren't even going to be able to explain it. I wasn't overly distressed about President Trammel's concern.

I followed Micky into his office, thinking that Jamison's killer would probably never go to trial, even if I figured out who it was. The feds wouldn't want a public trial for the killer of one of their protected witnesses. That would put a real damper on anyone's willingness to come forward.

"Micky," I said, as his door swung shut with a soft thump. "Do you know much about this case? I remember your insistence that anything for public issue must go through you first."

"Hey, Jack." His hands came up, palms out. "Whoa. All I know is what I was told. Anything relating to Jamison had to be cleared through us. The great journalism 'why' was not covered. I don't want to know any more, either. I tell you, though; I didn't like the sound of what I heard in there." He jabbed his thumb at the wall in the direction of Trammel's office.

I walked to the window and looked out at the now leveled block D, where several decades of human existence had been obliterated in the space of a couple of weeks. A few low mounds of gravel lay along one side. A single narrow path of old, dark red street paving bricks wavered along one end. They gave just a hint of what had been. It was apparently now too cold to pave the block; that would wait for spring. Over the winter, Urban Renewal Block D would remain barren, flat, and silent under its cover of dust and snow. I turned back to watch Micky Nelson fingering his Scots plaid tie. He had a worried look.

"Micky," I said, "that's a good attitude you have there. Stay as far from this mess as you can." I waved a hand casually and walked out, wondering how Anita was coming with her code breaking.

CHAPTER 25

*I have been threatened first with
one thing and then with another;*

Friday afternoon and no rehearsal. I was working late, catching up on the mail–mostly junk, recent administrative memos–mostly uninteresting, and reports of faculty committees–mostly arrogant, and nearly all of questionable value.

Somehow, intelligent faculty members, when assembled together in overheated conference rooms with a limited task at hand, lose their capacity to communicate effectively. The writing! Most reports issued by faculty and administrative committees wouldn't be tolerated for ten seconds by writing instructors in our classes.

Darkness comes early to the northern states in November. Daylight Saving Time was gone for another six months and the weak sun didn't last long into the afternoon.

The building cleared out and I became aware again of the silence that really wasn't. The place began to speak in that special language of old buildings. I went down the hall to the bathroom to wash my face. The flushing of the toilet was a thunderous roar. The sound of running water in the basin was a waterfall of noise. When I shut off the tap, I heard footsteps in the hall. They went by the door to the bathroom and stopped. Hot air ducts sang overhead and creaked with temperature differentials. I dried my hands on the roller towel.

The footsteps came in slow, measured cadence, back toward

the door. *Oh shit!*

I slid quietly into the nearest stall and eased the door shut. More creaks from the building. I breathed through my mouth. The door to the bathroom squeaked quietly as someone pushed it open. Silence.

"Hello? Anyone in here?"

My breath rushed out in a relieved gust when I recognized the voice of Paul Aubergeron, our night security guard.

"Just me, Paul," I said stepping out of the stall.

"You okay, Mr. Marston? You look a little skittish."

"Sure. I was just startled."

He nodded and went out, saying, "You have a good night, now."

I returned to my office, making my own echoing footfalls, and stared out the window at the seamless gray sky.

I was still bothered by my lapse of good judgment in not telling the police about those files of Alissa's. I decided to come clean. I'd copy the files and turn the originals over to the police with some excuse. The telephone rang. It was Anita. I was surprised she was still in the building.

"Jack, we've cracked more of the codes and translated two more files." Her voice fairly crackled with satisfaction. "Like Fred said, the codes weren't all the same but they were similar. He and his computer helped."

I felt my stomach muscles harden. "You want to tell me what you found out?"

"Most of it is just like your file, notes on the person named. Where they went, who they saw, stuff like that. Did she hire a private detective? She must have spent a bundle for all this information. She couldn't have been in all these places herself. Lot of references to dates and towns. Tidwell seems to have roamed the suburbs a lot. In some files there's a bunch of question marks or exclamations after a reference. Like she used the symbols for emphasis or to remind her of something. I don't know, maybe they were to remind her to check something further. Like here, in Tidwell's, there are two or three question marks after a note that must mean she was with someone."

"With whom?" I asked.

"Yes, well, that's a question, isn't it?" She used single letters like a Z to indicate a person, instead of a name. "Maybe Constant didn't know the names, or maybe she wanted to cover them up inside her own code. Maybe there's a key somewhere in her stuff, but it isn't here. Fred says she was pretty devious."

Was that a suggestion of a giggle in her voice? I grunted something unintelligible into the phone and then said. "So, what's your general feeling?"

"Nothing illegal, I guess. Unless the single letters go somewhere. It sure looks like she was building piles of information on all these people to have some kind of hold on them. Blackmail maybe? I haven't a clue what for. Or if she ever actually used it that way."

I already had some ideas along that line. I remembered the verbal dancing I'd encountered when talking to some of Alissa's former colleagues. "Good work, Anita. Will you have time to translate the rest?"

"Sure, we'll just keep going on it." Now she seemed eager to stay on the job.

I wondered if I could give her some of the remaining files. "Okay. Is there anyone around who can bring me what you've finished?"

"Sure, my student worker is still here. He'll bring it down on his way home."

I closed my eyes briefly as a wave of weariness passed over me. For a moment I hated Alissa Constant. In spite of our casual tone, I knew Anita was learning things about people she had no business learning and didn't need to know. Soon, I would know those things as well. Some of the people whose names were in the files were people we worked with every day. Our relationships with those colleagues, however casual, would be forever altered. It wasn't a nice feeling.

Twenty minutes went by. Where was that messenger? I called Anita, but the telephone rang and rang. Either her voice mail was down or she'd switched it off.

Just when I really started to worry, there was light tap on my door.

"Where've you been?" I snapped at him.

He handed across a heavily taped brown interoffice envelope. "Sorry, Mr. Marston. I didn't know it was urgent. Anita never said anything. I ran into a woman I know in the elevator. Rode down to the street and then came back up. Sorry."

I thanked him and sat down with the brown envelope. Talbot or somebody had taken the precaution of carefully blocking out all the previous addressees with a felt marking pen. The color of the ink was the same as that on the anonymous note I'd received.

Anita's assessment of the contents of the coded files was accurate. It was the kind of information I recalled writing down as field notes when I was doing investigative work in the Navy. Tidwell's file was a lot like mine. It covered a similar time span. The earliest date was only two weeks after Constant started working here at City College. If this file was to be believed, Tidwell spent a lot of her free time attending concerts by obscure groups and relatively unknown plays. There was no mention of embarrassing incidents but why the frequent question marks and few complete names? Nearly all Tidwell's companions were referred to only by single capital letters. D appeared most often. Always assuming, of course, my ad hoc decoding group was correct.

I locked the file away.

Among the memoranda I'd been reading earlier was a notice of the fall college reception. Twice each year, in the fall and again in the spring, the administration organized a reception to welcome back the old, introduce the new, and to have a relaxed, casual couple of hours. It was often the only time we saw some employees of the college. Occasionally, if there was a reason, meritorious recognition of select members of our little community occurred. The memorandum reminded me that, as an administrator, my presence was mandatory.

CHAPTER 26

*Who the devil cares whether
there's any risk or not!*

Wednesday afternoon, we slowly assembled in the enclosed glass-roofed garden courtyard of a nearby hotel. The printed schedule indicated we would begin with a brief welcome by the academic vice-president, but I suspected there'd be a substitution. It was interesting to me that some people can't bear to change schedules once they're committed to paper. They're probably the same ones who believe as gospel anything appearing on a computer printout.

The short program was to start promptly at four, but everybody knew that wouldn't happen. We who work in academic settings seem to be infected with a late-gathering virus. When the meeting is called for ten, say, expect it to start no earlier than ten-fifteen. This afternoon I didn't expect whoever was to make the opening remarks to start before four-twenty or even four-thirty.

"Jack, how are you? Haven't seen you in some time. Matter of fact, I haven't seen any recent memos about student peccadilloes, either. Things must be running pretty smoothly this fall, eh?" The speaker was old Professor Bently. He'd been with the college just slightly less than forever.

We stood on the highest of three levels, near the top of the last escalator. I could see the stairs that also connected the garden levels with the commercial mall below. Everyone entering the court would pass me or pass within waving distance.

The escalator filled with staff, chatting with each other; most looked forward to the end of the program and release for the evening. Nearly everyone either nodded or said hello as they passed. A few avoided eye contact with me, even when I spoke to them. One in particular who ignored me was Harvey Johnson, the business professor.

Lori brushed by, smiled, and touched my hand. Over Lori's shoulder as she passed, I saw Professor Emma Tidwell striding confidently toward the escalator, her long subdued skirt billowing about her. She hitched her big purse a little higher on her shoulder and stopped. I watched her gaze sweep over the people rising on the escalator until her eyes reached me. She swung to the right, choosing the stairs instead of the escalator. Had she done that to avoid me?

Behind me I heard the pop and crackle of the speaker system as somebody adjusted the microphone at the podium.

"Ahhh. Ladies and gentlemen," the ghostly voice reverberated over the stone parapets, bounced off the glass roof overhead and filtered through the many palms and split-leaf dieffenbachia that clustered in artful groupings and edged the twisting walkways and small turnouts.

"We'll get started in just a moment. Please gather in the ahh, amphitheater. Will Jack Marston come to the podium...ahh, to the podium, please?"

Me? Why did they want me? I wasn't on the schedule to make remarks or introduce any new employees to the assemblage. I turned and headed toward the rostrum. In a central part of the garden park a stone amphitheater had been created that held two or three hundred people. The stone risers on three sides were set with wooden benches separated by narrow walkways. On the main garden level, spreading out behind the back wall of the amphitheater, were walkways and small turnouts where tables and benches had been placed. At the base of the amphitheater, surrounded on three sides by the seats, was an open space where a microphone and lectern had been set up. This was the focus of the formal action this afternoon.

On one side of the space, nearly filling the side entrance to the amphitheater, were three long tables loaded with the buffet which the administration laid on at these things. A line of people wandered back out onto one of the suspended walkways. The line shuffled slowly forward as the attendees picked up plastic plates and cutlery and selected their snacks. From the look of it, we would be talking to a lot of people still in line if we started right away. I brushed past them and headed across the cleared space to the podium. A small knot of administrators stood nearby.

As I approached, Mrs. Grant, one of the president's administrative assistants, detached herself from the group and met me at the lectern.

"Ah, yes, here you are. President Trammel hasn't arrived yet, but we should get going, don't you think?"

I nodded and she leaned closer. It was just then I realized the microphone was still on.

"Vice-president Marshall has wisely decided to relinquish his duties as master of ceremonies today. I thought you might take his place and begin with a brief report on the progress of your investigation. Yes?"

I was startled dumb. Report on my progress? Whose idiotic idea was that?

I slapped my hand down on the microphone and its switch at the same instant I said, too loudly,

"NO!" The sound of my voice boomed out. I leaned in and whispered fiercely at her. "That's nuts, Mrs. Grant. It's a confidential matter!" I wondered if Trammel had put her up to it. Was there some kind of political gamesmanship going on here? Or was I beginning to see conspiracies where there weren't any? In a slightly quieter voice I agreed make a brief introductory remark.

Mrs. Grant turned from white to pale red and her thin lips quivered. I was sure no one at the college had ever before spoken to her with such vehemence. I glared and turned toward the assembling crowd. The rotund figure of our esteemed president waddled into view.

I clicked on the microphone and said in a loud voice, "'Proceed, proceed: we will begin these rites, as we do trust they'll end in true delights'. President Trammel." I gestured to him and turned away. I stalked out of sight, ignoring everyone around me. Still seething, I rounded a turn in the passage just beyond the buffet table, colliding with Emma Tidwell and nearly upsetting her. The plate of snacks she carried almost fell to the floor.

"Goodness! You just might watch where you are going!" she said sharply.

"Excuse me, Professor." I looked at her and made a quick decision. "May I have a moment of your time?"

She turned away and spoke over her shoulder. "If you must. Come over here." 'Here' was several steps away in one of the small private alcoves, almost completely screened from the stone walk. Close behind us, through the thick plantings and rising nearly two stories toward the vaulted glass roof that covered the whole place, was the buff-colored granite wall of the amphitheater I'd just left. Tidwell shifted her commodious leather bag off one stone bench to make room for me. We sat across the tiny round table from one another, knees almost touching.

"I'll remind you I have already said more than I intended, and will have absolutely nothing further to say on the matter of Alissa Constant and her relationship with Vice-president Marshall." Tidwell pursed her lips and stared at me, ignoring her plate of food.

I nodded. "Are you aware that Alissa Constant was keeping

tabs on you? That she had a file devoted to your off-campus activities?"

If I had intended to shake her up and breach that formal reserve–and I had–the reaction was all I could hope for, and more. She blanched and started with a violent rejective motion of her free hand. Her hand struck her bag and dumped it on the floor at our feet. She focused briefly on the plate she held to avoid spilling it. It gave me a slight edge as we both reached for her fallen bag. I picked it up and held it out. Tidwell snatched it quickly away.

"Please! I'll take that."

It was heavy, heavier than I'd expected. What was she carrying in there?

Professor Tidwell regained her composure and stared at me again, lips parted, gray eyes boring into mine. A tendril of hair had escaped the tight bun she habitually wore. I wasn't happy, badgering the woman. I wasn't happy with any of the business surrounding Constant and Jamison, but I knew Marsh was falsely accused–even though I still had no proof. Incongruously, I wondered what Tidwell looked like with her hair down. Then I wondered what her body looked like. No one I knew had ever seen her in anything but those drab, loose dresses like the one she wore this afternoon. Not that she was dowdy, oh no. Lori once remarked that Emma Tidwell spent a considerable amount of money on her clothes to avoid revealing any hint of her figure.

"Mr. Marston!" Her sharp tone cut into my thoughts. "Exactly what is your point?" She'd regained her iron composure.

"My point, Professor Tidwell, is that Alissa Constant apparently hired private detectives to spy on several members of this college at various times during their non-college lives. You're one of the lucky ones. How do you feel about that?"

"Exactly what do you know? What kind of information did you find in her files?" I detected a note of concern in her voice.

"I have dates, places, and indications of who your companions were when you attended various functions. For example…." I took a small piece of paper from my shirt pocket and looked at it briefly.

"On June 8th, and again on July 15th of last year, you attended concerts by a small wind ensemble in Shakopee. With a companion. Do you remember those concerts?"

It was plain Emma Tidwell did recall them. I wished I had a better idea of their significance.

"And your companion? Here's a small hint. The first initial is 'D'. Now my question is..."

Tidwell jumped to her feet, towering over me. Her eyes glistened. "Damn you, Jack Marston, and damn Alissa Constant!"

Before I could say another word, she swept out of the alcove and strode rapidly down the stone walkway toward the stairs. It appeared my efforts to goad her into revealing at least one of the people noted in the decoded file had gone awry. By the time I started after her, she was halfway down the steps. I increased my gait, wondering what I'd say when I caught her. As I turned onto the stairs, Merrill Swanborg took my arm. "Let her go. I want to talk to you right now," he said.

Startled, I stopped abruptly on the top step. What was he doing here? We watched Professor Tidwell continue down the stairs and across the lower level of the indoor garden court to the outside doors. There she paused and raked the foyer with her gaze. She raised her head and fixed me with a look that even at that distance had the impact of a physical blow. She wheeled and disappeared.

I slowly turned my head and looked at Swanborg. He too tracked Emma Tidwell, a bemused expression on his face.

"This had better be important. I have the feeling I may have provoked more than I expected."

Surprisingly, he nodded, "Yeah, you may have. That's a potentially dangerous woman."

"What?"

"Marston, we've been doing some detailed checking on your colleagues." He gestured vaguely at the scattered clots of people who were drinking, gossiping, and eating. The short formal program had gone on without my participation or notice.

"So?"

"So, Professor Emma Tidwell is a nationally ranked pistoleer."

I gaped at him. "A what?"

He smiled briefly and shrugged. "She shoots competitively. Pistols. And she's very good. Ranked among the top fifty in the country."

I remembered the heft of her bag. Did she carry a weapon? "So, you think she could have been the one who tried to kill me the other night at my place?" I found it hard to believe, even as I said the words.

"Well, it is something we're looking into."

"Merrill, do the initials A.L.G.Q. mean anything to you?" I showed him the letters on the scrap of paper I had in my hand, the same scrap I'd referred to when talking to Emma Tidwell. He tried to take the piece but I didn't let him.

"I'm not your personal research person, Jack. I think you're holding out on me. What exactly have you learned? What's going on? And I don't mean this little gathering." He waved a hand at the garden court.

I looked at Swanborg. He was a good cop and I was still bothered that I hadn't told him about the files. I made another snap decision. I told him. The telling lifted a weight from my head.

He heard me out without comment. When I stopped, he looked thoughtfully at me. "I ought to arrest you for obstructing justice and tampering with a possible crime scene. But I won't, just yet. Where are those files?"

"Locked in my cabinet at the office. We haven't decoded all of them yet."

"Which means what?"

"They're in some kind of code. I enlisted the aid of a colleague to crack the code."

"Jesus," Swanborg rubbed his bristly jaw, "I'm surrounded by an army of amateurs. Well, let's go get 'em."

We left the waning reception and walked the two blocks in the crisp night air to my building where Paul, the night security guard, let us in. I asked him if anyone else was in the building. He shrugged a negative and pointed at the logbook. The page was blank.

In my office I unlocked the cabinet and turned over the originals of the files I had. I didn't tell Swanborg that we had copies. I figured he wouldn't hassle me about something of which he was ignorant. He studied the files, first the translations, then the coded sheets.

Finally he looked at me and said, "You be very careful with your copies. And I want to be the first person you call when the rest of this stuff is translated. Looks like your Ms. Constant was not a very nice person." Without allowing me to respond, he turned and stomped out of the office.

CHAPTER 27

*I have never changed, except
perhaps to become a little more moderate–*

After Swanborg left, I sat at my desk thinking. I wondered what I should do next. So far, I didn't seem to be helping Marsh. All I'd accomplished was to irritate some students and faculty, and of course the president was unhappy with my progress.

I was stirring up something, or somebody with my poking about. Two attempts to kill me indicated that. But what? Who sent me those pictures? Damn it! The more I poked about, the more questions I had and the answers weren't keeping up. My frustration and the strain was apparent. I was short tempered with staff. I even snapped at Lori. At least she understood, thank God, and tolerated me. But for how long?

The building creaked and sighed, just like the other night when the security guard had almost given me a heart attack. I heard someone in the hall but I felt secure. Only during the day could strangers enter or leave without being checked. After six, street doors were locked and everyone signed in and out.

I stared at Emma Tidwell's file, looking again for something– anything that would help me understand the cryptic entries Constant had made. Damn her caution anyway. Codes and a personal shorthand. I called Lori, hoping she was home from the reception. She was.

"Hi babe. How was your reception?"

"Huh. Wait a minute, my dress is snagged on an earring." I heard her put the phone down and then a moment later, a faint sigh, "Ahh, that's better."

"What?" I said.

"Just removed a few garments."

The vision that popped into my head was considerably more attractive than what I had just been thinking about. "Perhaps I could come over and help."

Her low chuckle came through the connection. "The reception was–the reception. What happened to you, anyway?"

"I had a talk with Emma Tidwell which was more interesting than I expected. Then I got entangled with detective Swanborg. Have you ever heard of an organization with the letters A.L.G.Q.?"

"A.L.G.Q.? Sorry, nothing comes to mind. What's the context? Could it be a professional organization? You know, the Amalgamated Lodge of the Great Quail? I think I have a directory of academic professional groups right here, assuming it's an academic group." I heard pages turning and a clunk when she set the handset down again. "No, nothing even close. You're sure it's not just separate letters?"

"Nope."

"Are there periods after each letter?"

I looked again at the translation. "The letters are all caps. With periods." I glanced at the copy of Tidwell's file. "Oh. Anita made a mistake. All caps, but no periods in the original. We found these in one of Constant's mysterious files."

"Wait a minute," Lori said. "There is something, a club, I think, or some kind of organization. It's called the Allegheny. No! Algonquin. That's it. ALGQ. Sure. Hey, I solved that mystery. Can I join the firm?"

"Any time, babe, any time. I don't recognize the name."

"I think it's some kind of private club, out in one of the southern suburbs, possibly toward Shakopee."

"Yeah? Eden Prairie or Burnsville?"

"Sounds about right. Whose file are you working on?"

"Emma Tidwell's. Do you remember why you heard of it? I

don't think I ever did."

"Not off hand. I'll have to mull it over some more. Are you coming over? We can play word association games, put things together."

Now there was an offer I wasn't about to refuse. "Love to. 'Bout thirty minutes?"

When I cradled the receiver and looked up, the door to my office was open and Emma Tidwell was standing there. She still held her big leather bag, tight against her side. The one that had seemed so heavy. I looked at her face. Her eyes were red-rimmed, the lids puffy. She looked haggard and older than I knew her to be. I started to rise as my eyes were drawn to her bag. My heartbeat increased.

"Stay seated, Mr. Marston." Tidwell's voice was flat, almost toneless.

Suddenly I did recall something about the Algonquin Club. My thought must have been in my face, because Emma nodded and said, "Yes. The Algonquin Club. A place that was established to cater to the arts community, particularly creative gay and lesbian individuals."

I vaguely remembered there'd been a story in one of the weekly tabloids and a little gossip when the place first opened.

"It's a small, very private club. I go there frequently. I'm a lesbian, Mr. Marston." For a moment neither of us said anything, then she sighed. "I overheard you talking to that detective when I went down the hall. I waited until he left. I can see from the look on your face that you've figured it out, at least part of what Constant put in that file of hers; what she deduced a long time ago and later confirmed by spying on me."

I nodded slowly, wondering where this was going. Emma sounded calm, but her white knuckles where she clutched her bag betrayed her tension. I couldn't see her right hand. "I suppose I have figured out part of it. Constant learned you're a lesbian and figured it might be useful, since it isn't common knowledge."

"Yes." Tidwell's lips twitched in a bitter grimace. "I'm not out of the closet, as they say. Several months ago Constant started dropping hints that she knew something about my private life."

I leaned back in my chair, trying to appear relaxed. Tidwell remained where she was, alert, tense, clutching that leather bag.

"I have to say, I didn't know that about you, Professor Tidwell, and to be blunt, I don't care. What's more, I'm sure the college administration won't care, either."

"I know that. Unfortunately Dean Constant discovered something else, something that made me vulnerable to her blackmail."

"I'm afraid I don't understand."

"There are a number of reasons why I haven't revealed my leanings. Most important are because of my family. Both my aged, conservative, and ill, parents in Illinois would be devastated if they were to learn I am a lesbian. I cannot, I will not, let that happen."

I didn't like the way this conversation was going. If Tidwell was working her way up to confessing killing Constant and she had a gun in her purse, I didn't want her to feel she'd talked herself into a corner, with me barring her way out.

"Aren't you overstating the situation?"

"Mr. Marston, have you ever spent time in the border states? In small town America?"

"Not really."

"That's where I grew up, where my parents still live. About some things, they are unalterably bigoted. They live in a community of bigots. I don't wish to imply everyone in small towns is bigoted or homophobic, but the reality is that many people are and my abilities to continue my professional activities as I wish to do would be unalterably hampered if I were to be discovered to be a lesbian."

"You studied history. You must recall the hysteria of the Communist scare in the fifties."

I nodded, breath rasping in my throat. My heart thudded in

my chest.

"There was a phrase, a slogan. 'Better dead than Red.' That's exactly the situation. My father is extremely ill. The embarrassment of learning that his still unmarried daughter is a lesbian would kill him. Literally. And my mother. Dear God, my mother would be left alone for the few years she has left to face the scorn and pity and the backbiting–isolated from her old friends."

"Aren't you exaggerating things?"

"You people up here just can't understand. I've known I was different since early in high school. There weren't any programs, there was no support for women like me. I had to suffer alone. A close friend died when I was a senior. Then I heard the jokes, the whispers about queers. I tried to–this is all irrelevant. My parents would rather learn I'd been killed in an accident, murdered even, than discover I'm a lesbian."

She shifted her stance and hoisted the sagging bag a little higher. I still couldn't see her right hand.

"Mr. Marston, I would have killed Alissa Constant to protect my family. I'd have done so, if killing that despicable woman would have protected my secret. I did not, although I don't know why you should believe me."

"Assume I do believe you. Earlier you refused to gossip about her. Don't you see that if we catch the real murderer quickly, we can keep a lid on Constant's files? Protect you? If you know something, won't you help me?"

"Why should I trust you? You couldn't wait to turn those files over to the police as soon as you knew what was in them,"

"Professor Tidwell, I've had the files since the day Alissa's body was discovered and some of the translations for two days. The files are cryptic. I have no idea of the identities of most of the people mentioned in the file. I'm not even sure if all of the references are people. Some could be places." I switched subjects. "Did Constant approach you with a specific request or try to pressure you during the last year or so?"

She shook her head. I watched her carefully. I thought she was coming down from her emotional high, relaxing a bit. I experienced an almost lightheaded feeling of relief.

Then as quietly as she'd appeared, with her bag still clutched tightly to her waist, Emma Tidwell turned and left my office. I glanced at my watch. Only ten minutes had passed. It seemed much longer.

The night had turned colder and the mist seemed poised to turn to snow if the temperature dropped much lower. The heavy air turned the street lamps to glowing auras of sodium-yellow. Only a few lights bloomed in the dark office buildings squatting along Hennepin Avenue. First Avenue was even quieter. Two cars passed, tires hissing on the wet pavement. In the middle distance I heard the warble of a police car or ambulance siren. I periodically checked behind me while I walked to my car. There was no one, but the city looming over me in the speckled darkness, had become an oppressive presence.

It took only moments for the heater to fog up the windshield. I wasn't comfortable just sitting in the dark empty lot waiting for the windshield to clear. I found a rag to wipe the glass so I could get going. I wiped and shifted, then drove off the lot, turning north toward Brooklyn Center and Lori.

Twenty minutes later, Vivaldi's soft violin music and Lori filled my ears, my eyes, and my arms. It was warm and comforting and for a time I was able to forget Emma Tidwell, Alissa Constant, Stuart Jamison, and City College.

CHAPTER 28

*He is quite excited about
my discovery.*

Snow fell Sunday night after a peaceful, calm weekend. In spite of the mounting pressure I felt, Lori had insisted that I stay cosseted with her the entire weekend and avoid, as much as possible, any consideration of the murder investigation. I was not unwilling.

This was the first real snowfall of the season, a thick, heavy, wet covering. Early-morning radio announcers predicted dire adventures for anyone incautious enough to venture into the world this morning without adequate preparation, both physical and metaphysical. There were a couple of inches on the ground and more falling through the gray air. Snow covered the grass, bent tree branches, and began to melt into grimy slush in the streets. The first serious snow of winter always created mild panic in the motoring public. Minnesotans have short memories of standard winter driving techniques. This would be a morning of fender benders, traffic delays, and short tempers.

Breakfast over, Lori and I made our way gingerly to our cars. Since I had no overshoes, my first step out the side door of Lori's apartment building filled my shoes with cold wetness. The building maintenance supervisor had not yet ventured forth from his warm bed to shovel the walk. Fortunately there was no wind.

The snow melted on my shoulders and bare head, and by the time I had the car cleaned off, my thin topcoat was moist and leaking a little at the seams. Lori pulled out first. My wipers chattered streaks across the windshield. I was convinced that the manufacturers of automobile wiper blades had secret computer programs that told them how to make blades that failed just when they were most needed.

Snow dampened the usual sounds of the city while we struggled south. The slow-moving traffic gave me time to re-engage my thoughts about the murders as I drove carefully down the freeway into the heart of the city. Fortunately, the firm that contracted for snow removal in the city parking lot was more prompt than Lori's super.

As I made my way by elevator and foot up six floors and down the hall to my office, through increasing crowds of students, their chitchat was mostly about the weather. There was a noticeable hesitation in the murmur of conversation among some of the clusters of people when I passed. I surmised they were also talking about the murders.

"Good morning all," I caroled brightly as I entered our offices. "I trust we all still retain our share of good sense so no one has tales of accidents on the way in this morning?"

There was a murmured response. Teresa was out for the morning on personal business so one of our two student workers was already ensconced at her desk, fielding calls and trying to figure out how to log on to the computer terminal.

"You can't access Teresa's files, remember, but you can work on files in the common drawers," I said.

He nodded in response and punched more keys.

I hung up my coat and surveyed the wreckage of my office, not that it looked any different than it had when I left it the previous Friday.

Maybe, I thought, I should just give it up as a bad job and dump everything in sight into the wastebasket. Then I could start over.

Eddie Macon, our other student worker, came in and handed me the morning mail. "I thought, since Teresa isn't here, you'd wanna see most of it." It was a large, untidy pile of envelopes. Eddie had bright red hair, like our PR guy, Micky Nelson, only he wore it in a long spiky brush cut that stuck out all over his head. Occasionally I wondered if he used gel or mousse to get that effect, or if he just didn't wash it very often. He was short and slight of build. The top of his red spikes only came up to my eyes.

"Uhh, Mr. Marston?"

I looked at him. "Something you want, Eddie?"

"Some of us were talkin' the other day, you know? And, the guys were sayin', some of the guys anyway, that all this stuff about the murders was hurting the building fund. And the college. That people won't wanna go to City College 'cause they think it's dangerous or we're all a lotta weirdoes. I heard that a lot of people are canceling and transferring to the U or other places. You know?"

I nodded encouragingly. He obviously had more to say.

"Anyway, I can't afford to go somewhere else and my dad is on my back about City College again and I don't know what to tell him."

"Eddie," I said quietly, "sit down." I dragged a second side chair over so we were close to each other beside my desk. I always tried to avoid creating a barrier like a desk between me and a student.

"First, there's no rush of transfers to other colleges. I see the weekly stats on incoming and outgoing students and the numbers are normal. As a matter of fact, we're just about to announce another jump in enrollment. FTE, you know, full time equivalent students, is up again. What's more, none of the faculty or staff has resigned." I avoided mentioning the drop in donations to the building fund he'd already touched on.

"You tell your friends and your dad from me, that we talked. No question, this isn't a normal fall term, but the college is in good shape." I smiled at him. His face cleared and he smiled back.

"In fact, Eddie, things are a little too good. This fall we've enrolled almost ten percent more students than we predicted, so some of our resources are a little strained. But we'll get through it. Staff will handle things. We always do."

I stood up and stuck out my hand. Surprised, he stood also and took my hand. We shook, like comrades facing a hard, possibly even a dangerous task, who both knew without saying it, that somehow we'd win out in the end. Echoes of John Wayne and the marines invading some remote South Pacific island wafted through my brain. Sure.

I scanned the mail Eddie had handed me. After a few minutes, my wastebasket was half filled and my mind was clearer. My conversation with Eddie led me to wonder if he was an early warning of a ground swell out there. Maybe I'd better circulate this morning, I decided. I bypassed the good coffee in our office pot and decided to go to the caves. I called Lori, hoping she could meet me there, but she was out.

I was alone in the elevator and slowly dropped from the fifth to the fourth floor. Just as I passed the fourth floor I heard an unusual noise filtering into the elevator shaft. Somebody was screaming, barely pausing for breath, a high terror-filled skirl; the kind of wordless shocking scream that can only be a prelude to horror.

I mashed the big red emergency stop button and the elevator doors eventually opened at the third floor. I raced back up the fire stairs, fumbling for my keys in case the security guard hadn't unlocked the fire doors. On the fourth floor there was bedlam. The scream had stopped, apparently exhausted of emotion for the moment, but now replaced with cries and shouts. The focus of the uproar seemed to center on the cluster of offices where humanities and literature faculty had established their liberal arts beachhead against an encroaching tide of business and accounting majors.

Walking quickly down the hall, I shoved through the clot of people crowded around the entrance. The screaming and shouting subsided and now I heard sobbing. Inside the reception area, five people sat or stood in shocked immobility. One of them, the department office manager, looked up at me, her eyes glazed, and pointed at the only open door. Inside, two female students were collapsed in side chairs, crumpled over and hiding their faces. There was a lot of blood on the wall and Emma Tidwell's body lay slumped in her desk chair. Her head hung over the chair back. My stomach turned over and I put a hand on the doorframe to steady myself.

I dragged in a deep breath and said, "Who found her?" I looked at the two students. The blonde nodded without raising her head. I looked back into the reception area and sucked in more calming breath.

"You," I ordered the department manager, "Please take these students into an empty office and stay with them." She nodded and shuddered. I urged the two shocked students up and into the hands of the manager.

A young man shouldered his way through the crowd and said, "Mr. Marston, I'm Alan Carstairs. I'm one of the secretaries here." He wiped his mouth with trembling hands. He didn't look at the body crumpled in the chair, but focused his gaze on the wall beside the door.

"Did you just get here?"

"No, sir. I was at my desk. When the girls screamed, I rushed in and saw Professor Tidwell." He gulped and leaned on the desk. "Then I yelled for help."

"Okay, Alan. Did you call 911?" He nodded. "Good. Now call the police station and ask for Detective Merrill Swanborg. Tell him, or whoever takes the message, that you're calling for me and we've got another death at City College." He nodded again and wiped his mouth once more as he retreated to his desk.

"The rest of you, try to be quiet and stay out of the way." I looked at a tiny, outwardly calm woman sitting silently at the third desk in the room, staring at nothing. Lavinia Reynolds had been Emma Tidwell's personal assistant and office manager for several years.

"Lavinia? Are you all right? Were you here? Do you know what happened?"

She blinked, nodded, and explained in a low wavery voice that when she and others arrived, the door was closed but they could see lights on through the glass door panel.

"Professor Tidwell often got in hours before the staff. When her door was open, we could chat, or ask a question. Sometimes she'd be reading. When the door was closed, that was a signal she didn't want to be interrupted.

"The door was shut when I got here. Sometimes we wouldn't hear anything until her first appointment arrived." Tears trickled down Lavinia's seamed cheeks, tracking through her rouge.

"How long have you been here?"

"About two hours, Mr. Marston. When her students arrived the door was still closed. I told Marci to knock and stick her head in. Marci rapped on the door and went in, and found the professor" she gulped.

A quick series of questions helped me establish who had been there when Professor Tidwell's body was discovered and who could be encouraged to clear out. As we developed some calm, the police began to arrive. I sat on the edge of the receptionist's desk to give my weak-feeling legs some relief.

Two uniformed policemen showed up first. Detective Swanborg appeared moments later. He looked at me and I nodded at the now closed door of Professor Tidwell's office. He glanced around at all of us and snapped on a pair of thin latex gloves. They made his hands look dead. Then he opened the door and carefully entered the office where Emma Tidwell's body lay.

Paramedics with stretcher and assorted paraphernalia and more uniformed and plain-clothes cops arrived next. I explained who I was and what I had done since arriving on the scene. I told my story at least twice.

"Marston," called Swanborg, interrupting his partner, who was asking me more questions. He jerked his head and I joined him in Emma's office. A plastic sheet had been draped over the body, but the blood-spattered wall stood out starkly in the slanted sunlight pouring through the single window. Part of my mind noted that the snow had stopped and the sky had cleared.

"Here's what we have." He pointed at the body. "She was killed by a bullet fired into her mouth. She died instantly. A weapon is on the floor beside her; it's a .38 caliber Smith and Wesson. We've verified the pistol has been fired, so I'll be surprised if it isn't the weapon that killed her. There's also a note here." He pointed at a sheet of college stationery on the desktop. I leaned over and read it.

This may appear to be a coward's solution, but I can no longer withstand what will inevitably descend from recent events. I only hope that god, if there is such a being, will, in her ultimate wisdom, show me an understanding face.

It was written in Professor Tidwell's hand, which I readily recognized. At the bottom, below her signature, was printed

A4TP11.PVT.

"Do you know what that means?" Swanborg asked, pointing at the note.

"She recently revealed to me that she was a lesbian," I said sadly, "but that her parents don't know it. She said she'd do almost anything to protect them. They are old, ill, I gather, and she was sure the knowledge would kill them. She was not about to come out of the closet."

"So, when Constant found out and started to blackmail Tidwell, Tidwell killed Constant? Is that your theory?"

I shook my head. "I don't know, Merrill. I don't think Emma's sexual orientation is such a big deal. But she wasn't persuaded. She told me her parents would rather learn she'd died suddenly. She denied killing Constant, but she was a troubled woman when I talked with her Wednesday night after you left–after the reception. Constant was putting pressure on her, hinting at blackmail. And, as you told me, she's very familiar with handguns."

"Constant wasn't shot," he reminded me. "Look at this, Jack," he said, pointing at the symbols below her signature. "What's this line at the bottom?"

"It looks like a computer code of some kind. Wait a minute." I turned and went out. In the next office, Lavinia Reynolds sat quietly with the two still trembling students.

"Miss Reynolds, d'you have access to all the computer files in this department?"

"Yes, I do. Well, except for the personal files several of the faculty maintain."

I nodded and went around the desk with Swanborg at my heels and logged on to the computer. Then I punched in the code we had found on the suicide note. The response was instantaneous.

ACCESS DENIED

I called Fred Coper. "Fred, I need the personal access code for Emma Tidwell."

"Hey, Jack, I can't give you that. What's going on?"

"Fred, I haven't time to explain, just trust me and do it. Or log me on as Emma Tidwell. Whatever, but do it now."

He grumbled again, but something in my voice convinced him and moments later a message scrolled across the terminal screen. This time, when I tapped in the letters and numbers, the computer thought I was the dead woman and the file appeared. Before she died, Emma Tidwell had provided us with the security code for her private computer files. There was a single document in the file, a duplicate of her suicide note.

"Merrill, look here. I think she did this to insure that we, that you, would find this additional evidence that she wrote the note you found on her desk."

"That's a possibility, but if you can get into her private files, couldn't someone else?"

"Yes, but some things can't be faked without a lot of time-consuming effort and detailed knowledge. Look at this index line." I pointed at the screen.

"Here's the date and time this note was entered."

I turned to Lavinia Reynolds. "Was Professor Tidwell here in her office on Sunday afternoon?"

"Oh, yes. She must have worked hard for several hours at her terminal. There was an awful lot of stuff for me on the printer and in my electronic mail when I got here this morning. She did it all on Sunday. I remember looking at the date line on the computer that tells when she sent the messages and files."

Swanborg looked at me. "So now we know she was here and the autopsy will probably tell us she died sometime on Sunday. You know, Jack, except for the file from Constant on this woman, we have absolutely nothing to connect the two of them."

"It's true," I replied, "but if I'm right and Marsh didn't kill Constant, and you're right that Emma Tidwell didn't, what does that leave us?"

He stared at me for a moment. "I'm left with Marsh. You? You still got nothin'."

CHAPTER 29

It is a splendid vocation you have chosen–to smooth the way for the march of unappreciated truths–

From the moment Emma Tidwell admitted to being a closet lesbian and obsessed with keeping her secret from her parents, I thought I might have found Alissa Constant's murderer. If Constant had learned of Emma's sexual orientation and tried to blackmail her, and it appeared that she had, and it supplied Tidwell with a motive to kill Constant. Now, it seemed likely that my investigation, coupled with that of the police, which might have led to Emma's unmasking, was at least partly responsible for her suicide. Never mind that Professor Tidwell had seemed on the edge of a breakdown the last time I talked to her. That I was even peripherally responsible was an appalling idea and it depressed me even more on top of my frustration over lack of progress in finding the real killer.

Lori did her best to help me deal with my profound unease. "From what you've told me about your conversation with her, I'd surmise Professor Tidwell may have become severely depressed, even suicidal in the past. It's possible her school friend killed herself, which would have been a major influence on the professor.

"It doesn't really matter that we don't care one way or another about her sexual preferences. What's important is that she felt vulnerable. Suicide must have seemed like the only way to resolve what had become, to her, an intolerable situation."

"I understand what you're saying, but I can't shake the feeling that if I hadn't been poking around, Emma might still be alive."

"Jack, why don't you call Doctor Abram? He's an excellent therapist and it'll do you good to talk with a more objective professional. You met him once, remember? He's the senior psychologist at our clinic."

"You aren't being objective?"

"Well, I'm trying, but you know as well as I do that I'm too close to the principals."

Doctor Abram made time for me that evening for an hour, which helped me begin to establish some perspective. He suggested that I could help resolve my own feelings by doing whatever I could to protect Emma Tidwell's reputation in the coming weeks.

The next morning when I arrived at the office, among my telephone messages was a call from Fred Coper. The message suggested that I drop by the Computer Center before noon, if it was convenient. It wasn't, but I went. I walked in thinking that I should resign and go away. I hated the thought that I had contributed to Emma Tidwell's suicide.

Seven students sat at computer terminals in the quiet, low-ceilinged room. I could faintly hear fans humming in the machines. Fred's office was in a corner carved out of the big room. It had waist-high hardboard paneled walls with glass panels above on two sides so he could monitor the place with an occasional glance.

His secretary, a pretty dark-haired woman, sat at her desk just outside Coper's door. She told me Coper had been called away for just a moment. She was right. He reappeared, swinging through the door in a great rush. Coper never seemed to saunter or walk calmly anywhere. It was as if he was always late. Now that I thought of it, he frequently was late to staff meetings, sometimes even those of the all-college computer system committee he chaired. Even his clothes seemed to be in a hurry. This morning he wore a bright purple shirt that shimmered when he moved.

"Good morning, Fred. I got your note."

"Wait, wait," he made a pushing motion with his hand. "How about a cup of coffee first? It's fresh."

I sighed, thinking this was shaping up to be a protracted meeting. I liked Fred and I respected his knowledge and expertise with computers, but he was tediously lengthy at times.

Without waiting for a response, he wheeled around behind his secretary's desk and splashed coffee from the pot into two mugs sitting on the shelf.

"Say, darlin'" he said, to his secretary, "we're runnin' short on clean mugs. Would you take some of these down the hall and wash 'em?" I winced and watched for her reaction.

She slowly raised her head and looked at me with no expression on her face. Then, still staring at me but speaking to Fred, she said, "Sure, sweetie. If you think you can manage the phones, it is my turn. I was just waiting until you got back." Then she winked at me. "But I still don't do windows."

I smiled at the raillery between two people who obviously respected and were comfortable with each other. Coper turned around with a grin, a shrug and two brimming cups of hot coffee. He led the way into his office. I shut the door behind us and we sat in two more of the college's ubiquitous hard side chairs.

Coper's desk was an interior door panel laid on two ancient green two-drawer file cabinets. A tall dark wooden cabinet of shelves stood in one corner. It was nearly filled with fading computer printouts. The shelves looked oiled, in contrast to the satiny urethane-coated desktop.

A computer sat on one corner of his desk, its color screen saver glowing and winking. The dumb terminal wired directly to the college's central computer radiated its emotionless green signals at me from the other side of his desk. A tangle of wires that connected the computers to printers located on a table against the wall trailed across the carpet.

"What was that about washing windows?"

"Several years ago, right after we hired her, one of the techs wanted Traci to wash these windows." He gestured at his glass walls. "She asked him very politely if he could show her that duty in her job description. We all get along pretty good and she gives back as good as she gets. 'Course, window washing isn't in his job description, either."

"One of these days you'll get slapped with a harassment suit, if you say something like that to the wrong person," I suggested.

He shrugged. "Well, we remind ourselves all the time." He sighed then and shook his head. "Terrible thing last night. Professor Tidwell?"

I nodded.

"I hear she committed suicide. Is that right? Any idea why?"

"Did you know her, Fred?"

"No, not really. Only enough to say hello to. Real shame, though. Nobody ought to go that way."

"Enough. Tell me what you wanted." Coper paused, pulling at his ear lobe.

"I'm still thinkin' about Jamison and the virus he planted to erase his records."

"We don't know that he did it."

"Oh, yeah, we know. I can't prove it, but I know he did it, and if I dig into it long enough I'll find out how he did it and even when."

"I guess it doesn't matter any more. Jamison is dead and if he installed the virus for his own protection, or to create a problem for us, I don't think that information will help." I wasn't as sure as I sounded, but until I knew whether Jamison had been a protected witness of some kind, I wasn't going to talk about it.

"Anyway, that's not why I asked you up here. See that fellow at the terminal across the room? I checked on who came to our seminars and computer workshops over the past year or so. There were three or four people who came to several of the same ones as Constant. Jamison, for one. A couple of people have graduated, but that kid over there was in several workshops with both of them. In fact, Jamison, Constant, and that kid worked on a couple of programming projects together."

"I think I'd like to talk to him. What's his name?" I asked.

"Johnson, Tom Johnson." Fred went to the door and called to the young man. He was one of our younger students, slight, sandy-haired, wearing a huge pair of dark-rimmed glasses that wouldn't stay in place. They slid down his nose and he'd push them back up with a forefinger. Then they'd slide right back down again.

"Go easy, Jack, okay?"

"'The quality of mercy is not strained. It dropeth as the gentle rain, upon the place beneath,'" I quoted.

"Yeah, yeah, whatever."

Tom Johnson came to the office door. He flashed an engaging smile at me over his green and white checkered flannel shirt. I glanced down. He had on scuffed penny loafers and argyle socks that clashed with his shirt.

"Tom, sit down. I'm Jack Marston, director of student services here at City College."

"Yeah, I know. You're investigating the murders, right?"

"Right." I shot a sour look at Fred who looked blandly innocent and shrugged. "I want to talk to you because you attended several workshops with Dean Alissa Constant and Stuart Jamison. What do you remember about those workshops?"

"They were really interesting, except the survey of different languages." He glanced at Fred. "That was too basic."

"What about this one?" I pointed at a title on the printout Fred had run off.

"Oh, yeah, that one was okay. We learned a lot about UNIX, but I guess I forgot most of it. I don't use UNIX at all."

"And, what about the two workshops on codes? That was last year, wasn't it?"

"They were cool. We had some neat discussions about cryptography and how the computer could help once you had a basic structure. Mr. Coper told us about Enigma, the code machines the Germans developed back in World War Two. We made up some codes of our own together, me an' Stuart an' Miss Talbot."

"Was Alissa Constant involved in the discussions?"

"Sure. She seemed really interested in codes."

"Did you ever talk about computer viruses?"

"What?" For a moment Johnson looked blank, then a sly expression appeared on his face. "Oh, sure, now I think about it, somebody had a magazine and showed us something about them. I guess we talked about them some, but not a whole lot."

I wondered what he wasn't telling me. "What do you remember about Stuart Jamison?"

Johnson thought for a moment, unconsciously pushing his lips in and out. "I don't know, Mr. Marston. Nothing I can think of. He was older, quiet, you know? We could tell he had some serious ideas. He knew a lot about computers."

"Was he a hacker like you?"

"Nope. 'Sides, what makes you think I'm a hacker?"

I smiled. "Just an impression. Thanks, Tom. I appreciate you talking to us."

"Well?" said Fred after Tom Johnson went back to his terminal.

"I think we know where Alissa got her codes. I'd be surprised if Jamison first got the idea to install a security virus during your workshops. I'm not sure how this helps find the murderers. Thanks for the tip, though." I left Coper's office.

On this floor, the layout was different from my floor. The hallways ran along the outside walls so there were windows evenly spaced along the wall. When I reached them and glanced outside, I discovered a city transformed. When I'd driven in that morning, most of the previous day's snow had melted and only the low, gray overcast remained to remind us that winter was close at hand. I now discovered it was closer than ever. What I saw out the window was a wall of white. I could just make out shadowy outlines of buildings across the street, but the densely falling snow obscured everything else.

From my own office window I had a similar view. It looked like a major storm. Behind me on the credenza, my little radio issued a stream of reports on the storm's progress, interrupted by periodic commercials. When I could see the street below at all, few vehicles were struggling down Hennepin Avenue and foot traffic was non-existent.

Teresa reported an increasing stream of calls from students, mostly from those who lived in the suburbs, wanting to know if classes were being canceled.

I called Marshall. When he came on the line, I said, "It looks as if we ought to close things up."

"I was just thinking the same thing." His voice sounded flat and heavy. "How bad is traffic on Hennepin?"

"It's barely moving when I can see that far down and there's snow building up everywhere. Have you been listening to the radio?"

"Yeah," he said after a pause. "They're saying this storm system is stalled over us and snow may fall for several hours."

"We're supposed to have rehearsal tonight, but if the college is closing, that'll be canceled so I'm going to head out early."

"You want to hit a few tomorrow? Assuming you aren't snowbound out there in the boonies."

"Sure." I looked at my appointment book. "Brooklyn Center's not exactly the boonies, you know. How about noon? That'll give Minneapolis's vaunted services enough time to get the streets plowed."

I was encouraged that he'd suggested a session of racquetball. We usually played a couple of times a week, but since his release from jail, our attempts to run each other into total exhaustion hadn't resumed. Marsh was avoiding all but essential contacts with the college community. I wondered how hard Trammel was pushing him to resign.

Marsh lived in a new high-rise building at the edge of the Loop. The twenty-story building was a complex-appearing jumble of roofs and courts, to make it possible for some tenants to have gardens, others to have more or fewer bedrooms. The apartments were built around a ten-story atrium filled with light, trees, and expensive marble. In the basement under the atrium, the developer had installed a two-story, state-of-the art gymnasium-cum-health spa, replete with racquetball/handball courts, a whirlpool, a sauna and a big collection of chrome-shiny exercise machines, some of which I couldn't begin to identify, much less use.

"Teresa," I called out my door. "The college will cancel classes, and I'm declaring a short day for the office."

"State just announced it's closing most offices and sending all but essential employees home," she said.

"See you in the morning," I smiled.

CHAPTER 30

*Truth and the People will
win this fight–*

I called Lori and suggested we make a two-car caravan to Brooklyn Center, leaving immediately. The radio crackled with the announcement that City College had canceled classes for the evening. The announcement also stated that most college offices would close early, so Marsh had moved promptly. An announcement of the state's decision to close up early followed. Lori agreed to meet me in the lobby, but I waited ten more minutes before she exited the elevator, bundled to the eyes in coat and scarves.

"Hey, looks like you were prepared for this storm."

"Not me, fella, that's why I took so long. I've been going through offices and talking to the few hardy souls still in the building, borrowing this stuff to keep me from the wet. Look, I even found some boots that almost fit."

I had no boots and by the time we struggled the snow-clogged block to the parking lot, my shoes were sopping and my toes were numb.

"Look at this." Lori waved her arm at the white-coated lot where more than half the slots were empty. "Let's just leave your car and take mine. You can drive. You know I hate driving in a snowstorm. I'll just close my eyes and hang on."

It was true. Lori drove with skill and dexterity, but she'd confessed that piloting an automobile in a snowstorm gave her the willies.

The falling snow had let up slightly by the time we scraped the accumulation off her Honda and skidded out of the lot. The gloom of the snowy early evening, punctuated by snow-shrouded streetlights, filled the road with soft shadows and an eerie half-light.

We struggled and slid our way to Washington Avenue where earlier traffic had made a few tracks. I opted to stay off the freeway which had a tendency to freeze up under these circumstances. It looked like more than an inch of the white stuff had already fallen. Lori wasn't much for talk and I concentrated on my driving. The snow fell more thickly again and the wind blew in hard gusts, sending big flakes at an angle across our route. Occasionally the headlights showed only what appeared to be dense swarms of flashing white insects. The wipers barely kept up with the accumulation on the windshield.

There was almost no traffic going our direction, which was fortunate. I allowed the car to wander up the avenue, avoiding nascent drifts that encroached on the paved roadway like sand dunes on an ocean shore.

As we struggled slowly into Brooklyn Center, the wind picked up still more, hurling the snow almost horizontally across the streets. I turned into the winding drive that led to the parking lot behind Lori's apartment building. Both the roadway and the lot had been recently plowed, making the surface much firmer. I reversed into Lori's assigned spot so the front of the car was accessible if the temperature really dropped and we had to jump-start it in the morning.

Inside, warm lights leading up the stairs were a welcome sight.

"What a miserable drive," Lori remarked.

"'When icicles hang by the wall, And Dick the shepherd

blows his nail, And Tom bears logs into the hall, And milk comes frozen home in pail, When blood is nipped and ways be foul, Then nightly sings the staring owl,'" I declaimed, opening the apartment door.

"Me for the shower. I'd welcome a little bourbon and perhaps a back scrub, kind sir," Lori said, flipping lights on as she moved deeper into the apartment.

I murmured assent and shucked my wet coat in the entryway, my shoes and socks a step later. The kitchen tile was warm to my numb, wet, toes. I found the liquor and built two drinks. Shedding suit jacket and tie, I carried the drinks down the hall. The apartment had two bathrooms, the larger opening off Lori's bedroom. I rapped on the bathroom door and stuck my head around the edge. Steam clouds rolled out of the shower stall.

"Come!" she called over the roar of the showerhead. I set the two heavy glasses on the vanity. The steam and water running down the door to the shower stall made it almost opaque. Then she slid the door partway open and smiled at me. I felt a rush of desire. Just looking at her rosy wet and sparkling face was enough to turn me on.

"Are you coming in or are you just going to stand there gawking?"

"'Behold! How like a maid she blushes here.'"

"Jack! Stop that!"

I shed the rest of my clothes and stepped under the hot stream of water.

Lori handed me her gel and a big wet terry-cloth mitt. "Here, slave. Do my back."

The gel bubbled up into a thick, fragrant lather under my long strokes up and down her back. After several minutes I dropped the mitt in favor of more direct contact with her smooth slick skin. The creamy gel sluiced off her back and puddled around our feet. I leaned closer, pressed my lips against her shoulder. Steam billowed around us. After a moment of full body spooning, Lori twisted around and folded her arms about me, open mouth reaching for mine. We kissed for a long moment, bodies pressed together, then she pulled back slightly.

"Hungry?" Shower spray sparkled in her dark lashes.

"Umm, for you" I said, reaching for her mouth again.

"Drink?" she smiled against my cheek a moment later.

I broke away to reach out and hook the cold glasses of bourbon. Protecting our drinks from the shower, we slid down the tile wall and crouched side by side under the spray, laughing and smirking at each other. City College, the scrapes and small triumphs of our separate days, disappeared in the pleasure of this shared moment and our anticipation of what was to come, all wrapped in our love for each other.

Bundled in thick terry-cloth towels, we sprawled on Lori's queen-sized bed.

"We need to talk, babe," I said. "About us." We'd grown closer over the months, but somehow serious talk about the long term, about careers, had never materialized.

We'd switched to wine and Lori leaned over to take a careful sip of her cold Chardonnay, then looked up at me. I took her silence for agreement and went on. "I've had the feeling, more than once in the last few days that you've had something on your mind as well."

"True, but it's never seemed to be the right time."

"Maybe it isn't now, either, but I keep remembering what we decided when we finally figured out that we were attracted to each other."

Lori smiled. "After you calmed down long enough to apologize for that very rude remark and I stopped interrupting long enough to hear your apology. After that, our relationship got lots better. Remember, we agreed that we wanted a frank relationship? We agreed to keep talking to each other."

I nodded, "To tell each other what we're thinking."

"I've been thinking these terrible murders are getting in the way."

I sighed. "You've got that right. I'm over my head and I'm getting obsessed by my lack of progress clearing Marsh."

"Frustration is probably a better label. I was going to wait a while but, maybe having something else to worry about will give you a fresh cut at your investigation." Her smile was impish and I realized I was being gently teased.

"Jack, honey, I've been thinking about the possibility of our being married. To each other. And I just want you to know I've been having such thoughts."

"Ah. Well." I rolled over and reached for my wine glass to give myself a little time. "I love you. You know that."

"Yes, and it's nice you keep telling me so. I also know your first marriage wasn't everything you'd hoped for. And this is not a proposal. And besides…."

I stopped her mouth with a gentle kiss and then stared into her lovely dark eyes surrounded by those long lashes.

"When we talk about marriage," I whispered, "I don't want distractions around like these damn murders. Just so you know, I'll happily admit to having similar thoughts. What it would be like to spend the rest of my life with you. I just don't know if I'm marriage material. After my first try, I feel a little skittish. Plus the thought of hurting you in the process is not a happy one."

"What I started to say was we have important things to sort out first. Things like career moves and children. But all of that has to wait until this gruesome business is done with. What was it we said, to just take things a day at a time?" We were nose to nose and her hands were busy below my range of vision. "Still no breakthroughs?"

"I'm making very little progress on this investigation. I don't seem to be helping Marsh, and now Emma is dead." I shook my head.

"It's impossible for you not to feel partially at fault for Emma's death. We all have to take responsibility for our actions and that has to include Alissa and Professor Tidwell. No one can give you absolution, and I know you don't want that.

"You, like everybody connected to this mess, are driven to a degree by circumstances. Sure," she shook her head to forestall my attempt to interrupt, "if you knew all the answers, or even a lot more, you might have prevented Emma's suicide by handling things differently. Who are you? Solomon?" She shook her head again. "No, you're just an intelligent, caring man who is trying to find some truth and help a good friend." She smiled gently.

"And, who happens to be the man I love." She rolled away to put down her glass, then rolled back, holding out her arms. I looked down to discover her towel had gone missing and mine nearly so.

"Neat trick," I murmured. "How'd you do that?"

CHAPTER 31

*I am a quiet and peaceable man
who believes in discreet moderation–*

My visitor's pass to the health and exercise club in the basement of Marsh's apartment complex was waiting at the front desk when I arrived.

Marsh wasn't in the locker room. I changed and slipped my combination lock onto the locker door and went to the floor half a flight below, where the entrances to the six racquetball courts were located. Those tiny, low doors reminded me of scenes from the classic Russian movie, "Alexander Nevsky." The grease-penciled schedule on a clipboard hanging on the wall said Marsh and I had court number three. It was empty so I let myself in and began to limber up with some stretching exercises. Then I hit a few easy lobs against the front wall. It was some time since I'd worked out and even longer since Marsh and I had played racquetball, so I forced myself through the boring warm-ups.

Then I hit three-wall combinations, finally getting the ball to drop almost dead, a foot or so off the front wall twice in a row, until the door banged open and Marsh came in.

I turned from the front of the court, where I had gone to pick up the ball, and watched him shuck his sweatshirt. He had on his usual dark blue nylon track shorts. They stretched tight over his buttocks and I could see the lines of his athletic supporter. Thick ropes of muscles rippled the warm brown skin of his thighs. He did a few fast deep knee bends and swished the racquet back and forth in his right hand, rotating his shoulders. He turned toward me with that big hard competition grin on his face and I realized that was one of the things I'd been missing.

I bowed slightly from the waist and grinned back. "'But soft, here cometh my executioner.'"

"C'mon, man, let's get to it," he said. For a time we forgot Alissa Constant, Stuart Jamison and murder. We played two fast games, immersed ourselves in the sounds of the ball caroming off the hard walls, the screech of composition soles on the shiny wood floor, the smell of our own perspiration. I won the first game going away, then Marsh hit his rhythm and he took the second by a close score. He was becoming more aggressive and I knew the rubber game would require all my cunning to come up with another win.

We took a breather. There was plenty of time left in our session. Marsh stripped off his wet T-shirt and I admired his broad shoulders and well-defined triceps.

"You look to be in just as good shape as when we last played," I said.

"Thanks. I'm a few pounds heavier than in graduate school, and just that much slower. This place helps and I use it often. The club's open twenty-four hours."

"Seven days?" I huffed.

Marsh nodded. "Unfortunately, the guys who staff health clubs always seem to be moving around, so there's a lot of turnover. I suppose we don't pay them enough."

I shrugged. "So? It must be fairly easy to hire somebody to hand out towels and keep track of court reservations. It's not exactly a high-skill job."

Marsh stood at the serve line, bouncing the little blue ball and eyeing his target spot on the wall. I crouched a little at the back of the court. He had a heckuva serve. His big arm came up and he smashed at the ball in a whistling arc. The ball somehow hit my racquet just right after coming off the front wall, then flew into the corner. We volleyed two more exchanges and he took the point.

"No it isn't," he continued the conversation, chest rising and falling, "but the kid who was here the night Constant was killed could alibi me, if we could only find him."

Again the big serve. The little blue ball zipped by and I tried to pick it up on a rebound off the back wall. My swing was off the mark, and the ball dribbled across the floor.

"You mean you were down here the night she was killed?" The next serve caught me flat footed and went right by.

"Sure. I thought you knew. The medical examiner set the time of death in a range of a few hours on October twenty-fifth. From early evening to around ten."

"But the tour finished before five," I objected. "That means she must have gone back on her own."

"Anyway, there are plenty of people who saw me off and on during the day, but so far we only have my word for what happened after four-thirty when I came home."

I had been so focused on finding Constant's real killer that I hadn't paid any attention to an alibi for Marsh. Finding that gym attendant could have re-directed police energies to look for other suspects. I'd made a mistake.

With a lunging run that took me hard into the side wall, I managed to drop a return volley out of his reach and we changed serves. I took two points with my soft serve. Marsh let his emotions, as he talked about the case against him, control his game. He charged the front wall too hard, and my volleys went by him just beyond the long reach of his racquet.

"Anyway, I came home, had a swim, and spent some time in the sauna. I went upstairs and ate, read for a while and came back down for a light workout on the weight machines. Rode the bicycle. I was down here late, working slowly through my routines. There were only a couple of others around. None of the residents who told the cops they were here that evening remember me, but I'm sure the guy who was on duty would, if we could find him. After I showered, he and I talked about college for a while. The dude quit a few days later and moved. Nobody seems to know where to. My lawyer has somebody looking, but she's not too hopeful."

"How does your lawyer feel about the case against you?"

"She doesn't think it's much of a case. It's all circumstantial. The state is talking second-degree involuntary manslaughter. I killed her in a rage, no premeditation. But I still could do time and you know what a conviction would do to my career." He grimaced in disgust and slashed at the ball. It caromed off a side then the front wall and whined past my ear.

I wondered if Trammel had approached Marsh about resigning, but decided not to ask him. By now we were struggling to finish the game, neither able to get the necessary two point advantage. Finally Marsh fooled me completely with two nifty back-to-back serves and we collapsed to the floor against a side wall.

"Look, my friend," I said, when I got my breath back. Sweat dripped into my eyes and my vision blurred, "for what it's worth, you know I believe you didn't do it."

"Not even after you learned about those early incidents?"

I waved a hand weakly, not pleased to see faint muscle tremors. "So, you were drunk and passed out in one case and on the side of the angels in the other. The worst they show is that you have a capacity for violence. Who doesn't?"

"Yeah, well. It's been hard getting where I am, and I've always tried to be super careful. At least after graduate school. I'm still a little surprised that I got involved with Alissa, but she really came on to me."

I nodded. "It doesn't surprise me after what I've learned about her. Did she ever ask you for special favors?"

"As a matter of fact she did, but it was inconsequential, at least at first. Later on it got a little too frequent."

"Did she threaten you in any way?"

He thought a minute. "No, I don't think so." He shook his head at me. "Maybe I was just too dense to get it. No." He swiped at the sweat on his forehead. "She just wanted extra consideration now and then. Like when I came to you before Trammel asked you to get involved with the Jamison thing. She'd ask me to smooth the way, put in a supportive word here and there. Once in a while I did. She had some good ideas and it didn't seem to matter.

"Maybe six months ago, her requests got more serious. She wanted me to bend our personnel policies and get her appointed manager of that new grant project we start next month. That's when we began to quarrel seriously. We didn't fight very often, but she could get really angry. Had a real tongue in her head." Marsh's voice trailed off. He sat with his chin resting on his wet chest, remembering.

"Making up was a lot of fun, though." He looked up with a faint smile on his face. "C'mon, man. Let's hit the showers. I have to get back to work."

When I returned to the visitor's locker room, I put a hand on my lock and discovered it was open, not hanging open, but the lock wasn't latched. Hadn't I locked it? I thought I had. I yanked the door open. It looked like someone had gone through my belongings.

In the shower I said to Marsh, "Just how secure is this place?"

"Meaning what?"

"Well, I had to sign in for the pass you left and the guy in the lobby buzzed me through. How easy would it be for almost anyone to get past the guy at the desk?"

"Not very. On the other hand when this place was built, management handed out passes in every business downtown. Including City College. Every staff and faculty member got one. They were all short term of course. But every so often, so I hear, someone uses an expired pass or tries to. I assume a few get through. Why?"

"Just curious." Nothing was missing and I couldn't figure out what the intruder had been after. There was no sense in telling Marsh or calling the cops. I couldn't prove anything one way or the other but it gave me the creeps.

CHAPTER 32

*Tonight I have no intention
of dealing with all that filth–*

It was late when I got home and I hobbled around trying to loosen my stiff muscles. Our workout strained me a good deal. I checked the curtains to be sure they were tightly closed. It had become a habit ever since the shooting. Lori and I agreed she'd stay away from my place until this thing was resolved. She offered to have me move in with her, at least temporarily. I was tempted, but I decided not to chance making her a target.

I glanced through my mail, discarded most of it. I poured a small snifter of brandy and listened to the messages on my telephone answering machine. There were four. One wanted a pizza and someone else had to reach Georgia urgently. He sounded irritated when it sank in that he'd dialed the wrong number. The third was from Merrill Swanborg and the last was a computerized survey. It was too late to call Merrill so I drank my brandy, took another shower, and went to bed.

Morning was at last clear overhead and the air tasted sharp and clean. At City College, all was still serene so I immediately called Swanborg and left a message. Then I settled down to field incoming calls and study my lines. At eleven, Merrill called again.

"Good morning, Jack. I have the results of the autopsy on Jamison in front of me. I thought you might be interested."

"Sure, but you didn't just get the report, did you?"

He laughed, "No, but I just decided to share it with you."

"Merrill, we made an agreement, remember? I haven't got anything you don't know, except what we may learn from the rest of the coded pages from Constant's files, and I've already promised to turn that over as soon as we do the translation."

"Stuart Jamison was killed by someone shorter," he said, ignoring my comment. "The killer came up behind him, hit him on the head, and then slashed his throat as he fell. Apparently the killer couldn't hold him up and they kicked over those trashcans. Jamison was stunned, dieing from the throat slashing, and he fell, along with some of the cans, down several steps in the lobby. It must have been quite a racket. That's the noise that attracted you. Forensics found a boot print which might belong to the killer."

"Might?" I said.

"Yep," Swanborg went on. "None of the people who we know were on the scene, at the time, wear boots that fit this print. So there's a possibility the boot that made the print belongs to the killer. It's a small boot, with a pointed toe and small heel. Maybe a size seven."

"Cowboy boot?"

"Possibly. Do you know anyone who wears boots regularly?"

I pondered the question. "Not off hand, but it certainly can't be Marshall's," I said, an image of his large sneakers pounding about the racquetball court the previous day rising in my mind.

"We don't suspect him. We believe Jamison's murder is unrelated to Constant, or to City College. We've already been over that."

"Could it be a woman? How tall was Jamison?" I asked.

"He was about five-eight."

I thought about it. "So what we have is the possibility that Jamison was killed by a woman for reasons unknown. And you still think Marshall killed Alissa in a rage or a jealous fit. Are you looking for the missing gym attendant?"

"Yes, but not seriously."

"I understand that Alissa was killed some time after the tour ended."

"True. For which time Dr. Marshall has only the missing athletic club attendant as an alibi."

"Doesn't the timing strike you as odd?"

"No."

There was silence on the line for a moment.

"Merrill, could the prosecutor's staff guy be the mysterious McKenzie who's been calling around about Dean Constant? The guy I heard about earlier?"

"Nope. I already asked. Don't rule out the federal marshal's office, though."

"I think I want to talk with somebody down there in the sex crimes unit."

"Yeah? Does this have anything to do with our present subject? Are you gonna drop some new bomb on me?"

"That's why I want to talk with a specialist. I think it's separate, but I want to be sure."

"It would help to know what kind of sex crime you're talking about, rape, pornography, prostitution, kidvid–"

"What was that last?"

"Kidvid, pornographic videos of children." Merrill sighed in my ear. "That stuff bothers me the most. The kids usually aren't old enough to know what they're doing. They're abused, often drugged."

"I guess I want to talk with someone in that, in kidvid."

"You got some merchandise?"

"Yes, I think I may have."

"Okay, Jack. I'll have Detective Steve Castelano get in touch as soon as he can."

"Thanks."

I broke the connection and called Anita.

"Hi, Jack. I was about to call you. I have a little more decoded. I'm working on Professor Jellicoe's file. Constant seems to have used a lot of odd symbols and a kind of shorthand in this one which makes it even more difficult. It's like Emma Tidwell's code, but different, you know?"

She uttered a soft exclamation and then in the background I heard what might have been a hand smacking flesh.

"Anita?" I said sharply. "Is everything all right?"

She laughed softly. "Oh, sure. Did you want something else?"

"Yes. I want to show that pornographic videotape you found to a detective at the police station."

"Jack, you don't need my permission."

"I know, but because of the similarity in appearances, I want you to agree first. I hope you will. Maybe they can find the people using those young boys in the other piece. I think we should give them the tape, but I won't if you object." I held my breath. I couldn't predict how she'd react and I didn't want to argue with her. After a pause that stretched out several seconds, she said, hesitatingly. "Gee, Jack, thanks for asking. Will you have to tell the cops where you got it?"

"I don't think so. And then only if I'm convinced that's necessary to get to whoever made the tape."

"All right," she sighed. "You do what you have to. But please try to keep me out of it."

"Thanks. I'll come up and get it myself."

When I arrived at the audiovisual offices, I heard murmurs and laughter spilling from Talbot's office. I rapped on the door, disturbing the serenity of the moment. The door opened and Fred Coper came out, smiling slightly.

"Hey, Jack, howya doin'?" He kept on going down the hall. Anita was at her desk, also smiling.

I raised my eyebrows at her. "Well, I'm a little surprised to see Fred over here."

"It surprises me too, I guess. Here's the tape. Maybe you could erase it after you show it to the cops."

"We'll see. Thanks Anita. I will try to keep your name out of this."

I took the video cassette and returned to my office. My extension was ringing as I walked in, and I signaled Janet that I'd catch it at my desk. It was the policeman, Steve Castelano. He agreed to come to my office in an hour. I wheeled our stand with the video player and TV set into my office and plugged it in. Someone had disconnected all the cables so it took me several minutes to set up the rig and check it out. Castelano arrived early and Janet brought him in. He was a big, overweight, bald man, whose suit looked as if he'd slept in it several nights running. His tie was loose and a little askew. He had a hoarse voice and an expression on his face that almost immediately inspired confidence. Castelano slumped into a chair and I explained the situation, leaving out the exact details of how the tape came into my possession.

He smiled at me. "And this anonymous individual, not part of your staff, agreed to let you turn it over to us on condition that you not reveal who gave it to you, right?"

I nodded.

"Okay," he sighed, "we'll play it that way for now, but you gotta realize, your civic-minded citizen may have to come forward if we're not just going to waste our time. Well, let's see it."

I handed him the cassette and he looked at it closely for a few minutes. Wordlessly he handed it back and I placed it in the VCR. He watched intently during the few minutes of the recording of the young boys, but after just a moment of the threesome, he snorted and leaned back in his chair.

"Okay, enough. This is a different tape. I've seen the threesome before."

"You have?" I was surprised by his announcement.

"Sure. We probably still have a version of it at the station. Look at the quality. This thing is another copy that's a long way down the line." He was looking at me. "Why are you so relieved that the threesome is a tape I've seen before?" he asked abruptly.

"It came from a friend who could be mistaken for the woman on the tape. And one of the men might be mistaken for another friend. Has it been around long?"

"Oh yeah, five or six years, I'd guess. The version we have is quite long. We picked it up busting up a near riot at a college stag as I recall.

"It's the other piece that interests me," Castelano said, leaning forward. "That came after, recorded over the threesome. They used newer equipment and it may have been done locally."

"You can tell that from looking at the tape?" I asked.

Castelano nodded. "Expert analysis will tell us even more. We've busted several individuals who had home videos they made for personal use and last year we cracked a small distribution ring. You might have read about it."

I shook my head.

"Four perverts got together after they found out they had similar interests, and decided to import and distribute stuff from Europe. They were each making their own videos and then they decided to combine their talents and sell copies. This could be another case like that one." Castelano made an expression of distaste.

"They were dumb pervs in the bargain. They rented or borrowed cameras and VCRs to make and copy the tapes. We got onto 'em when one dummy left a tape in the camcorder he returned to a rental store. The clerk played it and called us." He shrugged.

"We grabbed the one guy and he rolled over on his buddies."

I took the envelope of photographs out of my lap drawer and laid it in his hands. He shuffled through them, holding them by the edges. "I suppose you've handled these a few times?"

"Not after the first time. You think they might have fingerprints?"

"Probably not, but it's worth checking. We could get lucky."

I explained how I had acquired them. Castelano told me he thought they too were locally done, bundled tape and prints into his briefcase and left, promising to get back to me if he turned up anything useful.

I called Anita. "There's good news and not so good news. The detective has known about the *ménage a trois* for several years. This is a bad copy of only part of the whole thing. That's the good part. The bad part is the same. Copies of the tape keep cropping up here and there."

She sighed. "Okay. Thanks for filling me in."

I picked up my playbook and went to early rehearsal.

CHAPTER 33

*They are truths that are of such advanced
age that they are beginning to break up–*

"Well shit!" cried a voice from one side of the auditorium. "Somebody oughta do something!"

"*Shhhh,*" came another voice. I could see two heads leaning toward each other in adjoining seats in the middle of the auditorium.

"I don't care who hears," responded the first male voice, but he moderated his volume. "He was really out of it today, and he's been like that all week. I think they oughta retire him."

"Well, maybe he's under some kind of strain, or something," said his companion, also male.

I walked over and sat in the row behind the young man who was still complaining so bitterly, though at lower volume, and poked him in the shoulder.

"You having trouble with a faculty member?" I asked quietly.

The boy turned his head and stared blankly at me for a moment.

"Sorry." I smiled. "I overheard you complaining and I assumed you were referring to a faculty member." He just looked at me for a moment more, then shrugged,

"Uh, no, thanks, Mr. Marston, I was just shooting off my mouth. Frustration, I guess." He turned back toward the front of the auditorium.

Delton was waving his hands. The sleeves on his coat were

too long and almost hid his fingers, except when he raised his arms overhead. He was shouting across the stage, trying to rally his cast to rehearse once again the critical moment in Act IV, wherein Dr. Stockman, now shunned by most of the town's leaders for his insistence in telling the truth about the pollution of the town baths, takes his case to the townsfolk, confidently expecting their support. Of course, he finds that truth, when it threatens the economic health of the community, is not so welcome. There is a good deal of shouting and surging about in the scenes. We worked hard and in surprisingly short order, the fabric of the act came together and we could see the shape and drive of the piece.

Time fled and before long we were listening to the assistant director's notes at the end of rehearsal.

Later at my apartment, I looked up the boy, Roscoe Barnes, in the student/staff directory and noted that he was an economics major. I wondered if he'd been talking about Matt Jellicoe.

Monday I had an interesting visit. Actually there were two of them, tall, well dressed in dark suits and carefully barbered. Almost in synch, when they came into my office, they went for inside pockets and flashed ID documents at me. FBI. Wordlessly I gestured them to chairs. The two men replaced their ID wallets and sat. They sat carefully and adjusted their pants legs to avoid stretching the knees or adding wrinkles.

"Gentlemen, how may I be of assistance?"

"Mr. Marston," said the older of the two, "we have a problem."

No kidding, I thought. I raised my eyebrows at them. "How can I help?"

The man nodded as if I had just confirmed a private theory. "You are involved on an ad hoc basis in an investigation into the deaths of two individuals associated with City College."

"That's correct," I said evenly.

"We've checked you out and we think there's a good chance you'll see things from the government's point of view." I opened my mouth to say something but he held up a hand, boring right in.

"This is a matter of some concern to us, so we are here to ask you in the most straight forward manner to forget about Stuart Jamison. Continue to liaise with Detective Swanborg if you must. In fact, we think it's probably a good idea to do so, but concentrate on the woman. That line of inquiry is likely to be much more fruitful. We can assure you there is no connection between the woman and that unfortunate student, Stuart Jamison."

"The woman has a name," I said flatly.

The FBI man ignored my comment. "In return, although the Bureau has no jurisdiction in a murder case, we have some information developed in another line of inquiry which may have value for you." He nodded once and his companion reached into an inside pocket and extracted three sheets of paper filled with typing. The agent leaned forward and gently placed the pages on the edge of my desk. When I made no effort to pick them up, he sat back again. There was just the faintest trace of a smile on the face of the older man, the one who had done all the talking.

"Well, gentlemen, I could make a statement here covering my reaction to your request, but I'm not going to do so. It occurs to me it may be in my best interest and the best interests of the college, not to say anything at this point. Was there something else?"

"No, I don't believe so," said the agent. They rose together and went to the door. I stood and watched them leave the office. *Well well.*

I looked at the papers they'd left. A quick glance told me they were notes of calls made to several people around the country who had known Alissa Constant.

I picked up the phone and called Merrill Swanborg. When he came on the line I related the incident.

"Interesting," he said. "How do you see it?"

"I think it's a sister agency helping out the Marshals by trying to get me to lay off Jamison in return for a little help with Constant."

"Yeah, I agree. Looks like your intuition about Jamison being a protected witness was right."

"What about the cops?"

"I don't think the Bureau will talk to me. I suspect they've already talked to the Chief."

We disconnected and I went back to a report I was scanning from our office of institutional research. There was federal money available for support of student services aimed at helping 'at risk' students, students who had demonstrated a tendency toward trouble of various kinds, including academic troubles. I was interested in determining how many of our students could qualify for the kind of help the bill supported. It was part of the regular routine of midlevel managers at academic institutions, searching for federal money. The report was not very helpful. Apparently, our students were not prone to the kinds of difficulties Congress had addressed. The telephone rang.

"Yes?" I muttered, still trying to decipher the language in the summary paragraph of the study.

"You are really popular with the PD today. Here's another one," came the voice of our secretary through the speakerphone.

I mashed a button and picked up the handset. "Hello? Jack Marston at your service."

"Glad to hear it," came the growly voice of a man who hadn't had enough hours of sleep in the past twenty-four.

"Who's this?"

"Detective Castelano, Mr. Marston. I wonder if you could come down to our office in city hall this afternoon."

"What about?"

"I want to show you some pictures."

"What?"

His back-of-the-throat chuckle rattled over the phone. "Not that kind. Since you received that stuff in the mail, I thought it might turn out you're acquainted with some of the players. Won't take any time at all. I'll even send a car."

I assented. It was only a four-block walk to the station, but twenty minutes later when I stepped outside, the raw November wind cut deep and I was glad for the warm squad car. I saw curious faces watching as we pulled away. It occurred to me at that moment that I would probably be the subject of all sorts of rumors by the time I returned. The squad's radio squawked and grumbled as we made a fast left turn and headed down sixth toward the old turreted city hall that housed the jail and the police department. The slender cop, who drove skillfully over the rutted street, wheeled the unit into the underground garage and directed me to the tunnel entrance that took me under the street and into the ground floor of the echoing old building.

One flight up I found Detective Castelano sitting in a small gray conference room with a single window that looked south at a gray city. There were several black ring binders stacked in front of him and he held another as he hunched over the table. He glanced up and nodded. I slid into the seat beside him and looked at the binder in his hands.

"What I have here is a collection of most of the known and suspected sex criminals in the city. I'd like you to go through them and see if you can pick out any familiar faces."

"Okay."

"You just sing out if you see anyone you recognize."

I took the binder and began to go slowly through the pages. Some were copies of mug shots, some were good quality color prints, and others looked like they had been taken from great distances and had been enlarged. Nearly all were pictures of men. There were men in restaurants, men walking on the street, a few apparently taken in bars. In many of them the subject was talking to other men. Sometimes to a woman. I was about three quarters through the binder when there was a knock at the door and another man stuck his head in. He nodded once at me.

"Phone, Steve."

Steve Castelano grimaced and heaved his bulk out of the chair. "Be right back, you just keep goin'."

On the next to last page of the third album I saw a picture that made me pause. It was very fuzzy and the man's face was partly obscured, but he looked familiar. I went on to the end of the binder and then returned to the fuzzygraph. The more I looked at the picture, the more sure I became that I knew that individual, or at least I knew the hat. Or the scarf. Who was he? It didn't come to me.

I set the book aside and looked out the window. The second hand on my watch went round and round. I drummed my fingers on the burn-scarred linoleum-topped table. After several more minutes, I picked up another binder from Castelano's stack. Idly I thumbed through several pages at random. These were young people. Again, some were obviously surveillance pictures; some color mug shots, mixed with black and white snapshots. Several had been cropped in odd ways and I realized that some of the subjects had been naked when the pictures were made. I turned two pages and there he was. I stared at the picture.

It was old, maybe ten or twelve years, but I knew the boy in the picture. The door opened and I dimly registered the fact, but I still stared down at the picture of a young Stuart Jamison.

"Marston? What is it?" Castelano had me by the shoulder, shaking me.

"I know this boy." He bent over me, looking at where my

finger pointed. "His name is–was–Stuart Jamison."

"You're telling me this is the student who was murdered at the college a couple weeks ago?"

"Yes. God! I'm sure of it. That's a really old picture, but I'm certain it's him."

"Jamison. I'll be damned. Just a minute. Carlson!" he bellowed, causing me to jump. "Sorry. Hey, Carlson! Bring me the open file from seventy-eight." He flipped the picture over to scan the back. A series of numbers was penciled there.

The other detective came in and handed Castelano a thick, ragged file. He stood there while Steve thumbed quickly though it until he found a single sheet of paper.

"Yeah," he said. "Listen to this. Oh, Carlson, this is Jack Marston from City College. I had him down here to look at the sex perp book, but he happened on something else. See, Mr. Marston, I gave you a collection of people we are convinced are doing child porn and kiddy prostitution around the cities. This book has pictures of kids we've surveiled in the same activities. They're street hustlers, and some are players in some of the porno pictures and movies we've collected. Juvies, most of 'em.

"We just collect these pictures and keep 'em in this book. A lot of 'em, we don't know their names, just dates and locations when the pictures were snapped. Some of them aren't even in the game. Sometimes, like now, we get lucky.

"This kid, Jamison? Well, he's got a juvie record and lots of suspicion that he was popular, selling himself in street trade and doing movies and pictures, but that was mostly street talk. We got no real proof. Then after eighteen months, two years, poof. The kid disappears. Now the next time we know him here in town, he turns up dead at City College. Very innaresting." He and Carlson looked at each other.

"I better tell Swanny," said Carlson.

"Yeah," replied Castelano, satisfaction in his voice. "By all means, notify Detective Swanborg that we have some new information on the background of one of his DBs."

Carlson hurried out. "Well, Mr. Marston, any more little surprises for us?"

I had nearly forgotten the other picture. "Umm, yes, I think so. Something about this picture is familiar, I think. I just can't quite put a name to the man."

"Don't force it. Let me tell you that this man is a suspected child pornographer who sometimes goes by the alias Cowboy. We haven't anything hard, just this picture and a lotta street talk. You think about him from time to time. If you press it, I've learned, the memory seems to go farther away. I appreciate you coming down here. Just call me if you think of his name."

Castelano took me down the hall to the elevator where I met the officer who had brought me to City Hall. Together we went through the tunnel under Third Street to his squad car patiently waiting in the ramp.

Back in my office, giggling Teresa and Ranae briefly related some of the more bizarre rumors that had come to their ears in the brief time I'd been gone. On reflection, more than one of the remarks seemed a bit malicious.

The gray afternoon moved swiftly toward evening. I wrapped up a few things and drove to my quiet apartment. I would stay home alone, Lori having professional responsibilities to occupy her for the entire evening.

I went inside and turned left to hang up my overcoat. Opening the closet door, a strong sharp odor assailed my nose. "Phew! What the hell?"

My gaze touched my gym bag and I remembered. I hadn't opened, cleaned, and aired it since Marsh and I worked out at his club two days ago. Now the sweaty clothes were wreaking their olfactory revenge. I took the bag into the bathroom and zipped it all the way open. Then I upended it on the floor. Out came shoes, socks, my shorts and jock strap, a wrinkled tee shirt, and a small sheet of paper. I banged on the bottom of the bag and other assorted detritus fell out. I set the bag aside and wadded up the soiled clothing, consigning it to the plastic trash bag in which I collected my dirty laundry. The shoes went into the corner with their tongues pulled up. The rest of the loose stuff I swept into my dustpan and was about to deposit it in the wastebasket when I looked again at the piece of paper. It had been folded into a square. I set the pan down and picked up the paper. When I unfolded it I found a cryptic note. I remembered then that I thought my locker might have been jimmied.

The note, in printed black ink, said, I have the answers. Call 555-8972.

I called the number. It was a professional answering service and I mumbled something inane and hung up. Then I called the cop shop for Merrill Swanborg.

CHAPTER 34

*You should never wear your best trousers
when you go out to fight for freedom and truth–*

Merrill Swanborg called me back.

"I found a note in my gym bag. It must have been put there while I was playing racquetball with Marsh."

"Do you have it with you?"

"Yes, it's here on my desk. I called the number last night. An answering service."

"What'd you say to the operator?"

"Nothing. I said I must have dialed wrong."

"Good," Merrill said. "Don't call again. We'll be over later."

Noon came and went. At two, he was standing in my office holding a police-issue portable tape recorder in his hand. We connected it by a suction cup to the handset of my phone.

"I didn't want to take a chance of calling from our phones in case there is some kind of high-tech gimmick that might trace the call," he explained. "You just call the number and ask if there are any messages." He pressed Record.

I dialed. When a woman answered, I identified myself and asked if she had any messages for me. "Yes," she said, and she gave me another number to call. The instructions, she told me, were to call within ten minutes of receiving the number. I wrote down the number and with Merrill beside me nodding encouragement I called the second number. A dark male voice answered on the second ring.

"Marston. If you have the cops with you, don't bother trying to keep me on long enough to trace this number. I'll only say this once. I have important information about Constant's murder. Meet me on the top floor of the Fourth Street parking ramp at two A.M. tonight. That means tomorrow morning, got it? No cops and no cover. You come alone. I'll be watching. I don't care whether you get this stuff. You do, so be there." The phone clicked in my ear. I cradled the handset and looked at Swanborg.

"Neat," he said. "No time to trace it, but at least we have his voice on tape." He patted the tape recorder on the desk, then disconnected the suction cup. "Maybe we'll get lucky. You didn't recognize the voice, of course." I shook my head. "Meanwhile you just ignore this. Don't go to the ramp."

"How can I do that? The guy might have something that will clear Marsh."

"Look, Jack. Remember the bullet holes in your window? The sandbag? Your feelings of being watched sometimes? Wise up. If this guy isn't the shooter, he's an associate. Forget the movies. Protection is very difficult, almost impossible. And no gun!" I shrugged. I didn't own a gun and wasn't about to buy one. My father had a gun once. He accidentally nicked my uncle with it. I never carried a gun in the service, either.

Swanborg looked at me. "You're still gonna go, aren't you."

I nodded. He nodded.

"Figures. Okay. I'll set it up and meet you back here around ten tonight." Detective Swanborg packed up his recorder and left.

Teresa walked in as Merrill was leaving. "Jack, the boy who used to be Alissa Constant's secretary just called. Seems some shoe repair store across the street had an overdue job for her. They called to remind Alissa to pick up the shoes. He went across and got 'em. It's a box, I guess. Do you want to look into it?" I did and went immediately to Constant's former office.

Jeffry, the young secretary, was at his desk in the otherwise empty office. A large pasteboard box tied with string rested on one corner.

"This the box from the shoe place?" I asked. He nodded.

Really sharp, I thought to myself, always asking the obvious question. "How much did you have to pay for it?"

He told me. I gave him the money. Then I opened the box. Inside I found a pair of short, deep russet, western boots. They had new heels on them. The boots were otherwise well worn with elaborate tooling over the toes and instep. They had very pointed toes.

I put the cover back on the box and said to Jeffry, "You did the right thing. These boots could be important. Call the police and tell them to come here to talk to you. I'll take the boots to my office and they can pick them up from me. Thanks a lot, Jeff."

While I waited for the police to arrive, I thought about the telephone call. Amid my growing nervousness about my upcoming rendezvous with the note writer, I wondered if these boots on my table would match the footprint from the lobby where Jamison was murdered. I couldn't shake the thought that a knife-wielding Alissa Constant was impossible to accept.

At four, after the police had collected the boots and interviewed Jeffry, I went to the Caves to have coffee with Lori and bring her up to date.

"Interesting business, those boots. If Alissa killed Jamison, why was she later murdered? Maybe the two murders are totally unrelated and it's all just a big coincidence."

"Sure," I responded grumpily, "and I'm the tooth fairy."

She laughed. "Well, let me give you another piece of intriguing information I came across earlier today. One of my clients in my other practice at the downtown clinic is having some pretty severe identity problems. It turns out she's been spending some time with friends at the Algonquin."

I looked up from my intense examination of the tabletop. "Is she gay?" We stared at each other.

Lori shook her head, saying, "That's not the point here, and I don't think you need her name."

I nodded. "What if her testimony is needed?"

"If it ever comes to that, she'll have to decide. She told me she recognized Alissa Constant from the newspaper picture. My client saw her more than once at the club, but she wasn't sure for a while because apparently, Alissa always wore some kind of western getup. Wore her hair differently, too."

"Ties in with the boots, doesn't it. Listen, I have another problem and I want your help."

I explained about the note and the call and the rendezvous that night.

"Jack! You don't have to do this. Don't do this. I don't care about Trammel and your investigation."

"Yeah, well, what about Marsh? This may be our chance to clear him."

Lori was not persuaded. She continued to argue against my going. Marion Lester stopped at our table to tell me that except for one or two recalcitrant faculty, he was now hearing approving comments on the careful way I was handling the investigation. I felt good that I hadn't created a huge fund of ill will, but I also knew that if things dragged on much longer pressure from the administration would rise to an intolerable level.

I looked around the room at students, several faculty, and some staff. Some of them glanced at us, but apart from Marion, none overtly acknowledged our presence. I wondered how many of them agreed with Lester. Professor Jellicoe walked out carrying his hat and coat. His secretary was with him.

Lori reluctantly agreed to stay home and wait until I called her after my meeting at the parking ramp. Back in my office I called the cops and talked again to Merrill. He was still against my risking the meeting. He explained to me about the officers who'd be stationed in buildings that overlooked the ramp and about the plainclothes cops who'd be inside the place.

I went across the street to have supper, but couldn't eat. I went back to the office to review my notes on the murders and sketch out a report in case…that didn't bear thinking about. At ten, the police arrived with a bulletproof vest for me.

"This is kevlar. If you're shot, you'll have bruises and maybe a broken rib or two, depending on the size of the weapon. Just remember that the vest doesn't protect you from a head shot."

After adjusting the fit, the cop with Merrill said, "You'll probably have to sit a while with the engine off. These people don't seem to like walking up to running automobiles."

"Damn," I said. "I didn't wear a hat today."

The officer looked at me and then said, "Here. Wear mine." I thanked him and gratefully took the heavy fur cap with thick ear flaps. It fit perfectly.

Sometime around midnight I found myself getting restless. Finally I called Lori for a little reassurance and then left the office to just drive around until time for the meeting. The walk to my car in the lot beyond First Avenue North was cold and I was glad for the officer's cap. There were few people about and I wondered, as I unlocked the car, if my caller was watching even now. If he was, was he cursing his lost opportunity to kill me, if that was his real reason for this meeting?

I decided such a train of thought was only depressing and of no help, so I tried to focus on more pleasant subjects. Like Lori, and our warm bed and her cheerful apartment. I wondered what my daughter Elizabeth was doing right now. I hoped she was still happy.

Cars passed, their headlights indistinctly delineated through the thickening vapors that rose as the city cooled. It was getting very cold. I could freeze to death. There I was again, thinking about my own mortality. I approached the parking ramp entrance. It was time to go to the top. I remembered my experience with another nearby garage, the one still under construction. I almost turned right instead of left and abandoned the whole idea. I almost decided to drive to Brooklyn Park instead; to the woman I knew anxiously waiting there.

The six-story parking garage was an older one, so it had none of the bright orange lighting required in new construction of these things. The owners would have to install the new lighting soon, but it wasn't in place tonight. There were several cars in the lower stories as I drove through. Up one level I went and then along the inclined floor past the stalls. At each end was a square brick column with its heavy steel door. Behind the door I knew, was the stairwell. I didn't see a solitary person and I wondered where my protectors were. Around a sharp turn, up to the next level, tires hissing on the salt and dirt encrusted concrete. A parked car, dark, silent. Two more on the other side, yellow lines on the concrete that marked the stalls. Out my right side window through the open walls I began to see more of the city lights and tall plumes of vapor rising in the chill night.

The temperature was six below zero and falling, the radio announcer said softly, urging us to bundle up and snuggle down. Another sharp turn and another level up. No cars. The low ceiling showed cracks in the pre-cast beams. Another turn and another empty level. Here most of the dim ceiling lights were out. My grimy headlights cast weird, distorting shadows on the stained walls at the end of each level. Almost to the top now, more sky, more lights, more vapors. One more sharp turn and I rolled onto the open roof. It had been scraped clean of snow. Under the sky, overcast and dark though it was, I felt somehow relieved, less vulnerable. As arranged, I drove slowly around the nearly deserted roof, my headlights sweeping faintly across taller nearby buildings. Flashes of light from the windowpanes reflected my headlights back into my face. I parked in the center of the roof, ignoring the yellow lines. I was three minutes early. Then I waited. I turned off the engine and listened to the ticking as the car cooled. The cold came quickly and touched my feet, my fingers, and the end of my nose. I readjusted the thick cap I had borrowed and sipped a steaming cup of coffee I'd brought with me in a cardboard container. Time passed. Except for the cold, I might have dozed off. Every time it got too cold, about every fifteen minutes or so, I restarted the engine and ran the heater on high to warm up the car, but I never really got warm after the first cold spell. I sat there alone for nearly an hour. I decided to stretch my cramped muscles and got out of the car. I did a quick jog around the idling machine, trotting through the billowing exhaust. It was damn cold, but fortunately there was almost no wind. I stopped at the front of the car and turned away to look out over the city at the twinkling lights. How much longer should I wait?

I went back to the car and opened the door. Warm air hit me in the face. I got a little more comfortable, a little more relaxed. He wasn't coming.

He was already there. I must have dozed briefly, because when I looked up a second later, there was the outline of a man's head in the rear view mirror.

"Hey," I shouted, twisting in my seat and reaching for the door. The next moment I felt intense pain and a blinding, momentary light when he hit me on the head.

The next recollection I had was of flashing lights, much movement and shouting, and excruciating, throbbing pain. Strangely, I couldn't hear anything. Later I discovered that the ambulance guys had wrapped my head to a board to immobilize my neck until I got x-rays, and my ears were covered. My vision was badly blurred and I could taste blood from my nose. I was on my back and several people hovered over me, sometimes looking down. I was very cold. I blacked out again.

It was daylight and my vision had nearly returned to normal. The shooting pains in my head were gone and if I didn't make any sudden moves, the dizziness stayed away. I was warm and comfortable, and when I slowly turned my head, Lori's dear face came softly into view. I felt pressure on my fingers increase. We were holding hands and now I understood that I was in a hospital bed. Lori leaned forward and gently kissed my cheek, worry lines in her face already beginning to soften. Suddenly I was very glad to be alive. I heard footsteps and Merrill Swanborg hove into view. He stepped up to the opposite side of the bed and peered down at me. Our eyes met but his stern look didn't change.

"What do you remember?" he asked quietly.

"Nothing much," I replied, my throat scratchy from tubes and oxygen.

"See your assailant? Nope? Thought not. We never saw a thing, either. Our men watched you through the scope, saw you get out of the car. They lost you for a second, then we saw the car door close. We figure he came onto that level and crawled across the floor to the car. After he whacked you he shut the car door. He must have left the same way, slithering across the floor, outa sight."

"What was the point?"

"Oh, we think he wanted to kill you. If he'd left the car door open he might have succeeded. Two things prevented your untimely demise." He grimaced at Lori. "She's one of 'em. Made such a fuss at the entrance to the ramp, we had to let her in."

I looked over at Lori. "You came down?"

"You bet. After an hour and you hadn't called, I drove down. I left Evelyn Jenner waiting for your call. She stayed with me the whole time until I left the apartment."

Merrill nodded and picked up the thread. "The other thing that saved your life was that thick cap the officer loaned you. The scumbag hit you over the right ear but the fabric cushioned your skull. No concussion. Even so you might have bled or frozen to death if Lori hadn't shown up."

"He must think I know something." Swanborg nodded again.

"I'm putting an escort on you for the duration, or at least until my superior calls me on it. There's a uniform outside the room until you go home." He left with a wave and a shake of his head.

Lori kissed me again. "You can come home tomorrow, if you promise to take it easy for a couple of days," she said, anticipating my next question. I nodded drowsily and drifted off to sleep.

CHAPTER 35

*Do you see any other way
out of it? I don't.*

After a day resting at home and missing a rehearsal, I still felt residual tremors if I moved my head too quickly, but the doctors said I showed remarkable recuperation. Lori's presence had a good deal to do with it.

I was at the window in Ranae Jannard's office looking down at the empty snow covered block across the street. The snow had softened the remaining mounds of trash yet to be carried away. Ranae picked up the phone on the first ring. "Jack, it's that detective." I took the phone from her outstretched hand.

"Merrill?"

"I thought you'd want to know, those boots of Constant's don't fit the footprint we lifted from the blood in the theater lobby."

"Now what?"

"Your ID of that old photograph of Jamison may help. Castelano is running his contacts. He told me he's shaking loose a few interesting things. How's your head?"

"Better if I don't move it too fast."

Ranae and I went back to reviewing our department plans for the upcoming quarter. We had mid-year budget requests to get in shape for the administrative council meeting next month.

I stood up from the table and went to the window for a brief break. I was staring down at the street in front of our building when a solitary figure came into view. He cut across the street mid-block and was walking away from our building, toward a small parking lot on First Avenue North where some faculty had reserved parking spaces. I recognized Professor Jellicoe from his hat and scarf. I watched him as he stopped, looked off to his left for a brief moment across the empty block, and then continued on. The phone buzzed again.

"Jack?" said Ranae. Teresa knew we weren't taking routine calls that afternoon. I frowned, took the handset, and turned back to the window. It was Anita Talbot.

"Uhh, Jack. I think I may have screwed up."

"What?" She sounded worried. I was immediately attentive.

"Professor Jellicoe came by and returned a missing camcorder he'd had checked out for a long time. I was working on the coded files. Sometimes when I concentrate I mumble out loud, you know? I think he may have overheard me."

"Whose file were you working on?"

"Jamison's. I dunno what I said, I just glanced up and there he was in the doorway, looking at me."

Down on the street a block away, Professor Jellicoe walked behind a car in the small lot and stopped again.

"What happened then?"

"Well, old Jellicoe just stopped in the doorway, and looked at me. His mouth fell open and his face got real white. I thought he was having a heart attack or something. Then he rushed off without saying anything. He just rushed off. I'm sorry, I know you said to be careful and not tell anyone anything."

Suddenly, watching Jellicoe over the car top, I had a flashback to a grainy photograph I'd seen at the police station. The hat was wrong, but the angle of view and the distance gave me a breath-freezing sense that the photograph had come to life.

I blew out my breath noisily. "Anita, I think you'd better be very careful until we resolve this. Don't be alone if you can help it and stay away from lighted windows."

"Geez. That bad? I'm sorry Jack. D'you think Jellicoe is involved?"

"I can't say for sure. I just don't know, Anita." But I did know. In my gut Jellicoe was abruptly linked to a nasty videotape of young, nude boys. "Anita, I'll talk to you later." I broke the connection and quickly dialed the police station.

"Steve Castelano," I said sharply. "This is Jack Marston." I glanced at Ranae who sat at her desk frowning at me.

"Sorry, he's out. Any message?"

"Yes! Tell him the man in the picture I couldn't identify the other day may be one of our faculty. Professor Mathew Jellicoe. Got that?"

"Got it," said the voice. I cradled the phone and said to Ranae, "Sorry, gotta go. We'll finish this tomorrow." I ran out and down the hall to my office where I grabbed my coat and gloves. Heading for the door again, I said, "Teresa, I have to go out and I'm sure I won't be back before the end of the day. You and Ranae will have to sort out whatever I've just dumped on you. Sorry." She waved dismissively as I strode swiftly out the door toward the elevator.

The sky was darkening under gathering storm clouds when I reached the parking lot. Already some cars had their headlights on. I headed out in the direction of Jellicoe's house. Then I began to think more carefully about what I was doing. If Jellicoe was a pornographer and a killer, who was I to chase after him? Why didn't I just call in the cops? Was this some macho play because he'd whacked me on the head at that ramp? Was it even Jellicoe who did that? I swore briefly at my apparent need to be in at the end. I didn't even know if this was the end.

The end could be my own.

Where was my proof? My mind jumped about as I wrestled the car along slippery rutted streets. I thought about that white room with the video camera at Jellicoe's house. If Jellicoe was the man in the police picture, had Alissa found out about his secret life? Had she tried to blackmail Jellicoe in some fashion? More questions than answers.

The temperature had dropped and snow squalls were spitting across my path as I drove northwest along cold city streets dangerously spotted with ice and rutted snow.

The light had nearly gone as I turned into the street where Jellicoe lived. There was no car at the curb and there weren't any fresh tracks in the snow that had fallen on the driveway. Where had he got to?

Several neighboring houses showed lights in their kitchens. Jellicoe's house was dark. I made a U-turn and parked across the street. Staring at the dark rambler, I killed my engine and listened to the ticks and squeaks as the engine and body contracted. Nothing on the block moved as far as I could see. Finally I got out of my car and stood there, shivering in the raw wind. The last light continued to fade.

I wasn't getting anywhere standing and freezing where I was, so I picked my way across the street and up the walk where I banged on Jellicoe's door. There was no response. I pounded on the door in a near repeat of the only other time I'd been there. This time no one responded to my hammering. My head started to hurt.

I decided to try the back door. I turned left off the front stoop. I found myself instantly in calf-deep snow. Having once again left my boots at home, my socks soaked up the melt and further chilled my feet. I struggled to the back door and started pounding on it. After the fourth try I discovered I was making longer swings. The door had come unlatched and was opening under my assault. Warm air filtered out and touched my face.

I leaned into the gap and shouted into the silent interior, "Jellicoe! Doctor Jellicoe! Are you in there?"

No answer. I pushed the door open wide enough to admit me and stepped into the dark kitchen. I was shaking almost uncontrollably and it wasn't just the cold. The back of my neck was damp and I could practically feel my shirt collar wilting. I tracked melting snow onto the kitchen floor, but I was past caring.

"Jellicoe! Are you here?" Silence.

I stepped further in, belatedly realizing that standing in the doorway I had been a perfect target against the evening sky. Two steps, three. My outstretched hand hit a wall with a soft thump. I had the impression of less density just to the left of my face, as though there was a doorway. Why did he have such heavy curtains everywhere? I could barely make out the lighter rectangles of the windows. I moved my hand slowly over the wall until my questing fingers encountered its vertical edge. I took hold with fingers of both hands. Then I made an educated guess and slid my right hand back and forth over the wall just above my waist. On the fourth sweep I felt a light switch. I pressed closer to the wall and flipped the switch.

Nothing happened. Oh, a sound started, a fan, probably, somewhere in the wall, but no light. I reached around the corner I was holding, no doubt leaving sweaty streaks on the wall and found a second switch panel with three switches. The hell with it. I flipped all three at once and bright lights came on all over the place.

After I calmed down a little and recovered my full vision, I went through the house calling for Jellicoe. I didn't search the place, breaking and entering were enough for the moment. I did locate the white room off the living room. It looked about as I remembered with the same equipment scattered about except the camera and tripod were gone. On a hat rack by the front door I saw a tan broad-brimmed hat with a low square crown. I had a similar one. A riverboat gambler, I think they called it. Not a cowboy hat. Cowboy. The name Castelano said was the nickname of the familiar but unidentified man. Was it really Jellicoe? I was becoming convinced it was. There was no evidence of anything else I was interested in, and not a clue to Jellicoe's whereabouts. Now what? I was stumped. I drove home to change my wet shoes and socks.

While drying out, warming up and listening to my stomach complain that I'd missed supper, I tried to call Lori at home, at the clinic and at the college. I came up empty. I left a message at the clinic and on her home answering machine. Finally I called the police department, hoping to catch Merrill Swanborg, but he'd gone to supper. I left another message. I barely got the handset back in its cradle when it rang. I snatched it up.

"Jack, are you there? God, your line has been busy for so long."

CHAPTER 36

*A man with a family has no
right to behave as you do–*

I heard a quaver in her voice. "Lori? What's wrong? I've been trying to locate you, leaving messages all around town. Where are you?"

"Jack, listen. He's here, or he's coming soon." Her voice was tense, controlled, but vibrating like a cello string.

"Who? I've been out to Jellicoe's but his place is dark and–"

"Jack, listen to me," she interrupted. "I know. Professor Jellicoe called. He sounded very agitated. He called and said he's coming here, to the college. He said he wants to see you. I called the police and asked them to find that detective, Swanborg? Jellicoe called President Trammel too and threatened him. At least that's what Trammel said it sounded like to him." She paused. I could hear her rapid breathing.

"Lori, where are you?"

"Oh, I'm here, at the college."

"Okay. If he calls again, try to keep him talking, maybe you can calm him down. I'll be there as quick as I can."

"I don't know," her voice communicated her doubt. "I'll try, but he sounds as if he's under enormous stress. He practically babbled. He could be having some kind of breakdown. Did he kill Constant?"

"I don't know for sure, but something happened when he was returning some AV stuff to the college. He may have overheard

Anita talking about those coded files I found. Anita said he looked shocked, then he ran out. I'm coming in right now."

I dropped the already cracked handset back onto the base of the phone and grabbed my heavy car coat. I was at least thirty minutes away, maybe more, depending on the traffic and the road conditions.

Outside, more snow fell, blowing in swirls across the city, dimming and dancing with the orange streetlights. Biting my lower lip and gripping the steering wheel in mittened hands, I raced for the center of the city.

Snow was falling harder as I reached the corner of Sixth and Hennepin. On my right, in the building I called my professional home, lights shown warmly in many windows on most floors. I drove slowly around the block, peering uneasily through the snow first at the dark, empty block, then at my rear view mirror, then at the few passersby, bent against the snow. I didn't recognize anyone. Nor had I noticed any vehicle tailing me, not since I left my apartment. Impatient as I was to get inside to Lori, I began to feel she was in no immediate danger, and if I intercepted Jellicoe now, I might prevent another death.

After another circuit, this time around the block, on which my building stood, I pulled slowly into the delivery spot at the back of the building. When I cut my lights and the engine, it got very dark. Somehow the streetlights on two sides of the building didn't penetrate back here. Funny, I had never noticed that before. Where was Jellicoe?

I locked my car and hurried to the small side entrance where the night security guard had his cubicle of an office. I rapped hard. The door was a steel fire door so I didn't hear the man until he unlocked and swung the door open.

"Hi there, Mr. Marston." His cheery greeting was belied by the permanent worry lines between his thick eyebrows.

"Who else is still here, or back again?"

"Lori Jacobs is here. She's up in your office." He shook his head in mock amazement. "There's a few others, plus the cleaning people. And some people up top in AV. No one else since I came on at seven and the log is empty for an hour or so earlier. 'Course, someone could still be here who never left, but I haven't seen 'em."

I nodded my thanks and said, "The police are on their way here. We're looking for Professor Jellicoe. If he comes in this way, or you see him before the cops arrive, call me. Don't do anything else, just call me. And don't get in his way." I took the elevator to my floor. Lori was on the phone when I went in. She hung up a minute later. She stood and we embraced.

"God, I'm glad to see you," I said.

"Me too, but I don't think Jellicoe is after me. With Wally downstairs and the cleaning crew and that pair upstairs," she pointed at the ceiling, "this is as safe as anywhere. Besides, when I talked with Jellicoe, it seemed obvious he wasn't in the building. What have you been up to?"

"I went to Jellicoe's house, but he wasn't there. The back door was open so I went in. Didn't find anything, though. I was too nervous to make a thorough search."

She nodded thoughtfully. "I decided to stay right here in your office after I intercepted his call to you."

"Me? He called me?"

"Yes, so I figure if he calls again, he'll be trying to reach you."

"You said he sounded as if he was on the edge?"

"He wasn't entirely coherent." Lori frowned in recollection.

"Okay. I'm going upstairs to talk with Anita. Be back in a flash." I went to the door and then stopped. "Wait a minute. What pair upstairs? Is that what you said?"

Lori grinned. "Go see for yourself."

I went up once again to the audiovisual offices. Talbot's office door was ajar and I could hear soft murmurings beyond. I pushed the door farther open. They were sitting side by side close together at Anita's worktable, behind and to one side of her desk. Anita was looking down at a paper in front of her and scribbling something. Fred was staring at the side of her head. It looked as though he was blowing in her ear. I cleared my throat. Both jumped a foot and looked up with semi-embarrassed expressions.

"Well," I said, uncertainly, "this is a cozy scene." Anita grinned.

"Your fault, Jack."

"My fault?"

"Yeah," Fred chimed in. "If you hadn't talked Anita into decoding these files, she wouldn't have asked me for help."

"And I wouldn't have discovered this bright, usually charming, Neanderthal," Anita finished, putting a hand familiarly on Coper's shoulder.

"Well, I'm learning. I may be a little slow, but you're having a positive influence on me." He grinned some more.

"Great!" I said enthusiastically, "but tell me again your conversation with Professor Jellicoe." She did. "Now, about the kidvid–"

"The what?" She looked at me, perplexed for a moment, then I saw comprehension dawn. "Oh, you mean the porno tape? I told Fred about it." He nodded affirmatively. "In fact," she blushed, "we looked at it…at the tape…well, at part of it." I just stared at her. Fred nodded again.

There was a pause and I finally filled it. "Did you make some notes for me about that tape?"

"Oh, yeah. I got 'em right here." She pulled some sheets of paper out of her desk and handed them to me.

"You got any more decoding done?" I asked then.

She nodded "Fred suggested we put some of this stuff into the computer and run substitutions of our own. He did, and it looks like we're on the right track."

I opened my mouth to compliment them when the phone rang. Anita picked it up and listened wordlessly, nodding. Then she stuck out her arm with the handset. It was Lori.

"Jellicoe called again," she said, skipping the preliminaries. She sounded tense. "He talked to me a little. He's very agitated, ranted about the city running their bulldozers over people and not caring about people, and about meddlers like Constant and President Trammel. Then he sort of sputtered and said something like stew ball something. Oh, he called Trammel again too. Trammel's in his office. I talked with him and he sounded very irritated at you, Jack. I think he blames you for letting Jellicoe get out of hand. He told me Jellicoe had just called him and threatened to kill him."

"Any idea where Jellicoe was calling from?"

"I tried to listen to background noises and I'm pretty sure he's downtown somewhere."

"I'm coming down. Call the cops again and tell 'em." I hung up and said good-bye to Anita and Fred, explaining as I ran out that it sounded like Jellicoe was coming after Trammel.

On the sixth floor, I stood in my office and stared out the window, down at the dark, empty block that had once been a vibrant, vital part of the city's nightlife. I listened as Lori repeated the essence of her conversations with Mathew Jellicoe and President Trammel while I was upstairs. She told me the police said they already had officers with Trammel. Then we rehashed the night's events, trying to find some clue as to what might be next.

"I don't understand," she said, "why he's complaining about the city and about Trammel."

"I don't either. It isn't as if Trammel denied him tenure or anything else, as far as I know. Trammel wasn't even here when Jellicoe received tenure." I shrugged. There was something, though. I could feel it just out of reach in some recess of my mind.

Then I began to feel something else. Just like the feelings I'd had that I was being watched. It was a growing awareness that Jellicoe was down there, somewhere close. I was sure of it. I tried to explain it. Lori just shook her head and I turned to my coat.

"Where are you going, Jack?"

"He said he wants to talk to me, right? Well, I'm not gonna let him in the building if I can help it."

"Jack, Jellicoe may be violent! He threatened the president, and he practically threatened you! He's probably the one who hit you on the head!" I put on my boots and started for the door. And the thing that had been at the edge of my mind moved a little closer.

"Wait!" I turned back to my office. From the locked file I took the documents I had collected on Mathew Jellicoe. There it was. "Jellicoe was a hometown boy, Lori. He graduated from high school here in the city."

CHAPTER 37

*I know I have represented
the facts truthfully and fairly–*

"You think there's a connection? That something here in the city, in his past, is the root of his problem?"

"Very good!" came another voice. Startled, both Lori and I whirled around to the door. "Do you also know that the Jellicoe family once owned a hotel in block D? The block where the new administrative center for this college will be built?" Detective Merrill Swanborg stood in the doorway, leaning against the jam, his hands thrust deep into the pockets of his heavy top coat. We stared at each other wordlessly for a moment.

"Sure," I said. "And Jellicoe was on the site committee. He pushed hard for an alternative site, as I recall."

"An uncle owned the hotel in better days and Jellicoe spent a lot of time there in the hotel." A small walkie-talkie clipped to Swanborg's belt scratched into life and captured our attention. He turned his head and spoke to his lapel.

"Swanborg."

Now I could make out the words. "We've just observed someone driving into block D. The vehicle has parked near Sixth, about thirty yards in from the street."

"Okay, I'm coming down now. I'll exit the front of the building and turn right toward the construction site. I have a civilian with me."

Swanborg and I started together toward the elevator. He didn't like it, I could tell, but he didn't bother to object. I looked back at Lori. She shook her head gently and frowned at me. "Be careful," was all she said.

When Merrill and I reached the lobby, the police radio squawked again. "What? I didn't hear anything in the elevator," Swanborg said to his lapel again.

The radio cleared up, "Shots fired by the subject. Not sure what he was aiming at. We're staying out of sight and not returning fire. We have a message for you to call Castelano on a land line."

Swanborg grabbed the pay phone in the lobby and dialed. He asked for the other detective and then listened for a long time.

"Okay," he said, "it all seems to fit," and hung up.

"What all seems to fit?" I asked.

"Steve has learned some interesting facts the past few hours. Stewart James was a teenager on the street ten, twelve years ago. He was picked up several times on suspicion of hustling, male prostitution, rolling drunks. He disappeared years ago. Stewart James, a.k.a. Stuart Jamison, a.k.a. Stew Ball, testif..."

"What!"

"That's right, he was a key witness on the west coast against a mob-connected child porno ring."

"No," I interrupted him. "What you called him, Stew Ball?"

"Right. That was his street name."

"That's what he told Lori. She said he sputtered something about a stew ball, but it wasn't clear what he meant."

"Who?"

"Jellicoe. Told Lori."

Swanborg nodded. "Sure. There's more. Stew Ball was known to keep company for a short while with an older man known on the street as the Cowboy because he often wore cowboy boots and a western style hat of some sort. Well, you saw the picture."

"Good God, Jamison and Jellicoe might have known each other."

Swanborg smiled. "Oh, we're pretty sure they did. The feds

didn't know about Jamison's history here or they would never have agreed to place him here. Castelano also learned about a bank box Jamison secretly had under another alias that was crammed with cash. I can imagine the shock to both Jamison and Jellicoe when Jamison discovered that his old lover and probable pimp, Cowboy, was also an eminent professor of economics at City College."

"Blackmail?"

"Yep."

"Where does Constant figure in all this?"

"Personally, I don't think she does. I still think Marshall is good for that one."

"Nuts. It's got to be Jellicoe."

"Let's go see if we can find out."

Swanborg looked at me as we stopped at the corner of the building, just out of sight of Urban Renewal Block D where Jellicoe presumably waited.

"Ordinarily, I wouldn't do this–take a civilian out there–but you might help us save this guy. The thing is, if I decide we've reached a crisis, you do exactly what I tell you and no hesitation, all right?" I nodded, already thinking ahead to what we might find across the street.

We stepped away from the shelter of the building, taking the full force of the wind that blasted down the street canyon into our faces. Across the street near the center of the block, I made out the dark shape of a car. Its rounded form stood out from the mounds of snow-muffled debris. Glints of streetlights reflected from its surface. I saw no movement as we crossed Sixth and entered the empty block in a steady, unhurried pace. My eyes watered, making everything difficult to see. A dozen strides into the empty darkness, Swanborg put his hand out and stopped me. Then he said so quietly I almost missed it, "Call him."

"Professor Jellicoe!" I called. "Are you here?" My breath was a bright plume against the dark sky.

Silence. I tried again. "Professor Jellicoe?"

"I'm here. You're here. Where's Trammel? He's the one I really want. You were getting nosy. Too close. Nothing personal. Just a job."

Now I made out the dark shape of a man rising cautiously from the other side of the car. He faced us. The snow lessened and I noticed that he had both mittened hands extended over the top of the car in almost a casual pose. The car protected most of his body from our view.

"I don't know," I said, "but I doubt very much he'll come down here, especially after you apparently threatened him."

"Oh, he's here, our esteemed president. I've seen him." Jellicoe's voice was steady and almost matter-of-fact in tone, if a little high in register. Maybe, I thought, just maybe we'll be all right. I turned slowly and looked up to the sixth floor of the building across Main. Most of the building was dark, but the entire sixth floor seemed to be awake. Then I saw the distinctive rotund shape of our beloved president against the lighted window of his office, the one in the corner that directly faced the building site.

I shivered and took a step toward the car. Jellicoe jerked and screamed at me.

"No! Don't come any closer! I'll shoot you both. You're meddlesome, Marston. Why couldn't you stay out of my affairs? Just like that stupid woman." His hands moved and I saw the uncertain length of something steely in his grasp. His voice rose again, "You get Trammel down here and we'll have a little talk."

"We already asked. Trammel refuses to come down," said Swanborg in my left ear.

"I'll ask him," I said loudly and reached for the walkie-talkie. Swanborg shrugged and handed me the communicator.

I pressed the transmit lever. "Do we have a connection to President Trammel?"

"Wait one," came a surprisingly clear voice. A moment passed, then I heard, "Sergeant Mark here. I'm with President Trammel."

"This is Jack Marston, Sergeant," I said into the mike. "Ask the president if he will agree to come down here and talk with Professor Jellicoe." For a moment there was only hissing and popping then the sergeant said flatly. "He refuses."

"See?" cried Jellicoe as if he'd heard. "He won't come. Just like he wouldn't listen when I asked him to head off the City Council so this block could be saved! I just wanted to explain. I just wanted him to listen to me. He sent me a memo, said it wasn't important! It *was* important!" Jellicoe's voice rose and rose and then suddenly stopped.

In the silence I peered at Jellicoe and said, "What about the woman, Professor? Did you kill Alissa Constant?"

He laughed. It had a chilling edge.

"She pushed and pushed. I warned her. She thought I could help her stupid career. Stupid, stupid. Just like Stew Ball!" His voice rose again in a tearing scream. He was losing control. My stomach was a hard knot. He swayed slightly and then I heard a keening, an ululation that rose and fell, cutting through the wind and the swirling snow. Deadly blossoms of red fire bloomed in the night. I thought I heard glass breaking far away and Swanborg's hand slammed me hard to the rough frozen ground. There was gunfire all around. Shouts. I covered my head and pressed into the cold ground. Then, silence. In the distance, muffled by the snow, a siren wailed.

When I looked up, Merrill was sprawled beside me, his head up, a revolver in his hand. His glare was fixed on the car. I looked but I couldn't see Jellicoe anymore. Cautiously, Merrill got to his feet, crouched, motioning me to stay down. I was miserably cold but I obeyed. Like a wraith, Merrill slid to one side, staying hunched over. His walkie-talkie hissed and popped and he turned it down. I watched him talking to his lapel again. Minutes passed and now I saw other shapes moving low, converging on the car. They stood up and I too got to my feet. I went around the car to the small group of officers.

"He fired the whole clip," said one of the policemen standing beside the hood of Jellicoe's car. "Pretty fast, too."

"He's here, Marston," came Merrill Swanborg's tired voice. I saw a crumpled shape on the ground beside the passenger door. "He's dead," said the flat voice of an officer crouched beside the body. "We hit him several times."

"Call in the teams," said Swanborg wearily. "And get me a tape recorder. I want Marston here to dictate everything he remembers about this event as soon as possible. I'll do the same." He scrubbed a gloved hand over his face.

"Look at this," came another voice. A flashlight flicked on and in its quivering light I saw the sole of a boot with a narrow high heel and a pointed toe. I glanced at Merrill in the reflected glow. He looked at me and nodded. "I'm not a bettor, but I'd make a small wager that boot fits the print we found in the blood in the lobby of the theater."

I blinked hard and turned my head to look up at the buildings. Kitty-corner across Hennepin and Sixth, up on the sixth floor, the bloated silhouette of President Trammel loomed there, motionless in the window. He stared down at us. Then, as more police cars drove into the lot and added the glare of their headlights to the scene, he slowly turned away and left the window. I wondered what he was thinking. I began to shake, harder and harder until I could barely stand. An officer got me around the shoulders and helped me across the street, out of that lot, away from the body, and out of the raw, ceaseless wind that moaned through the city streets.

CHAPTER 38

*And my school shall be in the room where they
insulted me and called me an enemy of the people.*

Warm air and clinking glasses blending with voices raised in laughter and song greeted us as Lori and I entered Maurie's from the crisp December night. Maurie's is a downtown restaurant, still hanging on even though not connected to the skyways. It's in the loop two blocks from the college and a block from the theater. The first public performance of "Enemy of The People" had just ended, and cast and crew were continuing a short tradition of celebrating opening night with drinks and late-night noshes at Maurie's.

I felt especially up. I was happy with our opening night performance; I was no longer masquerading as a private investigator and on my arm was my lady love, looking especially gorgeous in a clinging, long-sleeved burgundy jersey dress.

The stage crew, first to arrive since they had no makeup or costumes to remove, had pre-empted Maurie's back room. Through the open door I saw a small crowd around the battered old piano in the corner, singing camp songs. Others sat in pairs or temporarily alone at the round tables in the big room. Partway down the aisle between in the main dining room, stood Merrill Swanborg and Anton Marshall. They appeared to be chatting amiably enough.

"Why hello, Detective Swanborg," smiled Lori as we approached them. "How are you?"

"Fine, thank you, Lori," he smiled back. Then his gaze shifted to me. "Very nice job, Jack. I enjoyed the performance."

"You came to the show?" My surprise showed.

"Sure. I enjoy live theater, get to local productions as often as I can. I even manage to see a Broadway show once in a while." He grinned.

"Well, good." His laughter interrupted me. More and more cast members with friends and supporters who had attended the performance moved past, and I saw several curious glances directed our way.

"Homicide detectives also appreciate good wine and good food, Jack."

I smiled and shrugged an apology. "Yes, of course. I didn't mean to stereotype you. Come join us. I'm afraid you won't find any great wines here at Maurie's, but the company is terrific and the food ain't bad." We went into the back room.

Inevitably, as waiters scurried between the kitchen and the bar, conversation turned to the recent tragedies at City College. For two days after Professor Jellicoe's death in the swirling snow on Urban Development Project D, City College had been front page news, but interest quickly died, except among those who worked and studied at the college. A few wags talked about the creation of a folk legend, but somehow "Gun battle on Urban Renewal Project D" didn't have quite the ring of "Gunfight at the OK Corral."

No one else had been injured in the brief exchange of shots, but two bullets had passed through the window of President Trammel's office shattering the plate glass. Jellicoe had been shooting at the president.

"I have another reason for dropping by tonight," said Merrill Swanborg. "We've pretty well pieced the thing together, although much to my Inspector's displeasure, there will always be some questions."

"Jack, look." Lori, seated on my left nudged me. Fred Coper and Anita Talbot, arms around each other, had just entered the back room. They seemed to go everywhere together, these days. Anita had told Lori privately that they were about to get engaged. "Excuse me for interrupting, Merrill," she said.

Swanborg looked over at the couple. "Ah, yes, your cryptology section. Those two did a good job. Maybe the police department will call on their expertise again. There'll never be official confirmation, but I'm convinced Jamison was placed at City College by the federal witness protection program." He looked hard at me, reminding me that the revelations he had given me the night Jellicoe was killed were privileged.

I looked across the table at Marsh. He looked calmly back. I was sure he and President Trammel knew the truth about Jamison, but I wasn't going to ask.

"Castelano has collared two others in that nasty little porno group and they're spilling their guts."

"Did Professor Jellicoe leave that tape in the camcorder at the college?" Lori asked.

"We think so. You wouldn't expect him to be so careless. We think Jamison sent the note about Constant. He also sent you the photographs, Jack."

"You know that?" I was surprised. "They came after Jamison was murdered. He must have sent them the day he was murdered. It sure doesn't seem like something someone in the witness protection program would do."

"Criminals aren't necessarily the smartest people in the world. We assume Jamison got worried about the good professor. Maybe he discovered that Jellicoe had done some contract work for the mob. We know he did, although it's not provable in court. We know by inference and logical deduction."

"Ah, yes, logical deduction," said Marshall, smiling a little.

Swanborg cut his eyes at Marsh, smiled back.

"It's a legitimate way to make a case. But we make mistakes, sometimes. Jamison was a nasty piece of work. He may have realized that Jellicoe's role as a golden goose was at an end. Our psychiatrist believes the renewal of Block D was a major blow to Jellicoe's stability. After the trauma of seeing the family hotel torn down, to come up against both Constant and Jamison in such a short time may have tipped his grasp on reality. The existence of the hotel his uncle once owned was probably a kind of anchor. He spent a lot of time there as a boy. We think it upset him that he couldn't get anyone to listen to his complaints about the hotel's destruction, especially his own college president."

"Different reactions from different folks," I said quietly. They all looked at me. "I'm angry because the city tore down that block. I think we've destroyed the character of the street over the past few years in the name of progress, but I haven't tried to kill anyone because of it." Merrill opened his mouth but I held up a hand to forestall him.

"Yes, I know, the block was a nest of seedy rundown places where every criminal in the area hung out, but there must be other ways to deal with that."

"I was just going to agree with you, Jack," said Merrill. "Visually, the street has become really boring. The people who caused most of the problems have scattered. We'll hear from a lot of them in the future. Of course," he smiled, "that's just one civil servant's opinion."

"Miss Jacobs?" A waiter approached the table, a worried look on his face.

"Yes?"

"Can you help us? I was told you're a therapist. There's a young woman, I guess she's a member of the crew. She's sitting on the floor in a corner of the checkroom, behind all the coats. She's crying and won't come out. Could you talk to her?" Lori and I both started to rise.

"No, Jack," she said. "It'll be better if we don't crowd in there. It's probably just opening night reaction, aided by not enough to eat and maybe too much to drink." We watched her go off with the waiter to the front of Maurie's.

"Was Alissa Constant blackmailing Jellicoe?" I prodded Merrill.

"It must have been something like that. They knew each other back East, that's certain. We aren't sure Constant knew Jellicoe was a pornographer. She may simply have been planning to use him the way she tried to use Marshall here and the way she used others all along."

"I think he saw an opportunity to get rid of a dangerous irritation in his life. Jellicoe got her back to the hotel and killed her," Merrill finished.

"But what about Tidwell?" asked a student at the table. He was sitting right across from me, beside the costume woman. "How does she figure in all this?" I opened my mouth and then, looking at Merrill, closed it again. He was gazing calmly at me. Then he turned to the questioner.

"She doesn't figure into it at all. In a place as big as City College, there are bound to be people with a variety of personal problems. The timing of Professor Tidwell's suicide was unfortunate, but she was never under suspicion by the department. There's no file on her among the material we have from Constant. Now, of course, we've destroyed all those files." Merrill rose, shrugging into his overcoat. Lori was coming into the room with a very short, plump young woman. They were both smiling, talking and nodding at each other.

"Hi. I'm back. Oh, Merrill, are you leaving so soon?" Lori put her hand on his sleeve to forestall his move away from the table.

"This is Beth Williams, everybody. She's the assistant lighting director and technical director on 'Enemy of The People.'"

While those unacquainted with Beth introduced themselves, she took Merrill's empty chair and we sat down again. Merrill waved and walked out. The waiter brought more beer and Lori settled herself in the chair on my right.

She put a warm hand on my thigh and whispered, "I was right, it was just opening night reaction. Beth and I had a nice chat after she calmed down. She told me about her aunt in St. Paul who has a fascinating-sounding job at the Minnesota Historical Society."

I nodded and leaned closer. The fragrance of Lori's perfume covered for an instant the sour smell of old beer and older floor wax. I whispered a suggestion in her ear. She smiled and squeezed my thigh.

Before he became a mystery writer and reviewer, Brookins was a counselor and faculty member at Metropolitan State University in Saint Paul, Minnesota. Brookins and his wife are avid recreational sailors. He is a member of Mystery Writers of America, Sisters in Crime, and Private Eye Writers of America. He can frequently be found touring bookstores and libraries with his companions-in-crime, The Minnesota Crime Wave. He writes the sailing adventure series featuring Michael Tanner and Mary Whitney. The third novel is *Old Silver*. His new private investigator series features Sean NMI Sean, a short P.I. The first is titled *The Case of the Greedy Lawyers*. Brookins received a liberal arts degree from the University of Minnesota and studied for a MA in Communications at Michigan State University.

NORMANDALE COMMUNITY COLLEGE
LIBRARY
9700 FRANCE AVENUE SOUTH
BLOOMINGTON, MN 55431-4399

Printed in the United States
200640BV00001B/145-213/A